AMERICAN GIRLS

AMERICAN GIRLS

ALISON UMMINGER

FLATIRON
BOOKS

AMERICAN GIRLS. Copyright © 2016 by Alison Umminger. All rights reserved. Printed in the United States of America. For information, address Flatiron Books, 175 Fifth Avenue, New York, N.Y. 10010.

Portions of this book originally appeared in a slightly different form under the title "Anna Has Two Mommies" in *Waccamaw*.

www.flatironbooks.com

The Library of Congress Cataloging-in-Publication Data is available upon request.

ISBN 978-1-250-07500-0 (hardcover)
ISBN 978-1-250-07502-4 (e-book)

Our books may be purchased in bulk for promotional, educational, or business use. Please contact your local bookseller or the Macmillan Corporate and Premium Sales Department at 1-800-221-7945, extension 5442, or by e-mail at MacmillanSpecialMarkets@macmillan.com.

First Edition: June 2016

10 9 8 7 6 5 4 3 2 1

For my parents, with love and gratitude

These children that come at you with knives,
they are your children.

—Charles Manson

AMERICAN GIRLS

Preflight

My first Manson girl was Leslie Van Houten, the homecoming princess with the movie-star smile. She was on death row at nineteen for putting a knife into the already-dead body of some poor, random woman for the lamest reason that anyone gives for doing anything: all the other kids were doing it. I found her by accident, reading an article in the waiting room of the lady-parts doctor my mom was going to when she was trying to get pregnant with my brother. I'd been to the same office the year before, when I got my period, because my mom wanted a professional to lecture me about not getting knocked up. I was probably so traumatized that I forgot you couldn't use cell phones in the lobby—something about the radiation screwing with the pictures of the fetuses. This time, someone had left an old *Rolling Stone* next to the magazines about babies and pregnancy. Thank God. If the choices were between reading about psychopaths and "How I Fit Back into My Prepregnancy Jeans," then it really wasn't much of a choice.

The article was written by John Waters, a director who made a movie called *Pink Flamingos*. My sister's then boyfriend had insisted we watch the film the Thanksgiving before, because he had seen it as a boy in Poland and had had some kind of revelation about his life. After that, he just *knew* that he wanted to go to America. Nasty, filthy America, where you could put a person on trial for being an asshole and supersize transsexuals ate dog shit off of lawns, at least in the movies. Happy Thanksgiving and pass the peas! After seeing *Pink Flamingos,* I wasn't exactly shocked to learn that John Waters made friends with a Manson girl. He was out there. She was probably scared of *him.*

The whole morning had been stressful, because it was the day my mom was going to see if the baby inside of her had a heartbeat. The time before there hadn't been, and months of torture followed. It's not that I wasn't sad for my mom, I was, but she took so long to start getting out of bed again that I practically had to move in with my best friend, Doon, just to get a bowl of cereal in the morning. I never knew someone could get so upset about something the size of a quarter.

The *Rolling Stone* article was about what a regular person Leslie Van Houten was, if you could get past that whole murder thing. I knew for a fact that Charles Manson was not a regular person. I had watched part of a biography about him once at Doon's—he had pinwheels for eyes and a swastika carved in his forehead, which pretty much disqualified him from "regular." He had masterminded the murder of Sharon Tate, a very pretty, very pregnant woman whose face I couldn't remember, and that made me think of my mother and feel guilty for reading an article like that while she was having her big appointment. Manson did all of his crimes with a pack of women, girls who made it look like they'd found a way to clone crazy and dress it down with stringy hair, empty stares, lots of drugs, and lots of knives. Most people never thought about them as separate people at all. Definitely not as girls who went to homecoming once, or who got dragged to the lady-parts doctor by their moms.

Leslie Van Houten was a Manson girl, and she didn't help kill the pregnant one. She did, however, put a knife into the corpse of mother-of-two Rosemary LaBianca—and not just once but at least a dozen times. Then she watched while her friends wrote on the walls in blood. She also read the Bible to Charles Manson while he bathed, which was just gross and weird on top of everything else. Three things stuck with me about the article. First, that John Waters, the writer, thought that forty years was long enough for a person to be in prison for doing something stupid as a teenager—even something *really, really* stupid, like World Series stupid. Second, that Van Houten was tripping so hard on LSD that she thought that after they'd murdered everyone she was going to become a fairy and fly away—she even asked her dad if she should cut holes in the back of her jacket to get ready for the fairy-tastic new world. In school, meth was the drug they were worried we'd start taking, and they liked to scare us with pictures of homeless-looking people, toothless and aged a decade overnight. LSD sounded like a whole other world of batshit.

The third thing I remembered was that John Waters said that Leslie Van Houten would have been happier if she'd wound up in Baltimore, hanging out with shit-eating transsexuals and making movies about killing people as opposed to actually killing people. She would have been a different person if she'd washed up in Baltimore, not California.

I made it most of the way through the article before my mom came out, hugging me and practically making out with her wife, because they were going to have a baby. It seemed like bad luck to keep reading about murders after news like that, so I left the magazine and forgot about Leslie Van Houten. I only remembered her two years later, when I was in the airport getting ready to board my flight to Los Angeles, looking over my shoulder to see if my mom had figured out that I'd left. The flight next to mine was headed to Baltimore—it was twice delayed and the passengers looked tired and sad, the exact wrong look for people to have before getting on an airplane. For some reason, when I was finally on my own flight, with the main door to the airplane safely sealing out the life I was leaving behind, I thought about John Waters and what he'd written about Van Houten, how she hadn't just picked the wrong person but the wrong place. And I sent him a mental note, because it seemed like something he should have known, and because it was true: *No one runs away to Baltimore.*

1

I would never have gone after my mother with a knife, not while a credit card was cleaner and cut just as deep. It's not like I was going after her at all—mostly, what I wanted was to get as far away from her as possible, and her wife's wallet was sitting on the dining room table with the mail, just waiting to be opened. A person can only take so much. My mom had saged the house the week before and told me that she couldn't even enter my room, the energy was so vile. She spent all her time with my new baby brother, talking about how he was the real reason she must have been put on this earth, that the universe was giving her a "do-over," which made me what? A "do-under"? Once I added in the whole nightmare at Starbucks the week before—where my parents sat me down and put a price on my future like they were getting ready to list me on eBay—it seemed to me more likely that she *wanted* me to take the credit card. Was *begging,* even.

My sister, Delia, an actress in Los Angeles, told me last summer that everyone needs a "thing." She's beautiful, with silver-gray eyes and ink-black hair that goes halfway down her back, and a voice that sounds like she makes dirty phone calls for a living. She was almost cast as a Bond girl, but she told me that beauty isn't enough. *Everyone here is gorgeous,* she said, *so you have to figure out something else. You've got to be good at at least two things, and known for one.* She's a decent gymnast and can still cartwheel on a balance beam, so being able to do her own stunts is her "thing." I visited her last summer, and she took me to a boutique in Santa Monica and helped me pick out a new pair of glasses for when I started high school. It is safe to say that being beautiful is not what I am going to be known for, but she told me that with the right glasses I could rule the world of "nerd chic." I think she forgot that nerds are not, nor will they ever be, chic in Atlanta, or maybe in any high school in America. I bought a pair of thick black frames that you normally see on blind old men and wore the reddest lip gloss my mom would let me leave the house with. *Flawless,* my sister had said. *Very French.* The only person who noticed my makeover was my best friend, Doon, and she pointed out that I had lip gloss on my teeth. I didn't get beat up, but I didn't get asked to homecoming, either. I think my sister forgot that I don't live in a movie, or even in France.

Stealing, contrary to my mother's latest take on me, is not my "thing." Now, if you asked my mother, she would probably make me out to be a criminal of the first order. To hear her tell it, I'm no better than those actresses who shoplift from Saks and whine on the news about being bored with their lives. Blah, blah, blah, *You can't be trusted.* She was actually crying when my sister gave me her phone at the airport. Blah, blah, blah, *How could you have violated Lynette's privacy like that?* (Ummmm. Easy?)

Blah, blah, blah, *I wish I'd known more about how I was raising you when I was doing it.* Like I'm some kind of paragraph she wishes she could delete and rewrite, but she already accidentally e-mailed it to the world.

The good thing is that I was now in Los Angeles, while my mother was still in Atlanta with her awful wife and my new brother, Birch. *How?* my mother asked. *How did anyone let a girl who's barely fifteen through security at the Atlanta airport? Are you on drugs?*

She yelled at my sister for a while, who pulled the phone away from her ear and stage-whispered with her hand half covering the receiver, "Don't think this means you're not in a huge pile of shit, Anna. Because you are."

But huge piles of shit are relative, and it was hard to feel threatened in the Hollywood Hills, not in my sister's apartment, at any rate, which was all mirrors and white light. The space was carefully underfurnished. The living room had a Zen fountain, an oversize white sofa, a coffee table, and not much else. The doors between the living room and bedroom were translucent, and they slid to open. Her bedroom was like a crash pad from *The Arabian Nights,* with embroidered pillows and velvet curtains and a bed that sat close to the floor. I think if my sister were less pretty, her apartment would have seemed kind of ridiculous—there were too many pillows and candles in the bedroom and too few decent snack-food choices in the kitchen for your standard-issue human being. Instead, it felt like the inside of some Egyptian goddess's sanctuary, full of perfumes you could only buy in Europe, expensive makeup in black designer cases, and underwear that was decidedly non-functional. It had crossed my mind that my sister might be a slut, but a really nice-smelling, clean, and carefully closeted slut. Even I knew better than to ask if that's one of the two other "things" that she was good at, though Doon and I had some theories.

"Can we go shopping tomorrow?" I asked.

"Are you deaf? You're in some serious trouble," my sister said. Then she laughed a little; she couldn't help herself. "So you stole Lynette's credit card."

"I didn't steal it."

"Have you considered law school? You stole the number."

"I *used* the number," I said, annoyed that she even wanted to talk about it. "It was under five hundred dollars."

She kept an eye on me like I might make a break for the door as she leveled green powder and yogurt into a blender. "What does that have to do with anything?"

"What's that?"

"Greens and probiotics," she said. "Fish oil, B vitamins, acai berry juice, and herbs from my Chinese doctor. It's like licking the bottom of a compost pile, so let's hope it's doing something besides bankrupting me."

Dramatic, my sister. But at least she makes money for it.

"And don't change the subject. You could have gotten nabbed by some pervert. Mom was scared to death. Oh yeah, roll your eyes and make me another mean, mean grown-up, but

you're lucky you got here. What if I had been on location somewhere?"

"I'm fifteen, it's not like I'm twelve."

"And it's not like you're forty-two, either. People are disgusting, or have you forgotten?"

"How could I?"

My sister put on music and I checked to see what she was
playing: Pink Floyd, *Wish You Were Here*. Lonesome music that
seemed like it could only belong on the West Coast. My sister
only thinks music is good if it's a thousand years old. I sent her
some music by the band that Doon and I love best, Freekmonkee, and she told me that it sounded like bad Nirvana covers,
which proves she didn't even listen to it. They're British but just
relocated to LA. Doon had a shrine on her computer for the lead
singer, Karl Marx, and I was mildly obsessed with the guitarist,
Leo Spark. When I first got on the plane, I actually checked
first class to see if any members of Freekmonkee were on board,
but no luck.

My sister and mom always thought that something awful
was going to happen to me—they acted like the only option
for running away was winding up in pieces in some stranger's
freezer. My family was clearly the place where optimism went
to die. What about the hope that something amazing might
happen? Half the time I wondered if they weren't wishing for
the worst, then they could turn me into a sad story they told their
friends instead of having to deal with me as an actual life-form
who shared their DNA.

"What if the taxi driver had been a serial killer?" I said. "What if terrorists hijacked the plane? I did get here. I'm fine. I'd like to know how long it took her to notice I was gone."

"You laugh, but stranger things have happened. Did you know they found a severed head in Griffith Park last week? I jog there, or at least I did. And as to your second question, not long." My sister sipped the grass-shake. "Lynette's credit card company called a few hours afterward about a suspicious charge."

Lynette's bank called. I'll bet they did. Before my mom decided she was a lesbian, I thought lesbians were all these really nice, earthy, crunchy, *let's smother you with our twenty extra pounds of lady love and fight the power* people. But Lynette wasn't like that at all. She was thin and smart and mean, and probably slept with her cell phone to get bank alerts like that.

"So it's really their money they're worried about," I said.

"That's not what I said at all. That's how they found out. Are you depressed or something?"

I didn't shake my head either way. I hadn't really thought about it.

"I'm not taking sides on this one. Cora's clearly lost her mind and I regret that you're living the crazy, but you can't just steal people's credit cards. You can't. Okay?" She ran her finger inside the glass to get the last of the sludge while I reopened the refrigerator door to see if anything with refined flour or sugar had materialized. No luck.

But it wasn't really theft. It *wasn't*.

One thing I didn't tell my sister, and I wouldn't tell my mom or dad, or anyone, really, because it's the kind of thing that just makes you look sad when you're supposed to be having a good time, but when I charged the ticket I imagined that when I got on the plane I'd try to order a wine, or see if they'd upgrade me to first class, or at least spend some money on the snacks they make you pay for. Traveling with parents meant sad dried fruit and chewy popcorn in Ziploc bags. I was going to have Pringles! I thought it would be my reward for talking my way through security, but the crazy thing was that after I flashed my passport (stamped once from a horrible weekend "getting to know" Lynette in the Bahamas), they let me through security like a fifteen-year-old traveling alone was the most normal thing in the world. Maybe it was, but I'd never done it. They didn't even find the mini can of mace attached to my key chain. By the time I got on the plane, I felt even more invisible than I had at home, and I munched my sad peanuts like there were no other options. I had become the human equivalent of one of those balloons we used to send into the air with our name and address on the string in the hope that someone might mail it back, but no one ever did.

Maybe my sister was onto something, and I *was* depressed. A normal person would have at least bought an in-flight snack box. The thought did cross my mind that once I landed in LA, I could take a taxi to Disneyland, or hightail it to the Hollywood sign, or get one of those maps of the stars' houses and maybe even become the youngest member of the paparazzi and get accidentally famous for my pictures in a straight-to-Pay-Per-View-movie kind of way. I thought those were optimistic ideas, but maybe they were really depressing.

When we landed, my sister was waiting right outside the gate, inside security, plastered to her cell phone.

"Yes," she'd said. "She's here. I see her now. She looks fine. I know. Okay. Love you too."

"What are you doing here?" I thought about hugging Delia, but her hands were crossed over her chest and she didn't make a move in that direction.

"What am *I* doing here? Have you completely lost your mind?"

"No."

"I'll be the judge of that. Well, right now, I'm missing work because my phone rang this morning and I had to talk Cora off the ledge. Seriously, I've got to hand it to you. I thought I was a grade-A fuckup for not going to college, but you're leaving me in the dust. Is something happening?" Her voice lowered a bit. "Is anyone molesting you? Because I wouldn't send you back, and I would always believe you."

"No!" I said. "Gross. Who would molest me? Dad? Lynette? No, it's just . . . I don't want to talk about it."

"You flew all the way across the country and you don't want to talk about it. Fine for now, but I'm gonna let you in on a little secret, they're *gonna* want you to talk about it."

I hadn't seen my sister in almost a year. She'd always been pretty, but now she had the smoothed-down look of a Barbie doll. Her hair was straight and the glossy black of an expensive magazine cover. She had on a wifebeater, blue jeans, and five-inch-high dominatrix heels: black leather with silver studs. But she could still walk faster than me, in my Converse low-tops, Old Navy denim, and red Georgia sweatshirt.

"They wanted to send you right back home," she said. "You can thank me for the fact that you get to stay here to cool off for a couple of days. But you're under house arrest, okay? No running off to the Coffee Bean for celebrity sightings. I want to understand what's going on. You know this makes me feel guilty too, don't you?"

Just walking through the LA airport made me glad that I wasn't in Atlanta. When you go up the escalators at the Atlanta airport there's a mural on the walls that features a mystery-race toddler with creepy blurred-out genitals playing in a fountain. I think it's supposed to be friendly and *We love everyone, yay!* but it's just weird. The LA airport is the exact opposite; no one is trying to look friendly, and everyone we passed looked half starved and almost famous.

"You're not listening," she said. "Does it even bother you that I could lose my job for missing work today? Finding an actress to fill my shoes is like finding a clover in a clover field, okay? A thank-you would be in order."

"I'm sorry," I said.

Delia stopped walking and stared me down, like the old days.

"And thank you. *Thaaaaaannnnnnk youuuuuuuu.*"

"A little sincerity never killed anyone," she said, and then she gestured for me to hand over the bigger of my bags.

"So what are you working on?" I asked.

"Were you even listening when I called last weekend? It's an indie horror flick about zombies and the organ trade in China."

"Seriously?"

I hadn't checked any other luggage, so we headed straight for the parking lot. It felt like I was going on vacation.

"Did you know that part of the reason they won't get rid of the death penalty in China is the organ trade? And they don't just execute people in prisons, they have these vans that drive around and pick people up and do away with them on the spot. So I'm supposed to be this American woman who sees a body thrown from one of the vans"—she paused in creepy horror-movie style—"only it's not really dead yet. I think they're try-ing to make a point, the director keeps talking about human rights and Amnesty International, but I think that's to hide the fact that he can't write dialogue. Not my problem as long as he can pay my salary," she said. "You want to know what it's called?"

"What?"

"*Thief of Hearts.* I mean, unless your lead zombie is Internet dating, it's too tragically idiotic, right?" She was cracking her-self up.

"I guess."

We got into a BMW convertible that was definitely not my

sister's. It had magnets on the bumper that advertised private schools, or where someone vacationed, code letters that only other super-rich people would recognize.

"What's the HH for?" I asked. "Heil Hitler?"

"What are you *talking* about?"

"The sticker, on the bumper. And SSI? Is that Nazi too?"

"Hilton Head and St. Simon's Island. Vacation spots. Lord, Anna, there are more of those on bumpers in Atlanta than here. Where do you get these things?"

"I don't know," I said. "The Discovery Channel?"

For the longest time she was dating Roger, a film student who would have been hard-pressed to drive a '92 Corolla off a used-car parking lot. But now she's "just good friends" with the producer of the Bond flick that she lost the part for, and he lets her use his car when he's abroad. Because friends do things like that in LA, especially when one of the friends is extremely good-looking.

"Let me finish about the film," she said. "*Not* that you were listening. I'm practically the lead, only I'm down a kidney or something by the end."

It was three hours earlier in California and the sky hadn't started to get dark, but I felt tired. I leaned my head against the window and watched the traffic, the palm trees, the fruit stands on the sides of the streets. It was easy to be in California with my sister. She was the kind of person who people didn't just buy drinks for—they offered her their cars, their homes, their credit cards. I knew what the week would be like if I stayed here—Pilates and yoga, a trip to the old perv who balanced her energy, a few days on the set, a manicure or a haircut, and maybe a sip of a beer when we went out with the producer when he came back, just to prove how "cool" he was. People were nice to me when I was with Delia because I was her sister. My sister would never have to steal five hundred bucks—if she so much as looked a little sad, someone was there to open his wallet.

If only my sister were my mom. "Overrated," she said when I told her that once. "Cora was my sister-mom, and we're a real portrait of functionality, right?"

I'd heard stories about my mom in the old days, how she would take Delia on dates with her when she couldn't find a sitter, or the time they took off for the World Series of Poker in Vegas because my mom had a dream that she was going to win big. The mom I got, Cora 2.0, always made me call her Mom, and until their divorce she and Dad were sort of like the living room furniture—around, but nothing to notice. I guess they were fine, but they definitely weren't fun. When my sister talked about Cora, it was like she knew a totally different person.

I thought that maybe my mom was going to call back and I was going to be forced to get on the phone to apologize, but after my sister clicked off the second time, the phone never rang. While Delia was learning her lines, I sent Doon a message: "In LA. Hiding from Mom and Lynette. May have taken a credit card." Doon said I was evil for leaving without her, but she was on top of the credit card situation. She told me that I should Google "punishments for stealing" so that I would be ready for anything when I talked to my mom. Then she said that she'd read that Freekmonkee was recording a new album, and that the band had moved into a neighborhood not far from my sister's. She signed off with, "PLS buy me ticket! TRAITOR!!!!! JK. Not!"

We figured out a while ago that my mom likes to get advice from the Internet. After reading about how a child who steals probably already feels ashamed enough (please God, let her decide that I've suffered enough!), I found a site that showed a truck running over the arm of a boy who'd been caught stealing in Iran, only it turned out that the picture was a fake and it was just a scam for money. Then I searched those death trucks in China that my sister was talking about, and they looked like the kind of RVs that I used to think would be fun to take on vacation, where you could shower and poop and sleep and wake up in New Mexico, only in China they were sleek and black like giant police cars, and you woke up dead. I wondered if Doon had heard about those. I was pretty sure she hadn't, so I sent her a link to a page. China definitely sounded worse than Atlanta, even if my sister swore by Chinese doctors.

While I was surfing the Web, I started getting more and more nervous, like I was going to have a panic attack. So I Googled "panic attack" and decided that I didn't want to start having those at fifteen, but it didn't make my chest feel any less tight. I don't think I missed my mom and I know I didn't miss Lynette, but I wondered if Birch had noticed I was gone. At night, he liked to bring me this book about a duck and a cat and an owl who make soup out of pumpkins. I'd make these big slurping noises and he would die laughing, and when Birch laughs it's pretty disgusting in terms of cute. I wondered if he brought the book to Lynette, or what they told him had happened to me. He wouldn't have understood either way, but I kind of wished now that I had said good-bye, or left him a picture of me by a plane.

In the other room, I could hear my sister practicing her lines. *It pumps. It bleeds. But does it feel?* Her bed felt like the bed in a hotel, with white-white sheets and pillows everywhere, and the room smelled faintly of roses. *Do you love me? Or do you just think you love me? What is it beating inside of you?* From through the wall, those same lines over and over. Louder, then soft. Scared. Happy. Excited.

Alone.

2

When I woke up, my sister was already awake in the other room, doing sun salutations and drinking Chinese tea. There was nothing to eat in the refrigerator. Nothing in the cupboards, either. My sister had a blender that could pulverize the nastiest of vegetables, but only month-old apples and powders to put in it. If someone had wired her jaw shut, she probably wouldn't have had to change her diet. When I'd been away from my sister for months, I only remembered the good things about her—that she was funny and stylish and always had great stories about famous people. When reality sunk in, I remembered that she ate salads without dressing when she was *starving* and seemed to assume that I would just want to do the same. I found two peanuts in the crumpled bag from the airplane at the bottom of my purse. Delia had sworn she would take us grocery shopping, but I knew that meant "in this lifetime," not "this morning."

"Can we go get some breakfast?"

My stomach whimpered like a sad dog.

"Why? Are you treating?" My sister's ass was in the air, and it was pretty clear from looking at it that breakfast was not on her daily list of concerns. I should have Googled "flat-out evil" and crossed it with her butt to predict how she'd respond.

"This isn't a vacation," she said. "And I'm not made of money."

"I never said you were."

Delia had sunk back into child's pose. She let out a long, measured breath and shifted back into downward-facing dog.

"There should be an apple in the bottom drawer. You can have that."

"An apple isn't breakfast. Not even for horses."

"Well, today it's going to have to be. It's zombie day off, so we're meeting Roger at eleven thirty, and Dex comes back Friday, so we'll hit the market at some point, but there's not much I can do about breakfast this morning. Dex may have found a job for you, so make sure to thank him."

My sister moved from side plank position to side plank position, then effortlessly to upward-facing dog, arching her neck and talking at the ceiling. For someone who did a lot of yoga and had a peace sign tramp stamp on her lower back, she sure could be a bitch.

"There are three hours between now and eleven thirty. And please tell me Roger isn't Roger-Roger."

"Roger is Roger-Roger, and don't mention anything about meeting him to Dex. It's all professional between us now, but Dex won't understand that, and between you and him, I get tired of explaining everything."

Yeah, because it's so complicated to explain Roger.

"Who is Dex, anyhow?"

My sister broke her pose, wiped her brow, and looked at

me like I'd just ruined her workout. "Seriously, Anna, do you listen to anything? I've been talking about Dex for months. He's my boyfriend, you know, the one who's been filming in Hungary the last two weeks? The one who calls every night at ten forty-five?"

She was lying through her teeth, but if I wanted to eat again, I'd let it slide.

"How am I supposed to know who you're talking to? I thought your boyfriend was that bald European producer with the car. Do we really have to see Roger?"

"I'm just borrowing the car while mine gets fixed, and Roger is doing very well these days, I'll have you know. Did you watch those Burger Barn commercials? 'The Revolution Starts Now'? That's Roger. And now he's making a film about murders in Los Angeles, and so far, it's beautiful."

By "beautiful" she meant really, really, really boring.

"Because murder is so uplifting."

"It's a part of life," she said, like I was a total idiot from some other universe. "I'm playing a woman who is drawn to these places and doesn't know why. Like *Vertigo,* but there's a kind of spiritual kinship to the women who come to Los Angeles and never make it out. And it's all visual, no speaking."

I gave up and started eating the apple. "Dead women who don't speak. Sounds right up Roger's alley."

Roger was like the Edgar Allan Poe of stupid people. He'd been making movies about women who were dead or dying, who didn't have much to say, for as long as his stringy hair had been ponytailed into a cliché. My sister dated him for five years, and tortured us with as many Thanksgivings and Christmases where he reminded me how sad consumerism was and how unethical it was to eat meat, as if I asked, while I was just trying to have a second serving of dressing in peace. And he wasn't even American, he was Polish, which should have made him more interesting but actually just made him more annoying. When Delia finally dumped him, my dad and I did an actual dance of joy around the living room.

I must have been daydreaming, because next thing I knew Delia was in front of me asking, "Ready?"

She had twisted her hair into a French braid that wound around her head, glossed her lips, and wrapped a chic white scarf around her neck. It was disgusting how little it took for her to look beautiful.

"Sure," I said. "Just let me get my bag."

"We'll get some muffins," she said. "There's a holistic bakery on the way. Sugar and gluten free, but you'd never know it. I crave their blueberry flax cookies. They're like crack."

"Ass-crack," I said, but softly, because I was hungry.

Outside, the air was cold and the fog or smog or whatever it was hadn't lifted. In Atlanta, I always imagined LA as warm all the time, but this morning was cool and I'd only brought the thin jacket that I'd worn to travel. I wrapped my hands under the ends of the sleeves and hugged my fists close to my body. Delia was staring at her door. Someone had come in the night and taped a white envelope with her name handwritten across the front. No one had knocked, I was sure of that, and the handwriting was spidery, Delia's name in all capital letters.

She turned her back away from me while she opened it, and when she turned back toward me her face had lost some of its color. If she hadn't just gotten Botoxed, I would have said she looked worried. Maybe even scared. She folded the piece of paper and put it into her purse.

"Who's it from?"

"I have no idea," she said. "Not for you, okay?"

When my sister was finished with a subject, she had a way of letting you know. The letter had just been declared off-limits, but I was going to pretend not to care and see if I could fish it out later. That's what we did with information in our family—we squirreled it away and then dared someone else to lay claim. When my mom became a lesbian, I called Delia and she said, "That's the news?" like my mom had been batting for both teams her whole life. It made me mad, because I could tell she wanted me to be the last to know, or at least later than her. The note was probably just a bill for pizza, but as long as I couldn't see it, it was interesting.

We hit the bakery drive-through and though Delia didn't ask what I wanted, she did pay. I tried to eat around the flax-seeds, which only gave me less food and a lapful of crumbs.

"So," she said. "You haven't seen Roger lately. Be prepared for his hair."

I was listening with one ear, and searching for my phone to

see if Doon had texted me back. Since it was three hours later in Georgia, I figured she'd have something interesting to report. She had promised to low-level-stalk my mom and Lynette and remind Birch that he had a sister. For all I knew my mother was cutting my face out of pictures and reconstructing her perfect family, without me, from the ground up. I told Doon I would text her pictures every day to show him.

"Are you kidding me?" I said.

"What?" Delia said. "Are you okay?"

I was not okay, not even kind of.

"My phone. My phone is dead."

"You probably forgot to charge it." She was doing some kind of weird facial exercise while she drove, pursing her lips and then opening her mouth as far as it would go, like she was blowing imaginary bubbles.

"It was fully charged this morning. I checked."

"Just plug it in here."

She passed me the car charger and I hooked my phone in. Just the black-screen flatline of a phone with no pulse. Lynette. My mom.

"*Oooohmigod,*" I said. "Now what am I supposed to do?"

"Well," my sister said, and I swear she was half smiling, "phones don't pay for themselves."

"What if some maniac shoves me in his trunk? How am I supposed to call and let people know where I am? What if I'm drunk and at a party and need a ride? What if someone tries to date-rape me?"

"What if you can't text your little friend twenty-four-seven?" Now she was doing her breathing exercises, blowing air out of her mouth and making a noise that sounded like a dying cicada. I pretended to cover my ears.

"I can't *live* without my phone."

"Pretend you're a pioneer."

"It's not funny."

She popped a breath mint. "I didn't say it was funny. You can use my computer when we get home. It's not like you've been dropped on some deserted island to fend for yourself. Just chill."

We drove past billboards advertising new television shows and energy drinks that would have sounded made-up if they hadn't been real: Kwench, *Emergency*, *Volt*, Lifeline. An actress I didn't recognize loomed thirty feet tall in a tight-fitting tank top. A surgical mask dangled off the index finger of her right hand, and a pair of hot-pink lace underwear was half tucked behind her back with the other hand. Her eyes were wide and green, and she had that actressy look like someone had just whispered in her ear, "Pretend you have a secret," but you knew there wasn't any secret, not really, except maybe that the show was going to be even stupider than the billboard. The actress was naked from the waist down, and letters the same hot pink of her panties covered her lady parts with the words "GET SHOCKED!!!!! *VOLT.* SUNDAYS AT 9."

"I read for that role," Delia said, gesturing behind her. "But they wanted a blonde."

I didn't feel like hearing about the millionth role my sister had almost gotten. Not until we'd figured out the phone situation.

"I need my phone," I said.

I *really* couldn't live without my phone if I was going to have to be front row for the Delia-and-Roger show all morning. That was a punishment too cruel, even for Lynette. If she had ever met Roger, she would see why electronics were a necessity. Maybe I could just stare at the blank screen and ignore him while I slowly died of boredom.

We pulled in front of a hotel that looked like it should have been condemned a decade ago, and my sister parked her car next to a homeless man who appeared to have an open sore on his left arm. He sat next to a sleeping woman whose bare feet were tar-black on the bottom, and he covered her gently with what looked like a mermaid beach towel as we passed.

"Keep moving," my sister said, not even looking in their direction.

"That guy," I said. "He needs to go to the hospital."

My sister shook her head and checked her phone. "This is downtown, Anna. Watch the news around here sometime. This is where the hospitals dump the people who can't pay their bills. The hospitals won't have him."

Inside the building the lobby was more posh than the exterior would have suggested, but I still felt like we should be careful not to put our purses down, because any surface could have hosted a pop-up party for bedbugs. Doon got bedbugs at camp last summer, and her mother made her strip naked before she could come into the house; then her mom took all of her clothes and boiled them at the Laundromat before she would let her take them back into the house. Bedbugs can live for a year without eating. They're the zombies of the bug world—legion, tireless, and impossible to destroy.

"Okay," Delia said. "We're supposed to take the elevator to the top floor, then the stairs. Roger will meet us up there. Did you know that Richard Ramirez, the 'Night Stalker,' used to live here? It's like that hotel in *The Shining*, I think there was another serial killer here for a while as well, but I can't remember who. Can you imagine booking a room here on purpose?"

"Great," I said. I hated that I was more bothered by the homeless couple than by any long-gone psycho, that the thought of walking by them again made me decide against asking to go to the coffee shop on the corner. And it's not like there weren't homeless people in Atlanta; they just didn't seem to be openly wounded. Or maybe I wasn't looking as closely.

When the elevator stopped, we climbed a final flight of concrete stairs and stepped into the open air. The top of the building was dirty with bird crap and discarded cans. Three water towers sat toward the edge of the space, near a thin wall that looked like you could trip over it into the street, and about twenty feet away from us, dancing over his computer as he typed and held a hand up in our direction with a "No, no, don't bother the genius" wave, was Roger. He had on tight black jeans, a black leather jacket, and had shaved his head into a cancer-victim crew cut.

My sister rolled her eyes and pulled out her phone. At least she had an escape.

After a minute Delia gestured at the middle water tower.

"Anna," she whispered, "see that tower? A Canadian tourist was staying here and they found her body in it, but not until it was badly decomposed. The residents of the hotel had been using the water for weeks."

The wind picked up as she was talking, and I felt a chill.

"Are you serious? You mean that actual water tower?"

"Completely."

The water towers looked like oversize cans that should have been recycled long ago. They creaked to life every time someone flushed a toilet or ran a shower. I wanted to be home as much as I'd ever wanted anything in my life.

"*Gwiazdeczko,*" Roger said, and kissed my sister on the mouth. "*Misiu.*"

He was reaching for my cheek, but I put out my hand instead. My sister might have been confused about her relationships, but I was not even remotely confused about mine.

"Oh," he said. "You are so much bigger and formal now."

He was looking me up and down like I was trying out for some part in his idiot film. Hollywood people could be gross even when they weren't trying. Pimps and butchers.

"She looks more like you every day, you know."

"Rest assured she has a mind of her own," Delia said. "I figured it would be okay if she came today. She knows the drill."

"You are not in school?" Roger asked, like he cared.

"No," I said. "Keen eye for detail."

"Always the mouth," he said, and gave me a shut-the-eff-up smile.

"So I had a breakthrough," he said, and he took my sister's face between his hands, like he was going to make out with her or snap her neck in one swift move. "I *know*. I know who you are."

"That's reassuring," I said. "You did live together for five years."

My sister glared and Roger ignored me. Just like old times.

"Your character. Do you know how many children Charles Manson had?" he asked, like it was the riddle of the Sphinx. "How many grandchildren? He probably wasn't allowed conjugal visits, but no one knows what is really possible in prison. Could he have found a way around that? There were many children from his family who were placed in foster homes, who never knew who they were, let alone who their father was. And the sex was so promiscuous then, no? I thought she was going to be like Catherine Deneuve in *Repulsion,* right? So maybe it's in my unconscious, this woman who is victim and sadist. Manson. Polanski. I feel it out there."

I had to hand it to Roger, he was good at acting like he had an audience even when the two of us were pretty clearly underwhelmed.

"I'm a Manson girl?" Delia gave Roger her "Would you care to rephrase that while I melt your face with my mind?" look. I almost felt sorry for him. "Isn't that a little obvious?"

"No," he said, prickling. "Not a Manson girl, and not obvious. You are a child of California. All of those girls were children of America, reckless children. Heartless children. Cruel children who hated their parents. They confused love and hate, death and life. It may not be Manson, it may be one of the others at the compound, but it is part of that hot desert, that last summer of the 1960s. I need to think."

That was an understatement. I was starting to get cold, and I didn't like the sound of his movie. He was just the kind to pitch someone off a roof as part of his method, to scare up publicity for his latest failure.

My sister sucked in a long breath and exhaled. "Well, you need to shoot, because the light's changing and I don't think they're going to want us up here all week. Dex gets home Friday, and the rest of this week is zombies. Once he's back I can't just shoot anytime you like. You need to pick a schedule and stick with it."

"Dex," Roger said, and left it at that.

My sister turned her phone on and handed it to me.

"Just keep the sound off," she said, and gestured at a place for me to sit near where the elevator had opened.

I pretended to be texting, because I didn't want to give either of them the pleasure of finding what they were doing interesting, but it was hard not to watch my sister. I always learned more about my sister by watching her than by listening to her. If you ask Delia about her father, Mom's first husband who left and never looked back, she'll give her standard "That sonofabitch,

I'm glad he's gone" answer. But my mom told me that after he left, Delia cried whenever the doorbell rang. It didn't make sense, according to my mother, because it's not like he didn't have a key. *She would open her mouth and her eyes would get so open, and then they'd just shut. It was like a light went off, and she wouldn't talk about it.* That's what my mom had told me. I didn't get to see that much with Delia, any kind of openness, but she could bring it out when the cameras were rolling. I imagined that might have been what she looked like as she started wandering around the roof of that building, like she was waiting for a doorbell to ring, for someone missing to come home.

I'd been using Delia's bag as a pillow, waiting for her to let down her guard so that I could search the contents. If she saw me open it, she'd ship me back to Atlanta for sure. Roger had her posed at the edge of the building, sitting so close to the edge that it made my stomach drop just to look at her. They seemed to be disagreeing about which direction she should turn her face, so without moving any other part of my body, I slipped my hand into the side pocket of her bag and pulled out the paper that had been posted to her door. Inside there was one word, handwritten.

Whore.

The handwriting was ugly and aggressive, like it had been scratched with a knife, and I wished that I hadn't opened Delia's bag because that word was impossible to unsee, impossible now not to wonder who despised my sister enough to drive to her house in the middle of the night and leave personalized hate mail. Doon and I had joked about Delia being a slut, but the letter was hardly funny. And I had been sleeping in the living room while someone was just outside, doing what? Peeking in the windows? Waiting behind the bushes to see when Delia read it?

For a second, I thought that I was hallucinating hot-stalker-breath just behind me, but it was just Roger.

"I have something for you," he said. "I did not mean to scare you."

"It's okay." I folded the paper quickly and put it in my own pocket, nervous now that Delia would claim her bag before I could replace the letter. "So, genius," he said, "I hear you have time on your hands and need money."

Wow. Euro-subtlety there.

"Thanks, Delia," I said. "Maybe I should get a business card."

My sister took her phone back and wandered away from us. I pretended to be helpful, grabbing her bag for her, and slipped the paper back in when Roger turned to look in the direction she'd gone.

"I was joking," he said, half looking at me, half ignoring me. "You know, but really . . . you are not so different from these Manson girls. You steal money, take a plane, head out for California."

He handed me a worn copy of *Helter Skelter*, and then looked at me like he was waiting for a thank-you. Delia had wandered over to the water towers and was covering her phone with her hand while she texted—like anyone was looking.

"So what's your point?"

"I think you know my point."

My mouth felt dry, and as I looked at the ice-blue rings of his irises, it was like Roger was trying to work some mind-voodoo on me, to make me as blindly obedient to his so-called vision as my sister was. I might have borrowed a credit card number, but that did not make me a Manson girl. Not even kind of.

"You forgot the murdering-pregnant-women part," I said.

Roger waved me off, slipping further into his genius-at-work mode. Or just being his usual rude self. A rat bolted past us from beneath one of the water towers, and before I could react, Roger kicked it out of the way like he'd been kicking rats his whole life.

"I will pay you. You read about these girls for me. I am interested in how you see them, how they feel to you. Maybe you will let me know what was in their hearts. Or you make another one up, create a history."

"I don't want to read about murders," I said, trying to keep track of where the rat had disappeared into the shadows. A total lie. What I meant was: *I don't want to read about murders and then have to talk to you about them.* "And I don't see how I'm supposed to figure out what's in their hearts. That's just weird."

"Suit yourself. But I will pay you ten dollars an hour for research. You keep the billing."

"You can buy your own breakfast," Delia said, suddenly ten feet closer and stupidly cheerful. "Besides, last I checked, you love things that are graphic and disgusting. You seemed excited enough to hang out on the zombie set."

"That's because zombies are absurd. I'll bet no one on the zombie set accuses me of being a zombie."

For the second time since I'd left for California, I thought about Leslie Van Houten and how she'd started out a nice person, how something in the desert air outside Los Angeles had changed her.

"Oh for God's sake, Anna. Roger isn't saying you're some kind of cultish drone; you can stop being so melodramatic. And if you can't stand to hear what you did simply put, maybe you should think about behaving differently."

I hate, hate, hated when my sister tried to tell me what to do, like she was so perfect. I should have told Delia what she looked like from the cheap seats, but then she was already getting letters on her door with the same information, so what was the point?

Roger just smirked.

"*Bisous*," my sister said, kissing Roger on both cheeks.

"*Bisous*." He all but tongued her cheek.

They were gross. Whoever this Dex guy was, I already felt sorry for him. We took the stairs and then the elevator back to the lobby in silence.

3

The next morning, my sister let me use her phone to call Doon. Delia pretended to water her one sad plant for about fifteen minutes so that she could listen in, but being monitored was better than not getting to talk at all. I needed my cell phone situation remedied in the very, *very* near future.

"I have a hit out on you," Doon said. "You picked the worst week of my life to run away. I think my parents are shopping for bars for my windows. My mom just threatened to ground me until you get back from California. You *are* coming back, right?"

Doon was eating cereal. I could tell because she kept slurping between sentences, and whenever she and her parents were fighting she'd eat ten bowls of Corn Flakes at a time.

"I guess," I said. "It's that or move in with my lunatic sister forever."

I was a little nervous that Doon wasn't telling me something, that she'd been dead serious when she joked that I was a "traitor" the other night. A few weeks ago, I'd taken the fall for a bunch of texts that the two of us had sent together, texts that had been Doon's idea to begin with. Sending anonymous messages was the kind of thing that didn't seem so terrible at the time, but made my mom grow another head when she read what we'd written. On the scale of terrible things, if a one was sticking your tongue out at someone and a ten was flying a plane into a building, I think that what we wrote rated a 1.5. Maybe a two. But to my mom it was like an eleven. She waved a stack of printed-out messages in her hand and practically wailed at me, "How could you have such cruelty in you?" Like it was even my fault! If I'd really broken it down for her, all I'd done was let Doon use my phone to send maybe fifty words and a couple of pictures to one of the most popular girls in my school, Paige Parker, because Doon swore she knew a code where they couldn't trace your phone. Which, as it turned out, she didn't. If Doon hadn't spent half her life with her phone privileges revoked, it wouldn't have even been an issue.

"What is this?" my mom asked, pointing to the picture on top of the second page.

"A dog eating its poop?" I said. Underneath was written "TASTES LIKE PAIGE, YUMMMMM," and even though it was stupid and I was supposed to act like I felt terrible about it, the gleeful look on the dog's face cracked me up every time.

"You think this is *funny*? I don't even know you, Anna."

Maybe it would have been mean if Paige Parker were some kind of social leper, but she wasn't. Paige Parker could have had any guy she looked cross-eyed at, and she certainly got more than her share of invitations to slumber parties and dances. Yet somehow from my mom's point of view, Paige had become this tragic victim of her daughter the bully. I tried to tell her that my bullying Paige Parker would be kind of like a minnow eating a whale, but she wasn't having any of it. I guess that Paige's mom had some relative in law enforcement trace the texts back to my phone, and she called my mom in tears. Actual tears. I made the mistake of rolling my eyes when my mom told me that part.

"You don't seem to understand that she could get the police involved. I had to beg on your behalf. Do you know how that made me feel?"

I didn't answer. Who knew how anything made her feel? The whole thing was so much less of an issue than she was making it.

I had heard my mom talking to Lynette later about whether or not I was "you know, a sociopath," which I definitely wasn't. The one thing I couldn't tell them was that the whole stupid thing had been Doon's idea, not mine. Besides, Paige Parker was beautiful and popular and I was positive she didn't care what I thought about her, if she even knew who I was. Maybe her mom had been crying about the texts, but my guess was that Paige hadn't even read them. I tried to explain that much to my mom and asked her why she always rooted against me, but she went in her bedroom and closed the door while I was still talking. Like rude didn't count when it came from her.

"I texted you about a thousand pictures," Doon was saying. I'd missed whatever she said before that. "My hair is white now. I hope it doesn't fall out."

"I didn't get them."

"Are the guys a million times better-looking out there?" she asked. "I can't believe you left without telling me. And what gives with your phone?"

For a minute Doon was quiet and I could hear her typing. She liked to check e-mail while she was on the phone.

"Did they ask?" She hesitated. "About the texts?"

"They didn't ask about you," I said, because I knew that was what she meant, and for a minute it made me angry. "I wouldn't tell them if they did."

"Thanks," she said, but I couldn't tell from her phone voice how much she meant it. "I almost forgot, your moms were at the Kroger with Birch yesterday. They pretended like they didn't see me but I think they did. They were in the baby aisle, and they actually seemed kind of happy." I didn't say anything, and after a few seconds she said, "I mean, not really happy. I think they were probably trying to fake me out."

I couldn't tell whether Doon was trying to hurt my feelings or not, but when she said that my mom looked happy, I almost started to cry.

"My sister needs her phone," I said.

I felt a little queasy after the call, not better, not the way I'd thought I would feel. Delia had mercy and took her phone back without asking me any questions.

The rest of the week we were on the set of the zombie movie that was, according to my sister, paying her rent. The movie set for that film was real, not like Roger's sketchball, faux-indie home movie. Filming was like I had imagined it would be, from watching TV and reading magazines, only there was a lot more sitting around and waiting, and all the food on the fancy tables was bulk-food sad and stale. And the actors were short. There was one guy who I guess was kind of famous on a cable TV show, and his face was handsome, but it was like they made him in miniature, so I just couldn't see how people would get excited about him if they knew the truth—that he stood on a box for his love scenes with my sister. Sometimes, when it seemed like everyone was so busy-busy that I had literally become invisible, I would look at the whole mess of them and pretend they were telemarketers or dental assistants, and then it would crack me up—everyone walking around spewing fake blood and staring at their phones like they weren't just going to work with the rest of the world.

When we went home at night my sister would learn her lines for the next day, and the calls with my mother would start. *I can't even talk to you. You have no idea how much you scared me. How are we going to get you home? I can't just leave Birch, and I don't want you traveling alone again. How can I trust you to get on the right plane? Where would you end up next?* Like I was baggage just begging to be lost. *Do you know my milk almost dried up when I thought you were gone?*

Oooohmigod, I had to hand it to my mother, she could even make running away totally disgusting. *I expect you're spending your time away figuring out how you're going to pay Lynette back. You have to learn to think about someone other than yourself.* That was a little too "pot-kettle," as my grandmother used to say, but mostly she just yelled at me until she got tired and asked if I had anything to say, which I really didn't, except that I wasn't sure how I was going to pay the money back, which she said didn't count as an apology and just got mad again. Yesterday, I had asked her how Birch was doing and she calmed down a little bit and put him on the phone, but then he disconnected.

Aside from the call to Doon, Delia was being a real monster about letting me use her phone—even though she couldn't use it herself when she was filming. After the first day on set, the zombie film had lost its charm. My sister was right about the dialogue being idiotic. It was almost like the director had decided that if he filmed every scene at least twenty times, the words coming out of the actors' mouths might magically become interesting. Wrong. So I started to read the book that Roger had given me.

I found a relatively quiet place near the food table and cracked *Helter Skelter* open to the pictures in the middle: mug shot after mug shot of Charles Manson, lined up beside each other to show how he'd changed with each passing term in jail. The pictures reminded me of when parents lined up school pictures to show how their toothless second grader gradually became their peroxide-at-the-beach ninth grader. Over the years, the short-haired, clean-cut con man of the 1950s became the dead-eyed, swastika-tattooed, homicidal maniac of the sixties. There were also pictures of bad furniture, the rooms where the victims were murdered, and the various household objects that had been used against them: electric cords, beams in the ceilings, roasting forks from family dinners. The bodies were whited out, almost like after they were murdered they'd been erased from the scene.

And then there were the girls: long-haired and without makeup, looking like they all knew some juicy secret that they weren't going to tell you. A group shot of five of them talking intently, heads shaved, worried brows, like they were getting ready to go on a cancer walk, not waiting to be sentenced to death. It was hard to believe that crimes that horrible had actually happened, in regular living rooms on regular evenings. Manson's battalion of zombie-bimbos were the kind of slow-moving death that scared me more than any dumb Hollywood movie. If you wanted a go-to for "At least he's not . . ." and Hitler was taken, Manson was a pretty safe second choice.

I'd been reading for three hours, which meant thirty dollars. I would have to read for fifty hours to make back the plane ticket, and fifty more to get home to Atlanta again. Or maybe I'd be like some sleazy lawyer and start charging Roger for whenever I thought about the Manson family. I mentally gave myself five extra dollars for having to read about the murders twice, just to get the details straight.

On the night of August 8, 1969, Charles Manson sent Charles "Tex" Watson and three of the Manson girls, including head psycho Susan Atkins, to 10050 Cielo Drive with instructions to murder everyone inside in the most gruesome way possible. They killed five people, including the eight-and-a-half-months-pregnant actress Sharon Tate. But the murders didn't stop with Tate.

The next night, six more of his "family" members killed a married couple, the LaBiancas, in basically the same way but in a different part of Los Angeles. The killers even showered and changed into new clothes from the victims' closets at the crime scene. Then they hitchhiked back to the Manson compound and treated the person who drove them home to breakfast. The whole city of Los Angeles locked its doors, bought guns and guard dogs, and started concocting theories about orgies in the Hollywood Hills and roaming bands of Satanists. Everyone panicked. And those weren't even the only murders Manson was responsible for. Evidently there were plenty more, bodies in the desert never found, close friends who couldn't cough up money on demand. He sat around this abandoned film set, baking in the sun, like some psychopathic film director yelling "Do this!" and "Go there!" to dozens of hippies who seemed to think that they were making the world a better place by slicing off ears, gutting women, or just sleeping with the latest hitchhiker who stumbled by. Susan Atkins, the woman who helped kill Tate, said that it took "a whole lot of love to kill someone." Bat. Shit. Crazy. They left forks in the stomachs of the LaBiancas and on the walls of both crime scenes they wrote in their victims' blood.

Pig.

Healter Skelter.

Rise.

Death to Pigs.

And carved in the stomach of the last of the victims: *War.*

Healter Skelter, misspelled, made me think of the chicken scratch in my sister's purse: *Whore.*

When Delia put a hand on my shoulder, I jumped. The book was making me more nervous than I'd expected. Then when I looked at her face, I almost had a full-on freak-out. When I'd last seen her she'd had on her pre-zombie-apocalypse makeup, but now blood was trickling down her cheek and her left eye was completely black. A bruise that looked like a hand-print wrapped purple-blue around her neck.

"I know," she said. "The makeup artist is a genius, right?"

That was one word for it. Fingernail marks dotted her collarbone, and when she smiled two of her teeth had been painted gray. Another three had been blacked out entirely.

"Dare me to drive home with this on?"

I thought about the Manson family, driving around with blood on their hands, and how in Hollywood, you couldn't tell the killers from the actors. If there was a stranger place on earth, I didn't know where.

"Sure," I said. "Why not?"

When we came home from the set a miracle had taken place— my phone, which I had almost given up for dead, was plugged in and ringing.

"You going to answer that?" Delia asked.

I picked the phone up and looked at the number. Atlanta. My mom.

"I don't want to," I said.

"Well, if you want to keep the phone, I suggest you answer."

"Do you know something I don't know?"

"Of course I do. Now pick it up before it goes to voice mail."

It's terrible having an actress for a sister: traitor. Mental note made and filed.

When I answered the phone, it wasn't my mother's voice that I heard, but Lynette's. I hadn't talked to Lynette since I landed in LA, but it was her credit card that I used. I was guessing she took that personally. I would have.

"Hi, Anna," she said. Awkward.

"Hey, Lynette."

"I've gotta get the zombie off," my sister said, popping a black cap off her front tooth, and before I could figure out a way to make her stay, she was in the other room.

"Well," she said, "I can tell by talking to your mother that you have no idea what you've put us through on this end." Then she stopped, inhaled (long and loud), exhaled (longer and louder), and started again. "Sorry, that's not how I wanted to start this conversation. I'm glad that nothing happened to you. We both are. I want to say first, before we get into anything else, that I don't think the way your mother handled things, changing your school and all, was the best idea." She paused again, and I put the phone on speaker.

"When all of this happened," she said, "I tried to put my-self in your shoes. Your mother said that it didn't go well when she and your father talked to you, and I realized that I never got to say anything myself, and most of the time, we're so busy with Birch or work that we don't hear what you have to say. I think you know what questions I might have, so I won't patronize you."

Then she stopped. It was my turn, but I didn't want to talk. It didn't have anything to do with her, and I knew that she was being nice. If I'd had any sense I would have Googled "How to sound sincere when apologizing," but I hadn't, and it was too late.

"Okay then," she said. "I considered just letting the money go, but since you're almost sixteen I think that it's important that we take this seriously. I'm not going to lecture you about what you should and shouldn't have done, but the money needs to be repaid. With slight interest."

I wondered what she was doing on the other end of the line. Smiling? Waiting for me to tell her what an awesome per-son she was for wanting to turn me into a financially responsi-ble adult? She could wait forever.

"Here is what we decided. You're ahead on your studies, and it's almost summer, so we're going to let you stay with your sister until you've earned the money to pay me back and for a return ticket. You need to be back by the end of the sum-mer. This isn't a joke and it's not a vacation. We checked and saw that there are jobs you can do if you have a permit, and your sister has been kind enough to say that she'll help as much as she can with finding a job and transportation."

I was going to get to stay in LA! I bit my cheek so that I wouldn't sound as happy as I felt.

"Was this Mom's idea?" I asked.

"It was mine," Lynette said. "But that's not all. You can test out of your science and math classes, but your history teacher wants you to do a final project. He's going to be sending you an e-mail with details. Your teachers were all quite understanding. I hope you realize that you'll be missing all the end-of-year activities, the chance to say good-bye to your friends."

I was already thinking of the places that I would apply for jobs, maybe the candy store near the lot where my sister was filming. Or one of the ice cream stores with the trendy names and all the girls in line who looked like they kept that ice cream down for about 2.5 seconds. If Mom and Lynette thought missing some picnic at the aquarium was a punishment, they had read the wrong piece of Internet wisdom.

"And you can decide how you want to communicate with Birch."

You wouldn't think it was possible, but I'd really forgotten about not seeing Birch for three months. He was just learning to pull himself up on furniture when I left, and he could make baby sign language for "finished" and "more." He even called me "Na Na" when he really wanted my keys or to go through my wallet. He would probably start walking this summer.

"Do you think he'll remember me?"

Lynette let out a long sigh, like I was beyond hopeless, and I felt for a minute like I really was going to cry.

"Why didn't Mom call today?"

"Your mom has her own struggles," she said, but I didn't see my mom struggling. Instead, I saw her walking down the frozen food aisle with Birch and Lynette, having a grand old time and trying to forget that she even had a daughter. All the while, Lynette was blathering on about how much my mother loved me, and how she wasn't very good at expressing it, and how worried she had been. But I knew what Doon had seen— three people who did just fine on their own.

"It's a complicated thing," Lynette finally said, "the way mothers love their daughters. You don't understand it now, and I know it's not helpful when an adult says something like that, but one day you'll see. The way you feel about Birch is the way your mother feels about you, only she's had thirteen more years to know you and hope for you and love you."

Sometimes when Birch was doing something accidentally hilarious like trying to eat a shoestring, I'd ask my mom what I was like when I was his age. She told me that she wrote everything down in my baby book, but I wanted to hear what she remembered. *Well,* she said, *You were terribly smart. We could tell that from day one. And we could always see what you were thinking. Your eyes would get wider and brighter and you'd lunge for something, or start dancing like a lunatic, and your father and I would laugh and laugh and laugh.*

I could sort of see myself being like that, but the thing I couldn't picture was my mom and dad laughing like she said they did. It was like someone telling you about a trip they had taken, somewhere far away and fabulous, only when you went to visit it yourself the weather was lousy and all the good places were closed. I thought about the movie my sister was working on, and how it sometimes felt like my life was the transplanted part of everyone else's life. Something that could be cut out, or grafted on, but didn't really serve a purpose on its own.

"It's not the five hundred dollars, is it?" I finally said.

Lynette was silent for a long time. I listened to her take a deep breath.

"If you need to come home," she said, "just let us know."

Five minutes ago I'd wanted nothing more than to stay in LA all summer, but the longer I talked to Lynette, the less it felt like paradise. What I wanted, maybe, was for home to be real, for it to be as easy as taking a plane ride home to make anything better. But it wasn't, and I think we both knew it.

"Okay," I said. "Can I send Birch pictures?"

"Of course. Send him anything you want."

After I got off the phone, it was still working but I didn't feel like calling anyone. I didn't feel like doing much of anything except for staring out my sister's big open window and wishing there were someplace out there for me to land.

4

A garbage truck outside the bedroom window woke me up at six forty-five. My sister was already in the shower, and it was good to know there were signs of life on the roads other than stalkers leaving late-night messages. All the houses on my sister's street had high fences and thick trees, protecting private pools and tennis courts. Cars cruised the streets but half the homes seemed like the lights were on timers, the garages closed for the season. It was beautiful, but it wasn't neighborly.

I checked my e-mail and found the note from my history teacher that Lynette had told me was coming. Mr. Haygood was about a million years old, and he taught the one elective that I was allowed to choose—History and Culture, an excuse to read books, watch movies, and talk about America. He was bald and always wore polo shirts where you could see his outie of a belly button poking through, but he made history a thousand times less boring than in a regular class. When we studied the 1920s, he pretended that cell phones were illegal and made half the class narcs, and then he had us read *The Great Gatsby*. We spent most of the year talking about things like the Red Scare and the American dream, and whether or not America's really that great after all. Doon's dad said all the teachers at my school are communists. Delia, who had Mr. Haygood when she was in school, said he was an "acid casualty."

At first I thought that there was nothing attached to the e-mail he had sent, a mistake or an academic get-out-of-jail-free card. But then I saw there were two sentences: *Talk to me about something in the last fifty years that really changed America.* Duh, that was too easy. Hello, 9/11. Then after that he'd written, *And while you're at it, what's so great about Los Angeles?* This is why I didn't want to leave my old school, because Mr. Haygood wasn't afraid to ask a question that a person might actually enjoy answering.

Mr. Haygood said that we shouldn't be afraid of ideas or words or things that challenged us—not in movies or in the news or in school. When we finished *The Great Gatsby,* the last day of class, he asked, all sly and crafty, "While we're on the topic of all things prohibited: Is there any chance that Nick Carraway was in love with Gatsby?" You could practically hear half the class snickering, not that it was funny. I technically had two moms, and I could have told all of them that it wasn't exactly stand-up comedy. But Mr. Haygood waited the laughter out, and by the end we wondered if maybe he wasn't right. Gatsby sure was more interesting than Daisy, or that weird golf pro who was always lounging around and passing herself off as a love interest.

There were no classes like Mr. Haygood's at Doon's school, the school where I was headed in the fall since my parents had decided that sending me to private school was a waste of their ever-evaporating money. I knew what Doon read in her classes—boring books approved by the state of Georgia. She was always telling me about some book that got banned because a parent thought it was a scandal to read the word "damn" or "booger" or something stupid like that. All that was left in the library, Doon claimed, was young-adult lit as written by Barney the Dinosaur. No thank you. And there was no way they talked about which team Gatsby was batting for. Not on this earth.

"Worry about that later," my sister said, pointing at the door. "Move. Now."

Her boyfriend was back in town, and she was all hot and bothered.

Overnight, the BMW had vanished and the Jetta that my mom had sold my sister after Birch was born had materialized in the driveway. Delia didn't say anything about the switch, so I didn't ask. The inside of the Jetta reeked of cigarettes. Delia spritzed on some perfume that smelled like window cleaner, shook her hair out of the ponytail, and reapplied the plum lipstick that she had wiped off for the shoot with Roger that had evidently taken place before I even woke up. My sister may not have been a zombie, but she definitely didn't sleep.

"I think you should take Roger up on his offer," she said.

"Really, because I think you should stop taking Roger up on his 'offers,' or whatever you two are calling that movie of his. He doesn't even know what he's shooting. Why would you do this? He's an idiot. Haven't you figured that out yet? He probably just *wishes* he were Charles Manson. Did you know that if a girl wore glasses, Manson would break them because he thought they should all be 'natural'? He wasn't just a psychopath, he was an asshole. Who cares why anyone wanted to listen to him?"

My sister broke it down for me like she was some mafia boss. "I'm not saying you should care about Charles Manson, I'm saying it's a good business opportunity. Do you know they've hired television writers as young as seventeen? It'll be a great credit for you when the film gets released. Roger is going places. We stopped sleeping together at least a year before we broke up, not that it's any of your business. He thinks he might like men. Okay? You happy now?"

I wanted to say "*Ewwwww*," not because of the men part, but because it was my sister and Roger and *ewwwwwwwwwww*. The thought of the two of them having sex was scarring, then I wondered if maybe she was just dating our mother, but in reverse, which was doubly scarring. Third-degree-psychic-trauma scarring.

"So if it's so innocent, why can't you tell your new boyfriend?"

"Dex? You don't know men at all, do you, Anna?"

"Am I supposed to?"

Delia's phone was ringing and she answered in a completely different voice from the one she'd been using. Good morning, sunshine.

"Hey, honey, yup, we're on our way. Okay, I'll pick some up but they're poison and you know it. Love you too." She clicked off. "Keep your eye out for Doughnut Dynasty; it's coming up on the right."

"Actual doughnuts? Fried with real sugar?"

"You'll like Dex. You both have the palate of five-year-olds."

We pulled into Doughnut Dynasty, and Delia ordered a half dozen of the daily selection at the drive-through: one pink coconut, two chocolate sprinkles, what looked like a jelly or custard, a caramel pecan, and a Nutella banana.

"I'm just gonna have a chocolate sprinkle," I said. "There are two of them."

"Want to rephrase that as a question?"

"No."

The minute I ate the doughnut, I wanted all five more. I wanted a dozen, all to myself, in some closet where I didn't have to hear about what they cost or how many empty calories they had in them.

"Ohmigod, please tell me you've at least tried these." I was shaking down the napkin for any sprinkles I might have missed. They were that delicious.

"Sugar makes my face swell."

"Sugar makes my face smile." I was practically salivating at the thought of chocolate. Since Birch was born, my mom didn't even notice if I ate brownies for breakfast. Maybe my sister was right, maybe I was a sugar junkie.

"And then you'll crash and complain about how tired you are all afternoon."

"Do you talk this way to Dex?"

"Dex lives on sugar." Delia honked at the too-slow driver in front of us. "He never crashes because he's completely addicted. Sugar is as toxic as any poison."

"It's not that toxic. I remember when you used to drink Mountain Dews on the way to drop me off at school. You weren't, like, dying or anything."

"But my skin was terrible. It's your body, Anna," she said. "And I'm only concerned because I want you to be your very best self while I'm at work."

"You're not taking me with you?"

"This week you're going to Dex's work."

"Okay, so pretend that I've forgotten everything you've told me about Dex. Who is he and what does he do again?"

"See, I knew you weren't listening. Was that so hard to admit?"

Yes, I thought, because it is a lie. I couldn't hear something she never said.

"Well, where to start—he's biracial, but probably whiter than I am."

While Delia was equal opportunity about the BMWs she would borrow, when it came to actual dating, frat-boy white was last year's color. In high school, she was strictly interested in black guys. She found the one Nigerian exchange student to take to prom. She once broke up with a perfectly nice biracial kid from the suburbs because he was "too white." I think Roger slipped in because he had an accent and wore eye makeup on a semi-regular basis. By sheer virtue of his awesome command of Euro-weird, she must have overlooked the pasty glow of his flesh. Never mind that she herself had a lack of pigment rivaled by the walking dead. If I could have rolled my eyes, *Exorcist*-style, into the back of my skull, I would have.

"But he can't be whiter than you because you're actually white."

"Ha-ha," she said. "You'll like him. He's a writer."

"Roger is a writer," I said.

"I know, I know," she said. "You hate Roger. But he's not a writer like Roger is a writer. He writes for *Chips Ahoy!*"

It is a miracle that I didn't spit my doughnut onto her dashboard.

"You mean *Chips Ahoy!* with the Taylor twins? Seriously?"

She nodded her head, and we both started laughing at the same time.

"That is the worst show in the history of the world," I said.

Chips Ahoy! with Josh and Jeremy Taylor was a show about two very rich teenagers named Dan and Mickey Chip. For unknown reasons, they're traveling the world on a yacht with their butler, trying to find their parents, who have been lost at sea. And somehow they've brought friends along. It might have been the single stupidest show in the history of television. I'll bet even six-year-olds across America have turned their televisions off in disgust.

"How is that show even on television?" I said. "And how did you meet this guy?"

"At a movie," she said. "And he knows the show is terrible. He's working on his own pilot. The show pays really well. He's actually quite funny."

This is where I can never really trust Delia. Because she would talk about Roger's student film, saying, "It's actually quite deep," when the only thing deep about Roger was his voice.

"Well his show isn't."

"Be polite," she said.

My sister made a sharp right into the garage of a cardboard box of a four-story condo building that took up the entire city block. After she parked, Delia grabbed the box of doughnuts, checked her makeup one more time in the car mirror, and directed me to walk at a clip toward the elevator. "And remember, if he asks about last week, there was no Roger. Got it?"

"And I'm the family asshole?"

"No one's an asshole, Anna."

We rode the elevator to the fourth floor and walked to the last apartment on the left, 427. The door was cracked and a television was on extra loud in the living room, running classic movies. Marilyn Monroe in her fat phase was leaning over some crazy-looking sailor and fogging up his glasses. And not watching TV, but leaning over the breakfast bar eating an extra-large bowl of Cap'n Crunch, was Dex, who looked less like an LA writer than any boyfriend my sister had ever had.

"Boo," my sister said, handing him the box of doughnuts.

"I missed you," he said, and slapped my sister's ass like they were in a relationship where she was capable of being fun. She moved his hand around her waist.

"This is my sister, Anna."

"Cool," he said, nodding his head. "How's it going, Anna?"

I shrugged my shoulders like I had never met a boy before, like I was an unsocialized troll straight from Middle-Earth. Dex was about eight million times better-looking that most of the men my sister dated. He had a close-cropped 'do, almost bald with just a shadow of hair, and he was tall. Taller than Delia in her stiletto boots, so I'd say six foot two, easy, and slim but muscular. He had one of those superhero square jaws, and light brown eyes, and when he smiled the left side of his face dimpled. His teeth were spaced a little bit apart in front, and he wore a "Too Many Rich Crackers" T-shirt, with a box of faux Ritz crackers on it. I could totally, totally, totally understand why *Chips Ahoy!* was not a factor in the dating decision. He could have written in crayons, and I would have been like, "Go, Delia!"

"So you're a writer?" I finally said.

"I am," he said. "I just got back from Hungary, helping a friend with a documentary he's doing on the local music scene. Flying back into LA, it's a different earth."

My sister leaned over his kitchen counter, running her fingers over the tops of the doughnuts.

"You know you want one," Dex said in a voice that was

probably reserved for when little sisters were out of the room. "Do it."

"Poison." She closed the top. "I can't even look at it."

Dex mouthed *She lies* at me and I whispered, "I know." If he only knew the half of it.

"They're starting the summer season of *Chips* this week, and Dex said you'll be fine on the set, better than watching me do my herpes audition." Delia smiled her most commercial, plastic smile and made a *Wheel of Fortune* swipe over her mouth and lady parts. "Herpes. It's not just for ugly people anymore."

"Is that what you're supposed to say?" Dex nearly spit out his doughnut. His third doughnut.

"Of course not, but they should, right? I think they need to rebrand the herp, not make prettier commercials for some drug. I mean, it's just mouth sores on your ass, right? There are worse things in the world. It needs a better name. You're the writer. Suggestions?"

"Ass pox?"

"At least that sounds edgy," Delia said. " 'Herpes' sounds like something a really dirty Muppet would get."

Around Dex, my sister was a little less fake, a little more like the Delia I grew up with, goofy, even. She said that she'd met him when they were both stuck in line waiting to see the opening of *Three Girls to the Left,* a gag-worthy romantic comedy about a sports reporter and a wannabe cheerleader who keep meeting each other at the same basketball games. I'm not even kidding. Delia had three lines as "Bitchy Cheerleader," and Dex had worked on one of the rewrites. They were both ashamed to be seeing the film in the first place, since the party line in LA is that no one ever watches their own stuff. I imagined them as two chimps who'd caught each other looking in the mirror and decided it was *awesome*. At any rate, Dex bought Delia some Twizzlers, and she knew she liked him because she ate half the pack, even though she made sure to let me know that she wound up with a stomachache later that night. All of this I had learned on the elevator ride to Dex's apartment, though she swore she'd told me before.

"Are we allowed to talk like this around your sister?"

"Please," Delia said. "She's fifteen. It's the new thirty-seven, in case you haven't kept up."

"I have *heard* of herpes." I tried to be deadpan, and got a real smile from Dex.

"Speaking of," she said. "Gotta get the children home."

"I don't wanna," I whined. "Please, can I stay with you guys? Please, please, please?"

"I lied. Fifteen is the new two and a half. I haven't seen my man in a month. Look homeward, little angel." She pointed toward the door and Dex didn't object.

"I'll see you tomorrow," Dex said. "We're gonna be running buddies this summer."

"But . . ."

Delia had already opened the door, but she waited for a moment. "But what?"

I wanted to say, *But what about the note?* What about the fact that you're going to leave me in some house where someone's branding you "Whore" in their shaky, serial-killer handwriting and taping it to your door? I am not a whore and would prefer not to be confused for one in your absence. I don't know how to tell a sex maniac *Sorry, come back later,* because I'm pretty sure that sex maniacs are kind of like impulse shoppers—in a pinch, they'll take whatever happens to be around.

But I wasn't supposed to have seen the note, and I would have bet real money that Dex wasn't supposed to know about it, so I was just going to have to double-lock the doors, sleep with a phone by my head, and accept my fate.

"But nothing," I said.

5

When we got back to Delia's house, my mom called. She still phoned me every night, mostly to remind me about something she'd left off her laundry list of complaints: to tell me that my dad was going to have my head when he got back from Mexico, to ask me if I had a job yet, to bore me with more Internet blather about the importance of taking responsibility for my actions. She always signed off by reminding me that I wasn't on vacation, that she hoped I knew that I still had a paper to write. I was ready to tell her that I was going to be researching the Manson murders instead of working on my project, just to see if I could hear her overheat from Atlanta, but her voice sounded tired when Delia handed me the phone.

"Is your sister there? Could you put me on speakerphone?"

My sister was walking around her apartment, stuffing clothes into a gym bag, makeup, underwear from her special sexy drawer.

"You want to listen to the sound of Delia getting ready to go screw her boyfriend?"

Delia threw a pair of underwear at my head. So gross.

"Please, Anna. This really isn't a good time."

"For me either."

I handed the phone to Delia, and after brief hellos, I could hear my mom take a deep breath from her bedroom. The air purifier rumbled in the background and Birch was saying, "Dis, dis, dis," over and over again. He must have been rummaging through her jewelry or tearing books off the wall.

"Okay," she said. "I want to start by saying that I don't want either of you to panic, because this is going to sound like bad news, but it's all going to be okay. A few weeks ago I had to go in for a mammogram, and they saw something that made them nervous. It should have made me nervous too, but I had other things on my mind."

My sister looked at me. I kept looking at the phone. My mom continued. "I truly didn't think anything of it, because I'm nursing and I've had clogged ducts before, but they wanted the area biopsied."

I watched my sister while we listened. She wrapped her arms around herself and rocked slowly back and forth, silent.

"And it's cancer. There's no other way to say it. But they caught it early, and it's very treatable. They won't know for sure how to proceed until they've removed what they found, but the doctor assured me that we'd caught it early and treatment would . . ." Her voice wavered. "It should work. I have surgery next week and then some chemo to follow up, and it should all be gone by the end of the summer."

After the word "cancer" it was like I didn't hear anything else she said. A low, radio-static buzz starting to build in the back of my head, and my mouth felt sticky and walled off.

"Oh my god," I said. "I want to come home. I can help with Birch."

"Anna," she said. Another long pause. Another deep breath.

"So what's the prognosis," my sister said, "long-term?"

"Long-term I should be great. I don't have the gene. There's no way of knowing why this happened, and I"—now she was starting to cry—"I'll feel okay when it's all taken care of. When they have it out. It's hard knowing this is inside of me."

For the first time, I hated myself for being so far away.

"And I've been able to breastfeed for over a year. I'm trying just to be grateful for that."

"What about me? Can I come back?"

"Anna," she said, and it was her no-nonsense voice all of a sudden. "I just—we don't know how cancer works. I don't know what caused this. I don't know what would make it come back or make it spread, but I do know that I can't have any more stress in my life than I already have."

"Uh-huh," I said. Delia was staring at the phone on the living room floor like how those priests in horror movies look at calm little girls who have the devil inside of them. Waiting.

"I just—" she said again. "I can't take the risk that having you here might make the cancer worse."

My sister looked like she'd swallowed poison.

"What?" I said. I couldn't speak. I couldn't catch my breath.

"That's it," Delia said. "Conversation over. I'm so sorry about your news, but we can talk about this tomorrow. Good night, Cora. And thanks for handling this in such an adult fashion.

She's not old enough to handle your bullshit, you get that, right? You get that you're the adult?"

One of them must have disconnected because my sister tossed the phone across the room and then picked up her gym bag and slammed it against the floor.

"Please don't be mad at me," I said.

"Oh, Anna. I'm not mad at you."

She sat down across from me and collapsed into herself. I tended to think of my sister as a big person—tall shoes, wide smile, loud voice. But she was probably a hundred pounds soaking wet, and she looked kind of like a pill bug on her sofa, rolling into herself, almost disappearing.

"Don't cry," Delia said. "Please don't let her make you cry. Please. It's not worth it. She's like a selfish two-year-old. With cancer, yes, but, Jesus, God Almighty, is it so hard, such a terrible challenge, for anyone in this family to be normal?"

"Do you think it's my fault?" I could barely even say the words.

I knew I wasn't a perfect kid. I probably should have helped more with Birch, or complained less about the school thing. I should have walked to the grocery for her when she was pregnant instead of pretending I had homework to do and texting with Doon. There were about a million things I would have done differently if I had known.

"That's not how cancer works," Delia said. "Not even in her faux-hippie universe, okay? And if she ever says something like that again, tell her you are going straight to your therapist and not speaking to her again until your therapist gives you permission."

"But I don't have a therapist."

"Anna. I hate to tell you this, but you're gonna need one." She laughed, and went across the room to the television, where she removed a small box of matches from beside one of the candles. From it, she removed the thinnest joint I have ever seen and looked at it like it was her oldest, dearest friend.

"This is just lazy-ass self-medication," she said. "And I don't recommend it."

"Can I have some?"

I'd had one puff of pot a year ago when Doon sneaked some from her brother's stash, and it just made my lungs burn. Nothing interesting happened. Either the pot was defective or I was.

"Not a chance," she said, holding smoke in her lungs while she choked out the words. "But I will let you in on a little family gossip."

"Can I at least have the last doughnut?"

"You can have ten more doughnuts. We'll drive there later."

She tossed a pillow onto the floor, sat down, and focused her eyes on the ceiling. Then she started talking to the ceiling.

"So I never told you this, but the first part I ever got in a movie, it was a Japanese horror flick called *St. Succubus*. It was pretty twisted, I guess—you know how when you're on a set sometimes you can be doing the grossest stuff, but instead of seeming gross it just seems silly or stupid? Anyhow, there was this scene where I went down on a guy and then later I ate his boiled penis like it was, I don't know, a suckling pig."

"Can we stream it?" The thought of my sister cooking a penis for dinner was actually cheering me up. I moved my hands in front of my face like I was two-fisting some imaginary dinner. Dick a l'Orange.

"No way. It's disgusting. And my acting is terrible. But it was my first role, so I was proud and all convinced that it was artistic, so I let Mom know that I had made a movie, and I kind of warned her about it, and I thought, stupidly, idiotically, flying in the face of everything I know about our mother, that she would be proud. Because it was a movie and I was her daughter, and I'd been paid to go to Japan and act and all of that. It was exciting. I thought it would be my breakthrough role, blah, blah, blah. So I called Cora about two weeks after it came out, to see if she and your dad had watched it, and you know what she says to me?"

I shook my head. My sister stopped looking at the ceiling and stared me dead in the face.

"She says, 'I can't have sex since I saw that movie. It's disgusting and it's made me realize that sex with men is violent and predatory. I'm not sure that I can ever have sex with any man again.'"

"Seriously?"

"Oh, I am the deadest of serious."

"So it's your fault Mom is a lesbian?"

"And her marriage ended. Something like that. I didn't

speak to her for, like, two years. She's incapable of taking responsibility for any of her actions. Incapable. You must promise me to never, ever, ever under any circumstance take anything she says personally. Ever. Please. I'm making like it was funny, but it wasn't. She's my mother. I was devastated. I wanted her to be proud of me. I wanted her to be my mom. I mean seriously, isn't it, like, rule number one of your marriage breaking up that you don't blame your children? Don't even psychopaths follow that rule?"

I shook my head. My sister had finished the joint and in spite of everything seemed to be in a considerably better mood.

"It helped me to think of her as 'Cora' after that, not 'Mom.' I don't know. Everyone is different, but it worked for me."

I always wondered why my sister called Mom "Cora." I assumed it was because they'd had such a sisterly bond that back in the day they just broke down that mom-daughter distinction and rambled around the Las Vegas strip, chugging margaritas and putting dollars in the Speedos of cheesy male strippers. I should have known it was because my mom was batshit crazy.

"So what are we going to do with you, Anna?" she said, looking at me like I was a picture that needed to be hung. Only my sister would get stoned and then want to start doing things. "I thought Cora would mellow out after two weeks and you'd be back in Atlanta, but now it looks like you're here for the haul."

"I thought I was supposed to earn my plane ticket back."

"Technically," she said. "But they really just wanted to make a point. We'd talked about two weeks and then home."

"You're such a liar. You were just lying to my face, right? This whole time."

"It wasn't a lie, it was a lack of plan."

"Right. And Roger is just shooting some stupid movie with you because he's all business and loves dudes. *Riiiiight*."

The room had slowly darkened as we were talking, and Delia finally turned on the lamp behind her. Her apartment was like a cave, always ten degrees colder than it needed to be. My sister had zero body fat, but she never seemed to reach for a sweater. I wrapped my feet in a baby-blue fleece blanket that I was starting to think of as my own, and Delia scrunched her nose and turned her face to the side because she hated bare feet on anything.

"You can think what you want, but we barely had sex when we were in a relationship. Roger just likes the idea of things he can't have. He might even be asexual. The important thing is the movie. He's already talking to possible distributors and if it's a hit for him, it's a hit for me."

"I thought you told me once there was no such thing as asexual. Just a train from straight to gay with a whole bunch of stops in between. How will you explain that to Dex?"

I already felt sorry for Dex. I liked him, but he was no match for my sister. He was probably raised by normal people, and we were clearly raised by wolves.

"Dex doesn't quiz me about how I spent my day. Why

don't you help Roger by actually doing that research? I can get Dex to load up his Kindle with Mansonian weirdness and you can figure out my character."

When she said "character" she got all dramatic, flourishing with one arm and pretending to smoke an imaginary cigarette.

"He doesn't even know what he's making the movie about."

"He's a very intuitive artist and, honestly, the strength of his work is usually in the image. I know he's half full of shit, but I respect his process. And he's not afraid to ask for help. I think he really values your opinion."

"Because he thinks I'm crazy and lost. Great."

I pulled the blanket over my shoulders and tucked the corners underneath me.

"Because he thinks you're young and impulsive and you care. As you get older, you just care less. Or you care differently. I don't know which, but it's different. Never underestimate the power of youth—not in Los Angeles, at any rate. You can never be too young or too dumb."

"I thought it was 'too rich or too thin.' "

"That's the East Coast. I'll text Dex. I know he has some extra readers from when they were trying to get the twins to sponsor some kind of literacy awareness month. Like they read."

On paper, you would think that I would like Roger more than Dex. Dex should have been the bigger loser with his sad apartment and weird job writing for a lame kids' show, but every time my sister mentioned Dex, I felt a little jealous. He was normal enough to have a *Peanuts* comic strip on his refrigerator door, the one where Lucy keeps moving the ball and Charlie Brown keeps kicking. What was it Marilyn Monroe had said in the movie Dex had on when we were leaving, when she was breaking down how no man was a match for her mighty and heaving boobs? *"He's a man, isn't he?"* It worked for my sister like that as well.

"Will you be okay here by yourself tonight?" Delia asked. "It's perfectly safe, just don't do anything stupid like unlock the door or go for a walk. Remember, in LA pedestrians are just roadkill waiting to happen. I'll be back in the morning first thing."

Lying again, but at least she was trying to keep me safe.

"Where are you going?"

"For doughnuts," she said, giving me a wink and perfectly perverted look.

"Gross," I said. "I'm your sister, remember?"

"I'm leaving you twenty bucks, and ordering a pizza on the way. So you can open the door for the pizza guy, but that's it."

"Pepperoni?"

"It's your body to pollute."

She closed the door and locked it behind her, and I was really alone for the first time since my plane had landed two weeks ago.

On any other evening, I probably couldn't have read about the Manson girls, not alone in that house in the Hollywood

Hills. But I needed something to quiet the *wah-wah-wah* noise in the back of my head that was fast becoming a roar, something awful enough to trump the sad. My sister was right, in that normally I did like to read about awful things: leprosy, serial killers, global warming, flesh-eating bacteria, inbred babies from rural incest cults, etc., etc. For a while I even had Doon convinced that the real zombie apocalypse was going to be caused by the rash of dead armadillos by the sides of the roads; they were everywhere and they could carry leprosy—disaster seemed inevitable. Maybe I was morbid because it was easy to be morbid in the comfort of my own room, where my mom, however annoying, would be there to open my door if I so much as raised my voice. My mom. Just thinking about her made my eyeballs feel like they were made of cement and sinking slowly into my brain.

Earlier in the day I'd been reading about Patricia Krenwinkel, the only one of the Manson girls to take part in both of the murders. She wasn't a very pretty girl. That doesn't sound like a nice thing to say about someone, or like being ugly should have mattered, except that because they were girls, it mattered big-time. Krenwinkel had a face that was more dude than lady, and a medical condition that caused extra hair to grow all over her body. From what I read, her parents just made matters worse, which was starting to seem like the reason God made parents, to put the cherry on top of a shit-sundae. Her folks split when she was seventeen and pretty soon after that she met Charles Manson, and she stepped right out of her life to follow him around. As in, she didn't even cash her last paycheck before she hit the road.

Another Manson girl, Mary Brunner, who was also technically the first Manson girl, had a witchy face as well. And it's not like either of those girls had crazy written all over them—what they had written all over them was ugly with a big, fat side of alone. I kept kicking the same idea around my head the way I did a face that I couldn't match to a name—that the people that these women killed were richer, more attractive, more hip. Insiders. The fact that all the books mentioned how they looked meant that their appearances mattered, but no one ever said why or how. Before the carnage began, Susan Atkins herself said about Tate and the others, "Wow, they sure are beautiful people." Whether that made the rest of the night easier or harder, she didn't say.

I guess that Charles Manson had figured out why pretty mattered. Because he called Patricia Krenwinkel beautiful, even kept the lights on when they did the nasty, she chased down Abigail Folger and stabbed her so hard that she broke her spine in half. The murder was so brutal that Abigail Folger, her white nightgown soaked red, pleaded with Krenwinkel, "Stop! Stop! I'm already dead."

Such a creepy and sad thing to say!

All that death over nothing.

I was trying not to think about my mom, but that was impossible. She was going to need chemo. She was going to lose her hair. She might lose both of her boobs. She was going to look sick and sad and not like herself, and there was a chance I wouldn't even recognize her by the time I got home. My eyes were watering and I knew that if I started crying I probably wouldn't stop.

Then I remembered the letter outside my sister's door, my *beautiful* sister's door. For a minute I thought about Paige Parker as well, with her perfect skin and giant boobs, about how much boys liked her and how much Doon hated her. My head started to pound harder and I closed my eyes to make the letters inside the envelope go away, to squeeze them out of my mind. They weren't written in blood, but they felt just as sinister, and my sister just dismissed them, like the maid who told Manson he had the wrong house the day before he sent his followers back to murder everyone. And now I was living with Delia. And my mother thought I was as toxic as any zombie hippie. And she was probably dying and just not telling me. I took two aspirin and waited to feel better, but I didn't.

My sister's windows opened onto the valley below, with nothing but a sheer metallic curtain to shut out the night. The view could be beautiful, when she lit candles and watched the moon, but there was no telling who was looking in. I hunched down further into the couch and covered my head with a blanket, peering at the chalk-black sky through a pocket of light like I had done when I was a little girl and scared of the dark.

I wondered if my mom was feeling bad about what she'd said to me, or if my sister cared that she'd driven off and left me here with nothing but a pizza box and plastic silverware for protection. The dogs a few doors down started barking wildly at something, and I repeated to myself, *It's probably a rabbit; it's probably a rabbit; it's probably a rabbit* until they quieted again. I closed my eyes to try to sleep, but instead I just heard my mom telling me that it was my fault she was sick, that I was carcinogenic: a human cigarette without a warning label.

Finally, I gave up trying to sleep and opened the book again, because the only thing harder to think about tonight than the women in the Manson family was the women in my own.

6

My mother left a long message in the night. I played it three times before my sister finally came home from Dex's place. *Anna, darling, I'm so sorry. I don't want you to ever think that you can't come home. I just think you'd have so much more fun there this summer, spending time with your sister. Birch is going to be in the day care at Lynette's work, and I want to rest, to really heal and recenter myself. There's so little time for that. I'd like for us to talk; we're so far from how I want us to be as a mother and a daughter. Maybe we could write letters, or e-mails, or something to get to know each other again. And then when we're both ready, we can be friends. I'd like this summer to be about healing for all of us. You can call me later if you like, and your dad is coming back from Mexico soon, so he should be in touch. I'm sure that he would let you stay with him if you like. I love you so much. I don't want you to forget that.*

That's my mom's favorite MO: punch you in the gut and then tell you that she loves you. It's almost worse than being a garden-variety psychopath, because on top of everything you walk around feeling like you can't tell what's true anymore. My mom probably should have been the one to move to Los Angeles. *We're so far from how I want us to be as a mother and a daughter.* She was like something out of a bad Tennessee Williams play.

We read *A Streetcar Named Desire* for English this past year, and there were times when my mom seriously reminded me of a dyked-out Blanche DuBois. And it's not because she's so southern, but because she likes the idea of things more than the actual things, and she can't own up to anything she's actually done. Once she told me: *You were such an easy baby, a joy until you turned five or so. Then I just lost track of you.* Poor Birch. I wondered if he'd have a longer shelf life, or if she'd turn on him too when he developed an actual personality.

As much as I did not identify with Patricia Krenwinkel, it made me think of how after she was arrested her family wanted to make it like she had this perfect home life, when her parents were both AWOL while she was getting tortured at school for being fat; how her folks separated and Patricia felt like it was her fault. No one seemed to care that she was drinking and smoking pot, or that she'd run away, until mass murder in the news made them look back. They were an *awesome* family, the Krenwinkels—all you had to do was ask them. Maybe that was part of the appeal of the Manson "family," not as a family, but as a myth of a family, a clown-collage of bad parenting and anger focused in all the wrong directions. And batshit crazy— it was every bad headline you ever read, supersize—something you could point to at the end of the day and say, *Well, I'm not that bad, my life couldn't suck that hard.*

I'd meant to check out front to see if anyone had come during the night, but my sister's keys rattled in the door first. She had a dead-bolt lock and one of those chains at the top of the door that I'd seen kicked through in 3.5 seconds in true crime reenactments. The security system in the apartment was defunct, though she still kept the sign for it outside her door. Last night I thought I'd heard a car driving past, idling, and I turned on a light and slept with the covers over my head. My sister's apartment faced a large, sloping hill, and since the curtains were practically see-through, I had tried to maneuver a sheet to cover the glass with little success. Anyone determined could still look inside. I couldn't imagine how that never bothered my sister, who seemed to think it was no big deal.

Delia said that if you looked carefully, up the hill, there was a house that flew a rainbow flag on Sundays because that was the day they filmed porn, and people wandered around naked talking on their cell phones and eating pizza. She said that as long as people could look out their windows and see something like that, whatever happened in her living room was snoozer central.

"How'd it go?" Delia asked. "Did the pizza come?"

"Do I have to stay here every night?"

"Why? Did you find a hotel you'd prefer?"

She went in the bathroom and half closed the door; the hum of her electric toothbrush made it hard to hear what she was saying. Something about how she was doing me a favor.

"No," I said. "It's just kind of creepy."

"Anna," she said, "Do you know how much it costs to live in this neighborhood? There's nothing creepy about it."

"Did you know that Charles Manson didn't even kill

anyone? And those people that got murdered lived in neighborhoods even nicer than this one."

She switched the toothbrush off and started running water.

"I did. Are you reading that book at night? Of course you can't sleep. Manson is day reading, okay? Read it when you're watching *Chips Ahoy!* shoot this afternoon, not when you're alone waiting for the pizza man. Sometimes I think you like to be miserable."

I wanted to ask her about our mom, about how sick she thought she really was and if I should call her back, but I didn't want to be shut down, and Delia looked like she was closed for the season, emotionally speaking. My sister could do that, be broken down one day and then look at you the next like you were delusional and had hallucinated the scene where she had acted like a human being.

"I don't like to be miserable." I took a piece of cold pizza from the refrigerator and gnawed on one petrified corner.

"There are bananas in the bag," she said, gesturing at her tote. "Dex is going to pick you up at eleven. Are you okay with that? Don't attack him with a hammer because you think he's going to kill you. And please don't mention anything about last night."

"You mean the pot?"

"I mean Cora."

"Okay," I said. The bananas Delia had bought were too green to eat, but she'd also picked up vanilla almond milk and a box of organic chocolate chip cookies. "Why don't you want him to know about Mom?"

"Because I don't like having to explain our family all the time." She had washed her face and was patting the skin dry. The words came out like an accusation, like she'd already had to pass off one crazy and wasn't in the mood to explain another. Evidently, according to my family, I was pretty much responsible for all the evil in the world. But wasn't the whole point of having a boyfriend that he would help you out when terrible things happen?

No wonder she and Cora hated each other. They were exactly the same. Neither one of them had ever found a situation good enough that they couldn't find a way to wreck it.

"Don't worry," I said. "I wouldn't want you to have to lie."

"Then I'm glad you understand."

We had a sister stare-off for a good thirty seconds, and then we both let it go.

My sister was auditioning for a reality show, the herpes commercial, and a bit part in a feature-length. Dex had agreed to take me to work with him all week, and Delia would meet up with us whenever her day ended. At first I wondered whether Dex was a secret perv, not that I was so hot or anything, but it seemed crazy to me that anyone would do as much for Delia as he seemed to be doing. But since I hadn't woken up drugged and in a second location, I figured that he must really like my sister. Way, *way* more than she deserved.

I liked Dex, because he never asked me what I was writing

about, or told me to get off the phone. At eleven he picked me up, then doughnuts, then *Chips*. I met Josh and Jeremy on the first day, and they were typical actors in that they were both shorter and more handsome than they looked on TV. Everyone on staff seemed to realize that *Chips Ahoy!* was like the chest acne of children's television, best covered up in the hope of growing out of it soon. I guess if you have sixteen-year-olds making a show where they are supposed to be twelve-year-olds and marketing it to six-year-olds, there's bound to be some major rolling of the eyes.

However stupid the show was, the set was impressive. All the action took place in one of three locations—the deck of the boat, the living quarters down below, or an ever-changing island location that was really just the same place, only they moved the palm trees around. The three spaces were always brightly lit when they were shooting, but the minute the lights went out everyone deserted the set for a winding maze of half-furnished rooms where they did table readings and played video games. When they weren't filming, I liked to walk around the set, trying out the chairs and sofas for size like I was Goldilocks. Sometimes I took pictures to send to Doon so that she could show them to Birch: me outside the building where they filmed, making wacky faces, a lizard that wandered inside, or the spread of cupcakes on the snack table.

One afternoon, when everyone was on a break, I was snooping around the *Chips* living room set. I sat on the rocking chair where the butler/steward napped while hijinks ensued, and there

was a lump under the pillow so big and uncomfortable that I
was sure I'd broken something. I put my hand under the cush-
ion and pulled out a rubber penis the size of a banana. I'd never
even seen a penis except when Doon and I would sneak-watch
the porno channels, and I couldn't help it, I threw it off the chair
like it was someone else's used tissue. It bounced three times
before landing next to Josh.

"What's wrong, you don't like Pinky?" he said, picking it
up and waving it between his legs. "Did you know that makes
you today's lucky winner?"

He'd never addressed me directly before, and it sounded
strange, to hear him talking about a fake penis like we'd known
each other forever. Like we knew each other at all.

"Of what?"

"I don't know. Nothing, really. We hide it somewhere
every episode to keep from dying of boredom. You find it, you
get to hide it next." He held it out and handed it to me like it
was no different from a deck of cards. I took it, to prove I could,
and tried not to look too hard at the details, the veins etched
across the outside and the dirty pink lines that marked the ridges.
I walked over to one of the bookshelves and placed it there
sideways and dick-end-out so it would look like a toy or a weird
bookend from the audience.

"Nice," Josh said. "You get extra points if the audience can
actually see it." Then he walked away like we'd been talking
about the weather.

From what I'd seen, Josh was the more chatty of the twins

and spent most of his day playing host to various hipsters who lounged around and smoked cigarettes when they weren't filming. I hated cigarette smoke, and hid out in one of the hallways when I wasn't with Dex or watching them shoot. Every once in a while, Jeremy would come into the hallway as well and play video games on his computer. He was quieter than Josh, and when I looked up he would smile at me and ask what I was reading, or how things were going.

The other day we'd had an actual conversation about LSD. I told him about something crazy I'd read that afternoon, about how in the fifties the United States government had allowed tests to take place on unsuspecting people where they gave them so much LSD that the drug completely erased all memories of their past. And not only that, the doctors then convinced one of the men that they'd brainwashed that they'd killed his mother, even though she was perfectly fine. *X-Files* crazy and totally true, and Jeremy said it figured that the government would do something like that. The LSD talk was the longest conversation I'd had with Jeremy, and I think I held up pretty well. I pretended not to notice that television did not even kind of do him justice, that no matter how much I made fun of *Chips Ahoy!* with Delia, part of me was stupidly, ridiculously happy that he was talking to me.

Technically, Josh was the better-looking of the twins—he was about a half inch taller, and his features were perfect. Jeremy had a sliver of a scar over his right eyebrow, and his skin broke out along his hairline from the makeup they wore—tiny flaws that were visible in person, but not on-screen. But Jeremy had the better voice, low and calm, and when he smiled he raised the eyebrow with the scar. By day three on the set, I had developed an embarrassing crush.

The twins were part of a Hollywood dynasty. They had just turned sixteen to little fanfare in March, I guess because with their fan base it paid to seem younger. I had thought they were twelve or thirteen, but I really didn't watch *Chips Ahoy!* Their mom was a famous groupie who had written a tell-all about all the men she'd slept with in the early nineties. Doon and I had passed her mom's old copy of the book around at the pool last summer because the sex scenes were pretty detailed. It was strange looking at the twins and thinking, *I have read about your mom's genital warts. I know which eight-thousand-year-old Rolling Stone your mom went down on. I am trying hard to forget that you were conceived in the back of a tour bus during an AIDS relief show.*

And they had an older sister, Olivia, who was the result of a fling with a Japanese rock star that ended in a house burning down. Olivia Taylor was so popular when I was in elementary school that Doon had two Olivia Taylor lunch boxes, and convinced her mom to buy tickets for every night of her show when she played Atlanta. Only last week, she'd been in the tabloids smoking pot and pulling her eyes into an over-the-top Asian slant, which she said was *not* racist, since she actually *was* half Japanese, but it still wasn't doing anything to bring her half-dead career back to life. The twins were the ones on the rise, and you could almost see in the pictures on the gossip sites how much she cared, that it was killing her to see these two little shits riding the wave of her success, cashing in while she was going broke.

"That's the funny thing about fame," my sister had said. "It's not like she's ugly. She's not even that terrible an actress, but you can feel that shift. Once that shift happens, you're fighting an epic uphill struggle. Epic. You need some director to make you his darling and save you from the feeding to the lions that's going to happen in the press. You can see it in her pictures, that she gets what's happening and doesn't know how to stop it. It's despair, but she's trying her damnedest not to let it show."

"She's just a fucked-up kid," Dex had said. "Plus, she has money, which makes her a monster. And I mean that in the nicest way possible."

I wasn't really prepared for the full Olivia Taylor–ness of Olivia Taylor. I don't know what might have prepared me. Definitely not the tooth-rotting sweetness of the film she did where she found out her dad was king of some anonymous European country and she had to rescue a dog and make nice with the local prince. For sure not "Nice Is Nice Too," the hit single that Doon and I made out to the one time we kissed. Positively not *Kandy Kisses,* the biopic that Doon and I had camped out to see when we were ten years old, *Kandy* necklaces around our necks. And not the recent gossip-site pics either, which had her looking like she could as easily be sliding into a body bag as passed out in the backseat of her ex-boyfriend's SUV, waxed lady parts on display like a naked Barbie doll.

In person, she seemed both bigger and smaller than she did in her pictures and videos. Her hair was wound through with silver ribbons and braided in four sections that went down the back of her head into one large ponytail. She wore tight black jeans with silver seams, a fuzzy white sweater, and high-heel wedge boots that came just above her knee. If I hadn't known she was Olivia Taylor when she walked in, I would have at least known that she wasn't regular—her clothes, her hair, her skinny-girl slouch—without her having to say a word, her whole being set her apart. And if Olivia Taylor's star was starting to fade, the last person to know about it seemed to be Olivia Taylor. Even the nerdy "I hate Hollywood" writers took notice when she stormed onto the set, interrupting the tail end of an all-staff Nintendo marathon.

"If you two rat-turds know who leaked those pics, you better let on, or someone's going to let the rest of the world know which of you ejaculates spends all his Disney money on porn so he doesn't look like the scared little virgin he actually is. And don't pretend not to look at me. Don't forget, I know where you live, you cuntresses."

The twins didn't even look up from the on-screen zombie massacre, but gave her an almost balletic, synchronized bird-flip. I don't think I'd ever heard a girl use the word "cunt," let alone find a way to make it seem like poetry.

"I have no friends," she said. "And not in the sad way. Until I find out how those pictures got out, every one of those whores is on house arrest."

"Boohoo." Joshua macheted three zombies. "If you screw up my high score I'm putting *you* on house arrest."

"You wait," she said, pushing a pair of oversize sunglasses atop her head. "You wait until no one gives a shit what rotted-out beach your tired asses wash up on, when you get stopped in the mall and someone says, 'Weren't you on that show *Nutter Butter*?' Because it's going to happen, and the only person left on planet Earth who'll suck you off will be some prison guard with basic cable who thinks fucking you will make the president love her."

It was like she was training for the Olympics of swearing.

"So you're the klepto?" she said, and it took me a minute to realize she was looking at me. I stood up a little straighter and tried to pretend like she was just another girl in my English class.

"I'm not a klepto," I said. "I was taking out a loan."

"Right. Here's a tip. Own it."

"She's fine," Josh said. "Not everyone is a psycho like you."

"Is that the best you can do? 'Psycho'? Maybe you should lay off the video games. So Anna—it is Anna, right? Since you're a professional, or a loan shark, or whatever you want to call it, would you like to come shopping with me?"

It sounded like a trick question. And she knew my name, which meant that the twins must have talked about me when I wasn't around. Crazy.

"I'm supposed to be on a spending fast," she said. "They're doing a feature for some no-name sad-teen magazine, and I'm going to write some sermon about how not spending has saved my soul and is better for the planet and all of that, only I hate, hate, hate not spending and there is no way any sane editor could expect me to weather this shit-storm without at least a new bag. You need money too, right? I'll pay you a hundred bucks. Finder's fee and hush money. If you so much as tweet it to your best friend, I will destroy you, okay?"

Like anyone would believe me. Even Doon would think that I was making this up.

Seeing Olivia Taylor made me realize that everyone my sister knows is only kind of famous. Partially famous, faded around the edges, and potentially forgettably famous. Even Delia, if she works every day for the rest of her life, will never be Olivia Taylor. Olivia Taylor has sold out stadiums. She was on my television five nights a week and again in the mornings as reruns. I am pretty sure I know her birthday as well as her favorite color.

"I can work a credit card," I said, giving her a smile like I could own the crazy when the time was right.

"Perfect. See you laze-balls later."

I should have checked with Dex first. Jeremy gave me a look like, "You're really going to just walk out the door with my insane sister?" And I tried to let him know, telepathically, *Yes, because it's going to be about a million times more interesting than walking out the door with my own insane sister.* "The devil you know" may be the saying, but crazy is always a million times more interesting when you're just getting introduced, shaking hands, and deciding whether or not you're going to give your real e-mail address.

Even exiting the building, a man who looked like he was casing the parking lot pulled out a camera and started snapping pictures. Pictures of me and Olivia Taylor. I could be the blacked-out square in a trashy magazine in a grocery store checkout line. The question mark over the head on a gossipy Web site. I had arrived.

"Good luck getting five dollars for that," she said. "Shit-sniffer."

The man made a motion like he was tipping his hat, then kissed the air at her.

"Disgusting," she said. "They won't be happy until I'm dead and they're first on the scene to take a picture."

She ushered me to an SUV the size of small house. I climbed into the passenger seat like I knew exactly what we were doing next, like driving around with movie stars was something I'd been doing my entire life. That I did not pee my pants was probably a miracle. Olivia's laptop was open on her seat, and she fired it up after she sat down. She handed it to me so that I could see the pictures that were so offensive—three shots of her passed out at a party next to a half-eaten birthday cake, with her basically nonexistent belly hanging ever so slightly over her too-tight snakeskin pants, and her head angled so that it looked like she had the tiniest of double chins.

"Who would do this?" she said, and pointed at the screen. "An asshole of biblical proportions, right? The party was totally closed. Now I have to go all Agatha Christie on my five best friends and my brothers to see who murdered my career. And look at that cake. Grocery store cake. Assholes."

So these were the pictures she was so angry about. Not ones that made her look like a druggie, or a racist, or a *naked* druggie-racist, but the ones that made her look just a little closer to regular. The only shock was that it really wasn't all that shocking.

"Maybe you can pretend they're not of you," I offered. "They don't really even look like you."

"Tell that to the next casting director running a Web search." She closed the computer and tossed it behind her, then started the car and drove us off the lot. I was thinking about how much it would have cost to replace the computer if it had missed the backseat, when I felt the craziest sensation, like heavy rainfall thumping up my arm—but without the rain. The feeling traveled from my right shoulder and onto my head, and I panicked. Something from the backseat was attacking me. I must have let out a totally for-real scream, because Olivia almost drove us into a streetlamp by the side of the road.

"Are you completely psycho?" she asked. What I could now see was a large green lizard had jumped from my head and onto her lap. "You're going to give Iggy a nervous breakdown."

"Iggy?" I said.

"It's okay, *Iggyyyyyy*." She kissed the lizard on the head. "This is Anna. She didn't mean to scare you." The lizard perched on her leg, and she stroked its head delicately. I checked the backseat for more reptiles and tried to quiet my heartbeat. Olivia pulled the car into a parking space marked "Employees Only" behind a strip mall, and tucked the lizard under her arm.

"You have a lizard," I said.

"An iguana," she corrected me. "Did you know they can live as long as people? And unlike people, they never, ever fuck you over." She gestured for me to get out of the car. "You do have a credit card, right?"

The way she was looking at me, I seriously thought that she might leave me in the car if I answered wrong.

I had a card from my dad, just for emergencies, and there was a good bet it was still working since I hadn't heard from him since he went to Mexico last month. I could hear his voice while Olivia was still talking: *I can't take the time I need to get away with Cindy? Not even a weekend? This is what happens? Why doesn't anyone tell me anything?* And then my mother, who'd probably look on this as an opportunity to remind him just how much he sucks at being a dad: *It's a month you've been gone, not a weekend. And you are still technically her father, so you could tear yourself away from your piña coladas,* blah, blah, blah.

"It's just for emergencies," I said.

"Well, this is an emergency." She'd led me to a hole-in-the-wall boutique with a thick glass door and spare, headless mannequins in the windows. "You'll buy with your credit card and I'll pay you back. It has to look like we're shopping for you." After we entered the store, one of the women who worked there locked the door behind us. Olivia put her lizard on the ground, and he ran underneath the sale rack. The normal rules no longer applied. We had entered a parallel universe where her arrival meant that some whole other secret set of rules went into effect: Iguanas, good. Other customers, bad.

The store walked the line between chic and totally destroyed, and the clothes looked like they could have been from Goodwill, if Goodwill charged a hundred and fifty bucks for a T-shirt.

"This would look amazing on you," she said, holding up what I thought was a shirt but soon realized was a dress. "You would look like someone deserving of a solid bang on the third date, am I right? I heard that southern girls were all sluts at heart. Back-door gals because the front's for Jesus or your husband or something."

She stopped short and looked at me. "You're not a virgin, are you?"

The salesgirl nearest me was trying not to laugh. It was so embarrassing to hear it, and in that exact moment, as I felt the heat spread like brush fire over my face, I hated Olivia Taylor. She was a horrible, horrible person. I hoped my credit card was declined. I hoped someone scanned her toxic-waste-heap of a brain and leaked that to the press.

She, on the other hand, had already moved on.

"This," she said, and handed me a duffel bag with a geometric pattern across the front, two large metallic straps that went over the shoulders. "This is the one you *have* to have. I told you it would be perfect. Flawless. Love, love, love it."

She wasn't even looking at me, or anyone else in the store when she talked, she was like a tornado, swirling and touching down, but it was becoming increasingly obvious to me that her movements were arbitrary, that I was nothing more than some trailer park she might destroy before disappearing back into the clouds.

"You have to buy it," she said. "I know it's just what your daddy would want you to have for your birthday. She's turning sixteen." She mangled "daddy" like it was the filthiest word in the English language, like she'd finally found something that caused her physical pain to say. The clerk pretended to care. She probably saw this kind of mania three times a day, seven days a week. I always thought that people in LA must be in awe of the fame, of the random interactions with the people you only saw on-screen. Now I could see that it was probably just exhausting.

I pulled out the credit card that I was supposed to use only for emergencies and bought a $498 green python bag. It was more than I'd ever spent on anything in my life, including the plane ticket before taxes. My hands shook as I forked over the card. I'd almost wished the card had been declined, but now that it had gone through, I had visions of my dad getting a call in Mexico that there was a strange charge from Los Angeles. They were probably alerting the credit card police even as the store clerk slipped the bag into a felt pouch, and then a larger bag, and handed me the package.

"Do you want the receipt or should I put it in the bag?"

I looked at Olivia, who was pulling her hair across her face and practically making out with her phone. She waved me off.

"I guess I'll take it," I said.

The clerk handed me the paper, and I half tried to pass the receipt to Olivia, who brushed me off again and kept talking. I put it in my purse, and got the weird feeling that I had done something very, very wrong.

I tried to ignore her, to figure out something to do with myself that didn't look sad and idiotic and alone. The iguana was running laps around the front counter, and the salesgirls had stopped smiling.

I stood by the still-locked door to the store as two girls in cutoff shorts tried to open it, failed, peered inside, and moved on.

Across the street, above a salon that advertised fifteen-dollar manicures, another billboard for *Volt* blocked the sun. The same blond actress in the same white tank top stood with her hands in front of her, balancing a stethoscope against a handgun. She was trying to look serious and sexy and smart all at once, but mostly she just looked as fake as her fluorescent-green eyes—like every other actress on every other billboard trying to look serious and sexy and smart. My sister said that the show was about a neurosurgeon who had been hit by light-ning as a child and could see the future when patients were dy-ing. She could decide whether it would be better if they lived or died. At least, that was what the show had been about when she read for it. By now, Delia said, the show might just as easily have been about a nurse with an electric vagina. Looking at the actress's face, it could have gone either way.

"Texting your friends?" Olivia said. "I'll bet you couldn't wait to tell them who you were shopping with. Did you send pictures?"

She took the phone from my hand, like she owned it, and read aloud, "'Out shopping with Olivia Taylor.' See? This is why I have to check everything. You can't make any money for that, you know."

"I left without telling anyone where I was going," I said. "It's to my sister."

"Of course it is."

She handed me the phone the same way she had taken it, like it was more hers than mine, like she was entitled to anything she could put her hands on, just because. As the salesgirl unlocked the front door, she gave me a "Good luck with that" kind of smile. I gave a "Pray for me" widening of the eyes in return.

On the way back to the set, I watched Olivia Taylor text with both hands and her elbows on the steering wheel, and tried not to think about the fact that she hadn't made any mention of the hundred dollars she'd promised me, let alone how to pay me back for the bag. And as we drove farther from the store, the prickly unease that I had been feeling became something hard and dark. I felt something that I'd only read about in books, the kind of cold that ices your insides when something terrible is just about to happen. I remembered a picture that Doon had said we should figure out how to send but never did, a fake selfie of Paige Parker with rope around her neck and whited-out eyeballs, and I wished that someone could have done the same to the so-called terrible pictures of Olivia Taylor. I knew that part of me wouldn't have cared at all if something really bad had happened to Olivia—worse, part of me wanted it to. And just for a second, maybe because it was California and you could understand how truly vomit-worthy fame could be only when you were right up next to it, I almost, kind of, understood what it might have been like to be a Manson girl.

7

I was starting to wonder what I was doing in Los Angeles. As Olivia cruised past yet another billboard for *Volt,* I almost longed for the weird billboards of the South. It seemed like anyone in Georgia could afford to take out roadside advertising, and once you got outside Atlanta there was always some crazy billboard that let you know that people were made by God, *not* from monkeys, or that *demanded* the president's birth certificate, or—my favorite—a six-year-old with a crossbow advertising the "kids' corner" of the local gun store. Doon and I would text pictures of the best ones to each other, daring each other to call the number on the anti-evolution billboard and ask whoever answered to explain the hair on her chest, or to take Birch to the gun store to see if there was anything for toddlers. I wouldn't have even bothered sending her the *Volt* pictures, they were such an obvious and boring kind of stupid.

Besides, Doon was writing me less and less. I guess she was irritated with me for leaving her stranded. And it wasn't just her. My mom was probably going to throw a party to celebrate her Anna-free life as soon as she started feeling better, my sister was constantly busy auditioning, and to the rest of planet California, I was all but invisible. Olivia dropped me

back at the *Chips Ahoy!* set where—shocker—no one had noticed that I was missing. Dex was in a writers' meeting, and
the twins were playing Texas Hold'em with a few of the extras. I perched on a couch end near the edge of the game, trying not to take up too much space.

"So how'd it go?" Josh asked without looking up from his
cards.

I didn't answer for a full minute because it hadn't dawned
on me I was supposed to field the question.

"Oh," I said. "I think I just bought your sister a purse."

"I thought you were broke." Josh still didn't look up, but
Jeremy did, probably long enough to see that I looked dazed,
like I'd been hexed by a very beautiful person who'd cast a spell
on me so that I handed over my father's credit card without so
much as a "Why?"

"I guess I'm even more broke."

Jeremy laughed a little, and then he said, "Consider yourself lucky. The last person she took shopping bought her a car."

"Seriously?"

He raised his arm like he was taking a Boy Scouts oath. It
was a gesture that the "Chips" made all the time on the show,
bleeding into real life or vice versa.

"She's a whore," Josh said, and Jeremy frowned like he was
going to contradict his brother, but didn't. I saw the same word
from the letter on my sister's door for a second and squeezed
my eyes to make it disappear.

"You know how to play?" Jeremy asked.

"Kind of," I lied. I knew how to play, and I knew the first rule of knowing how to play is pretending that you only kind of know how to play.

"I'll buy you in," Jeremy said. He tossed a fifty-dollar bill across the table to his brother, who handed me a stack of chips.

My mom was a pretty serious gambler back in the day. She made it to the final table at the World Series of Poker once, and we played poker growing up the way other kids played Old Maid. I didn't really think of myself as a competitive person, but the minute someone passed me two cards facedown, I became a shark.

"I know the rules," I said. "But do you have a cheat sheet for what beats what?"

I was the only girl at the table and I knew that they would humor me. They would be on the lookout from then on for beginner's luck, but I could tell that the "Ohmigod, like, is that a spade or a club?" angle was going to go far. The nice thing about poker is that lying isn't really lying in poker, it's just playing a game. If you let on that you're a shark, that doesn't make you a nice person, it makes you an idiot. There are some great female poker players, and they might have played with a few, but I knew they wouldn't expect it from me.

I bet like a total moron and played extra dumb for the first two hands.

"I'll help you if you want," Jeremy said.

"No help," Josh replied. "You bought her in. That's it."

I shrugged my shoulders and Jeremy gave me an "I tried"

kind of half smile in return. He had the same almost fluorescent-blue eyes that made Olivia's face so impossibly beautiful. Only his eyes were kinder, the eyes of a seer, not a judge. If I hadn't been in shark mode, I would have felt bad that I was about to take his fifty dollars.

I started to play a little more carefully, won a few hands, and then lost big. Really big. I had three kings, but Josh had a full house. It was a miracle hand; he had an ace and the other king in the hole, and he cleaned me out except for my last three chips. I was barely going to have enough to make the blind.

"Sorry," Josh said, but I could tell that he loved it, cleaning out the already cleaned-out girl across the table from him. I almost said, "Golly gee, shucks," just to be an asshole, but I still had three chips and a chance. And in poker you make your own fate. In the next hand, I doubled my pile and then a few hands later tripled it again. Nothing crazy, but by playing tight I was holding my own while still being able to look "lucky."

Jeremy was dealing and I got a pair of eights facedown. There was an eight on the flop and a pair of tens. It was almost a dream hand, and I knew it but couldn't let it show. The twins were watching me like a pair of falcons. I willed my hands not to shake.

I put in half the money that I had left, which would have cleaned out anyone but Josh. Jeremy folded and the other two extras folded as well. One of them was out, but I didn't even notice when he left.

"I'll call," Josh said, looking me straight in the eye,

gladiatorial. He pushed his chips into the pot. Jeremy turned an ace, and I could see Josh smile, just the tiniest curl at the corner of his mouth, and I could feel it, he had tens. He was going to beat me.

"All in," I said, pushing my chips into the center.

Josh could barely contain his glee.

"You know there's no insanity plea in poker, right?" he said.

"I know."

He pushed the rest of his chips into the pot.

And then I caught that last eight on the river. It wasn't just statistically unlikely, it was a damn miracle, up there with the wine and the fishes and feeding of the multitudes. I had been prepared to go down in a blaze of glory, but now I was going to win. I was going to win and it was going to look like dumb luck, so I did what only a true shark would do.

"Double or nothing?"

"It's not even your money," Josh said.

"This is hilarious." Jeremy slapped his hand on the table, delighted. Even the extras had stopped texting.

"You realize I'm going to destroy you," Josh said. "Is it possible you just like owing people money?"

"Double or nothing," I said. "I have a job. I'm good for it."

By then I had forgotten that they were television stars. Jeremy fished fifty more dollars out of his wallet and handed it to me. I put it on the table.

"It's your life," Josh said, and matched me. He rolled out his cards, exactly what I thought, full house, tens and eights.

"Is this better?" I asked in my most bullshit girl voice and laid my eights on the table.

"I love this girl," Jeremy practically yelled, and it made me remember that he was one of the two biggest teen stars in the country, one of whom had just declared his extremely exaggerated love, and the other of whom I had just cleaned out.

"You bitch," Josh said, turning the slur into a term of great respect. "That's impossible."

"Possible," Jeremy said. "Happened."

"Shut up, douche bag."

I tried not to gloat as I moved the pot in my direction.

"I gotta go," one of the extras said, pointing at his phone as if that explained everything.

"Cool, bro," Josh said. "Later?"

"Mos def."

They bumped fists, and then Josh excused himself.

"That was evil," he said, turning around and pointing a finger at me. "How long are you here, again?"

"Most of the summer," I said.

"Rematch. Beware and be ready. No cheat sheets next time."

I smiled and shrugged like I had no idea what he was talking about. Jeremy stayed behind and I gave him the two hundred and fifty dollars that I had won.

"Thanks for spotting me."

"Dude, I would have paid five hundred dollars to watch that beat-down. How long you been playing poker?"

"I don't know. Since I was born?"

Jeremy made a dramatic "Thank you, God" gesture at the ceiling, and handed the money back.

"You won it."

"But it's not mine."

"An honest thief," he said. "We'll split it."

He handed me $125. I would have framed the bills if I didn't already owe everyone I knew.

"So what are you doing here?" he asked. "Really. We know now that you're a card shark. Are you some kind of media plant, too? Writing a story about the 'troubled Taylors'?" He tucked his chin into his chest and used his best old-man newscaster voice when he mentioned his family, like he was trying to make them something imaginary, something he wasn't really a part of. I knew the feeling.

"God, no," I said. And I must have sounded shocked enough for him to believe that it was the truth. Had he really been thinking I was some kind of mole?

"But you are a writer, right? Are you working on a screenplay?"

In LA everyone was working on a screenplay, and in a way, I guess I was.

"Kind of. I'm helping"—I had to think about this one—"my sister's friend. I'm doing some research. And I have this paper I need to write for school."

"I figured," he said. "You're always reading."

He smiled and tilted his head to the right. As he pushed

his shirtsleeves up his arm, one at a time, for a minute I saw my life from a distance and I couldn't believe it was really mine. How could I have been missing Georgia? Nothing like this ever happened there—not in Atlanta. Not to me.

"I'm not *always* reading."

"You read a lot. What are you reading about now?"

"Cults," I said. "You know, the kind where there's someone in charge and people listen."

"Oh, I know about cults," Jeremy interrupted. "My mom was kind of in one when we were little. We lived on this farm in Pennsylvania when Josh and I were toddlers, and we weren't allowed to talk unless we were singing."

"You're making that up."

"Uh-uh. And Olivia was, like, five, and they made her dance with these crazy flowers in her hair, and they'd already picked out some old dude for her to marry. Only they didn't call her Olivia," he said, and then made a nonsensical sound that made it pretty clear that his career was going to stay in acting, not singing. "That was her name." He paused and then made another ear-splitting noise. "And that was mine. I still remember."

"Seriously?"

He started laughing.

"Nah," he said. "But I had you going, hustler. My mom did almost make us become Scientologists a few years ago. But my dad threatened to sue her for custody."

I'll be honest, I didn't think Jeremy was capable of making

a joke, not a real one, at any rate. My sister was pretty and funny when you got her going, but I always thought that really beautiful people were kind of like stuffed animals, like they sat in corners and didn't say much of anything, because people loved them anyhow. But Jeremy was actually funny.

"I gotta go," he said. "I want to read the screenplay sometime."

"Yes," I said, "definitely," and I tried to repeat the crazy noise that he'd made.

He gave me a high five, and headed for the parking lot.

I was $125 richer, but it felt like a million. Next time we went to the hippie grocery, I could spring for some serious organic chocolate. Jeremy Taylor had made conversation with me like I was his favorite person in the universe, at least for a minute. And while it felt great, all I could think about was whether or not I would look better if I took off my glasses, if there was some way to slide them over my head and show that, look, *just like the movies,* I was secretly a knockout underneath. Only I wasn't one of those movie characters who wears glasses and pretends to be ugly, I was just a regular person who probably didn't look all that different either way. Not that I would really know, because I couldn't even see my own face clearly without my specs. I never could get used to putting contact lenses on my eyeballs, so the whole instant makeover hadn't been an option.

Normally I didn't care because I'd never known any different. I started wearing glasses when I was three years old.

One afternoon my mom was playing with me, and my right eye just kind of rolled in toward my nose. Freaked her out. My parents took me to the doctor, scared that I had a tumor, but I had just started showing the signs of being as farsighted as I had probably been since birth. They got me glasses that were hip and cute, the kind adults like, but glasses are glasses. No kid has ever said: "Look at the hot new girl with the glasses. Maybe she'll have braces and a clubfoot, too!" I think it made me cautious about other kids, because I was always one screwup from becoming "Four Eyes" on the playground. Those were the facts, like a card hand that you couldn't fold. But beauty wasn't everything. I could still be the kind of girl who beat a table full of movie stars at poker. If I couldn't be dateable, I could at least be respected. I was like the lady Godfather of plain-girl self-awareness.

But in that exact moment, I wished I were just a tiny bit more lovely. I wanted Jeremy to cancel whatever plans he had for the rest of the evening so that we could go waste our winnings together. I wanted him to look at me the way men looked at Delia.

"You been sitting here this whole time?"

The writers' meeting must have ended. Dex slapped me on the shoulder.

"Kind of?"

"You disappeared for a while. Not gonna ask. So long as I bring you home in one piece. And don't let those players take you for all you're worth."

I gave him my most angelic, innocent look and said, "I'll be careful."

On our way home from the set, Dex and I usually ordered takeout or went through the cafeteria bar at one of the health food stores to make sure Delia was fed and watered when she got home. Whether she ate or not during the day was anyone's guess, but I'd have put my meager winnings on no. Dex would let me sit in the car and read, or text Doon, or write notes to Birch while he shopped. I was pretty deep into my research for Roger. Every night I sent Roger an e-mail about what I'd been reading, and he'd send back some one-word response like "Received." All warm and fuzzy. I wasn't sure he was even reading my reports, but I was keeping a log of every hour that I spent working on the project. Last time I checked he owed me two hundred bucks.

Since I couldn't pay for groceries with an IOU, Dex bought just about all the food. He never complained about springing for things, not like Delia, which should have made me feel like less of a mooch but did the opposite. Maybe he had signed up for one of those 1-800 numbers that came on late at night— his heart moved by pictures of starving actresses and their siblings. For thirty dollars a night, you could sponsor two ladies in Los Angeles. Before he braved the hippie grocery, I offered him some of the money I'd won. He waved me off like I was the crazy one.

While Dex was in the store, I read the last book Roger had given me and listened to an interview that Doon had downloaded where Karl Marx, the singer from Freekmonkee, was talking about LA. Karl Marx *liked* that LA was trashy around the edges. He said in a whisper-soft voice that LA was always pretending to be something better than it was, and that made it always the same. The music they were recording was about the emptiness in the air. The emptiness was inspiring. *Fill the void with the void.* At the end of the podcast he played a song they'd been working on, and it was so dark and beautiful that I closed my eyes and forgot for a minute that I was in a car in a grocery store parking lot. I hadn't understood everything he'd said in the interview, but when I listened hard, I could feel that space they wanted to fill.

"It's like the Hunger Games in there." Dex slammed the door behind him and grabbed the steering wheel with both hands. "I almost had to take down a grown-ass woman. In front of her child."

I started to laugh.

"I have three items, three dinners in the ten-or-less lane, and she's behind me with her kid and she gets mad at me that I don't let her go in front of me with her twelve items and nose-picking kid. What is wrong with people in this town? Riddle me that, grasshopper?"

"You should just start going to the normal supermarket. People are much nicer when they're buying Doritos. I have no medical or scientific explanation, but it's a fact."

"Let's exit this hell."

"Crappy food makes people nicer," I said. "I'm telling you."

I have never thought that hippies were nice. One afternoon in the Whole Foods parking lot and anyone can see that once the patchouli clears, those vegans would slice you for a parking space. Lynette, the world's biggest ex-hippie, was the one who made us get rid of our dog. As a newborn, Birch cried for four months straight—and he didn't exactly chill out so much as dial the volume down as he got older. He had slowly driven the poor dog psycho. Tarzan, our boxer, tried to rip a teething biscuit out of Birch's hands, and she growled, and it was scary. I offered to take care of her, but Lynette sent Tarzan away to my aunt's house anyway. The dog I'd had since I was seven.

My mom met Lynette at her grief group, after her first miscarriage, the one with my dad. I didn't even know she *was* grieving until my mom sat me and my dad down one afternoon and told us about Lynette, the person who had helped her reconnect with her true self. Note to ghost-of-self-past: if your mother starts talking to you about the fluid nature of attraction and the joy of finding out who she really is, you should probably start saving for a plane ticket west.

In the parking lot, while I was listening to Karl Marx, I'd been half reading about "Squeaky" Fromme. She was one of the most famous Manson girls even though she didn't take part in any of the Tate-LaBianca murders. Her real name was Lynette, which was crazy since I'd never met a Lynette other than my stepmom and I kind of thought it was one of those names that people just made up. The two Lynettes were nothing alike on the surface, but I couldn't help trying to line them up, see if anything other than their names matched. My mom's Lynette was like some kind of yuppie superhero: banker by day, hippie by night. She ate part of my mom's placenta after Birch was born, even though she didn't actually pass him through her lady parts. That was a health hazard of global proportions if you asked me.

The Manson girls were all in with the hippie lifestyle. They upcycled food from the local grocery stores' garbage bins, they breastfed in public, they made their own clothes (out of their own hair at times, which was weird, even for hippies). Squeaky Fromme was probably the biggest tree hugger of them all, and what did she wind up doing, you know, after the Tate case had died down and there hadn't been any massacres for a while? She decided to go and shoot the president.

Trying to assassinate the president should not be funny. It really shouldn't. It's not like I was cracking up when we read about Lincoln or JFK. But let's face it, they were real presidents. Gerald Ford ranks right up there with Millard Fillmore and Bush the First on the list of unexciting white men who have run this country, made their way into history books, and otherwise been human sleeping pills. If all the presidents had been television shows, Gerald Ford would probably have been a PBS fund drive. So I'd bet the fact that anyone would try to kill Gerald Ford, Gerald Rudolph Ford, was kind of hard to get excited about, even back in the day. And Fromme sounded like something out of Monty Python, dressed all in red with a sawed-off shotgun under her sister-wife dress and fake-nun robe, muttering "He is not a public servant" before *not* firing her gigantic gun at the president. "It didn't go off" was her great defense as the Secret Service took her out of commission in Sacramento. *Sic semper tyrannis* it was not.

Lynette told me once that I was "part of a generation of the historically illiterate" when I told her that I thought the sixties were ridiculous. Not the civil rights movement, or any of that, but the free love and bad hair and half-baked philosophies. *Look at me, I'm naked and having sex with everyone and getting stoned.* Groovy. "Hair was political," Lynette told me. "Love was political. People wanted to change the world. Of course you'd only see the surface; that's all your generation really sees. Maybe you've all been medicated past caring." Lynette could go on forever if you asked her to, about "the apathy of the young," not like she did anything for the earth besides recycle her plastics.

"You're terribly cynical for such a young person," Lynette told me a few months after she and my mom shacked up. I hated it when adults talked that way, looking at you like you're a charity case for not applauding every idiotic choice they made. She wanted me to be happy for her and my mom. Yay, divorce! Yay, midlife sexuality changes! I told her that by the time my mom reached her fifties they'll probably have figured out another way for her to have a fourth baby, so Lynette should probably have a backup plan before they started monogramming the towels. That wasn't cynicism; that was experience.

"I don't expect you to like me," she had said. "But I will ask that you respect me."

I decided to do neither, but had the sense to stop arguing.

Still, for as much as the two of them drove me crazy, sometimes, when I looked in the mirror, I worried that my mom and Lynette were rubbing off on me. Neither of them wore much makeup, and they tried not to shop at the mall. Lynette had a friend who spun her own wool and made sweaters, and they were super soft and comfortable, but they weren't exactly fashion-forward. Lynette probably would have made a good Manson girl. I could see her picking "perfectly good food" out of garbage bins and embroidering her own shirts, weaving fringe out of her stringy, unwashed hair.

If any of my clothes said "Made in China" on the tag, I got a lecture about the conditions of the kids who had to cut the patterns or work the sewing machines. And it was a tragedy, I got that, but lately when I looked at my wardrobe I wondered if that wasn't some kind of social injustice as well—a crime against what I could look like with normal moms. And since Jeremy Taylor had taken to asking me what I was reading, or how long I was staying this summer, I was starting to care. My jeans were the wrong length for what people were wearing, and when I cuffed them I just felt like Huckleberry Finn, some ragamuffin from the South slumming around the corners of the set. I wanted something tight and knee-length, like Delia was wearing, and some T-shirts that fit better. I probably needed a haircut, too, but since I couldn't really even afford new clothes, that was out of the question. I knew I'd never look like Delia, but if she took me shopping, there was a chance that I could be Delia-lite, the affordable model to her sports vehicle.

"Looks like Delia's home," Dex said. Her car was parked in Dex's other space, even though she was supposed to be gone until ten.

"Good," I said. "I need to talk to her about something."

And it wasn't the Manson girls.

8

When we got inside, Delia was already there looking like death's torn-up sister. Half of her face was bloody, and maggots that seemed almost three-dimensional were eating out the side of her jaw. I knew that Delia had been reshooting some scenes from the zombie flick, but usually she had washed and changed by the time I saw her. Evidently, the director had gotten food poisoning, so the actors went home early. She'd kept on the makeup because she said that it made drivers much, *much* nicer in traffic. The sickest part was, she looked an almost creepy kind of sexy—bugs and all.

"You look like you saw a ghost," she said to me, laughing.

It wasn't her nicest laugh. Technically, we were still in kind of a fight. The night before, she'd dropped me off at her place, which I was liking less and less by the evening. No more notes had been taped to the door, but I heard noises in the driveway at weird hours and the nights felt long and lonely. Delia said the noises were probably squirrels, or some dog loose in the neighborhood, but that's not how it sounded when there was no one else around. And last night, there had been a bona-fide knock at the door, then a louder knock, which I didn't answer because I could hear the woman outside saying, "I know you're in there."

Maybe pre—Manson project I would have considered cracking the door, but after what I had been reading, no way. So I hid, and the woman said louder, "I saw you in there. I saw you by the door." I almost cried, I was so scared. I talked myself through how I had double-locked all the doors, then I remembered that the doors of the Tate residence had been locked the night of the Manson murders, but they had left a window open to allow the newly painted nursery to dry. I prayed that there were no weak points in my little fortress and called Delia from the bathroom, trying not to breathe because I was sure psycholady could hear that through the door as well.

Delia came home and while I guess she wasn't evil about it, she wasn't exactly nice. She pointed out that there was a roaring party two houses down, and couldn't I hear the music or was I going deaf as well as crazy? She figured it was just a lost partier who got the address wrong, and yes, that was probably scary, but maybe not scary enough to interrupt her evening. But that's what they said about Manson as well, that the people he murdered just happened to be at the wrong address. I told her as much and she said I was being hysterical, and that if she didn't get some time alone with Dex she was going to lose her mind or at the very least, her relationship, so could I please be more considerate. I thought about mentioning the note I wasn't supposed to have read, but worried that she'd ship me back home, whether my mom wanted me or not. I told her that she would probably be making excuses for how safe her house was as they chalked my outline across her apartment floor. She stayed the rest of the night, but left before I was up the next morning. I hadn't seen her since.

"That makeup is freaky," I said. "I don't remember it being that gross before."

"It wasn't." She was quartering an apple and cutting out the core, the same way she'd always eaten apples. "I guess they've decided to go a little more oozing with the zombies. Our fearless 'director' "—she circled her fingers before landing the air quotes—"is panicking because people were laughing at the rough cut. I'll probably still be getting calls to reshoot when I'm old enough to need the organs myself."

"Good," Dex said, and kissed her on the gross side of her face. "Let him suffer. I haven't seen you in daylight in a week."

I told my sister that I wanted to go shopping.

"Sounds like sister talk," Dex said. "I think I'll excuse myself."

"Are you making that much money?" Delia asked, knowing full well what the answer was.

"I thought you could help me; we could make it my Christmas present."

"I'm confused," she said, joking but not. "I thought all of this was your Christmas present."

She'd pulled some leftover chicken wings out of the kitchen, and as she ate them, the delicacy of her fingers next to the bugs painted on her face almost made me dry-heave.

"Are you going to keep your makeup on?" I asked. "It's kind of freaking me out."

My sister waved me off and cleaned the chicken wing down to the bone.

"What's wrong with the clothes that you have?"

"Nothing."

She chewed her chicken slowly, and I swear I could hear her thinking.

"Is this about one of the twins?"

"No," I said, embarrassed that she'd said it out loud. "Why, did Dex say something?"

"I don't need Dex to spot puppy love. Plus, you get all misty now when we pass the cookie aisle."

"Very funny," I said. "And I'm not in love. I just want to look, you know, better."

My sister narrowed her eyes and stared at me like I was a day-old doughnut, the fate of which was suddenly in her hands.

"Stop it."

"I think you've lost weight," she said. "Seriously. You do need new pants, and"—she lowered her voice—"Roger wants to see you. He had some questions about the write-ups you've been doing. I'm sure he'll pay you something, and I can cover the rest. Within reason."

From the bathroom, the toilet flushed.

"If," she whispered, leaning in and pausing for dramatic effect.

"What?"

"You have to let me know which twin."

I covered my face with both hands and told her.

"Knew it," she said. "He's the keeper."

Dex emerged from the bathroom and went into the kitchen.

"So we'll go shopping tomorrow afternoon," she said loudly. "You can tag along with me and we'll hit some of the boutiques on Melrose. I think they're your style."

"Thank you," I said. "Thank you, thank you, thank you."

The next afternoon we met Roger at a vegan restaurant on Sunset Boulevard, the same Sunset Boulevard that I had seen watching old detective movies with my dad, though it didn't look anything like it had back in the day. Old-movie Los Angeles always seemed more glamorous than dangerous, full of snappy dialogue and women in tight dresses, not douche bags ordering black bean burgers with their kale juice. Any femme fatale worth her salt would have arched her eyebrows and ashed a cigarette on Roger's plate in disgust. Any femme fatale except for my sister.

"You are in a good mood, no?" Roger asked. He was shooting a commercial nearby, and his hair was growing in. He looked the way I imagined someone might if they'd been slated to go to the electric chair and grown their hair in when they got a pardon.

"I'm taking her shopping," Delia said.

Roger smirked. He considered all shopping other than his own bourgeois.

I ordered something that was supposed to approximate a hot

dog and sweet potato fries, Delia ordered the flower-power salad, and Roger ordered black coffee, extra annoying since he had insisted on meeting here. He could have ordered that on the moon.

"So," he said, leaning across the table and pretending like he was gazing into my soul. "Tell me. Do you now have a favorite Manson girl?"

That was Roger, always with the most disgusting way of saying anything. Boxers or briefs? Bundy or Dahmer? Fromme or Atkins?

"No," I said. "They're all pretty weird."

"Understatement," Delia said, picking at her salad. "Don't play coy, Anna. You've been reading every night. Roger was thinking that maybe my character is reincarnated, or possessed, so it doesn't have to be literal. Tell him what you know."

"Well," I said. "For one thing, he made all the women throw away their birth control, so if you wanted her to be someone's niece or granddaughter or something, it wouldn't be hard or anything. Did you know that Susan Atkins and Charles Manson had a kid?"

"Susan Atkins," Roger said. "She was a Manson girl?"

It dawned on me that Roger might not have read a single word that I had sent him. Nada. Not a one.

"Yes," I said. "But she's too crazy. I mean, they're all too crazy, but she was extra too crazy. And then she became a born-again Christian, so I don't really think that would fit."

"No," said Roger, like fundamentalists were more repulsive than serial killers. "None of that."

I took a bite of my hot dog, which was salty but nothing a normal person would confuse for meat. Birch could have done better with a pile of mushy grains. The fries were okay, though, because it's hard to mess up fries, and they didn't have to pretend to be something else like the rest of the menu. At the table next to us, a greasy-haired thirtysomething dude was eating alone, fingering his food like he couldn't remember why he ordered it, all but spraining his neck to listen in on our conversation. He kept staring at Delia like he knew her, but she didn't seem to recognize him.

Delia pointed at my plate. "Just don't complain that you're hungry later."

I tried not to breathe through my nose and took another bite of the hot dog and a big swig of apple juice. I made eye contact with the creeper at the next table, and he smiled like he knew me as well. I looked away.

"Oh, for God's sake," Delia said. "You'd think we were trying to poison you."

Roger ordered more coffee.

"That reminds me," I said. "So I guess there were a few girls on the ranch who were less crazy and more scared. One of them, Barbara Hoyt, hid out in the brush for days while they hunted her down, but they didn't get her. And then she was supposed to testify for the prosecution in the trial, and she ran away to Hawaii, and one of the women fed her a hamburger laced with so much LSD that it almost killed her."

"You can't kill a person with LSD," my sister said matter-of-factly.

"Whatever. They tried to do it anyhow, but the thing was that it was like this inside joke, or punishment or something, because they were all vegetarians and they weren't supposed to eat meat." I pushed my plate away. Even the Manson girls knew that everyone needed a burger now and then. "Maybe if it were someone like her, who went crazy or something and was just wandering around, not knowing who she was . . . Anyhow, that seemed more interesting to me, since you asked."

"Only then the movie would have to star a senior citizen." My sister was irritated.

"Do not be so literal," Roger said. "I like this. It is a good start. I want you to find out about every woman in this case. More of these hamburger stories. More that we do not remember. Something . . ." He fanned his hands dramatically over the Formica tabletop. "Something will click." He picked up the check and opened his wallet, put his credit card down, and handed me three hundred dollars.

"Seriously?" I said. It was a hundred dollars more than I figured he owed me, and I was even counting the time I spent staring into space when I got bored.

"This is LA," my sister said. "People do way less for more all the time. Take it and keep walking."

If shopping with Olivia was kind of like accidentally being taken hostage, shopping with my sister was like watching a top hostage negotiator lay out a plan of attack. We crossed the street while Delia mapped out the order of shops we were going to hit—consignment, then low-end retail, then high-end with excellent sale rack.

"I think you're fighting what's attractive about you," she said. "Your hair, for instance—you should get better product and let it run wild. Everyone straightens their hair around here, so it makes you different, and you are different, so you might as well play it up."

My sister saw everyone, even people who weren't actors, as trying to create an image. Last summer she'd convinced me that I wanted to be like a French film actress from the fifties. Now she thought I should go boho chic, let my inner flower child out to play.

"This is the best secondhand place in LA," she said, and pointed to the entrance of a color bomb of a boutique where even the mannequins had posh green and blue wigs on their too-hip, size-zero frames. "But I'm swearing you to secrecy." The dresses in the windows were short and colorful, with layers of necklaces and rows of bangle bracelets.

"I'm going to look like I had a psychotic break if I show up tomorrow wearing this stuff," I said, and lowered my voice because it was embarrassing to even talk about it. "He's going to know that I went shopping to look different."

"Anna," Delia said. "I don't want to disappoint you, but your average guy won't notice anything you change about yourself short of missing limbs. If you came in armless, he might ask if you got a haircut, okay?"

"But I wear that purple sweater every day. I think he'll notice. He calls me 'Purp' sometimes."

"Oh dear lord." She raised her hands to the ceiling. "I have my work cut out for me."

Within minutes she had two armloads of clothes, and ushered me into the dressing room.

"I'll be here," she said. "And unless it doesn't fit, I want to see everything. Okay?"

"Okay," I said.

The first dress was crazy, and I do mean padded cell for the criminally insane. Electric purple with neon-pink flowers and green trim, it looked like someone had repurposed upholstery. There was no way I was walking out of the dressing room in it.

"How's it going?" Delia asked.

"Not this one."

Delia's hand rattled the knob. "Can I at least see it?"

I opened the door.

"Okay," she said. "You're right, it's a little loud, but look at the length. Halfway up the thigh is perfect for you. And I love the sleeves. We're in the ballpark."

I tugged at the back of the dress like maybe there was some secret panel that would drop down and cover my ass. No dice.

"This is a terrible length. I can't go to the set naked. I'm naked. You realize that?"

"It's not naked, seriously, look around this town. You wear this, you're still practically a nun."

She may have been right, but not right enough for me to bare my butt over.

"Don't they sell jeans?"

"Of course they do, but I want you to stand out. I'll bring jeans, too, but keep looking at the dresses, see if there's anything that you could tolerate, okay?"

There were racks and racks of dresses in my size, some used and some new, and I tried to find five or six that seemed like something I would not ridicule if I saw them on another human being. Sometimes I do better if I can pretend that I'm someone else when I look at myself in the mirror, just unfocus my eyes and act like I'm some random person wandering down the street, bumping into some chick named Anna who just started my school, then I'm usually a little more okay with how I look. I'm not actively offensive—in fact, there are times when I'd even say that I look nice, if it's not me doing the talking. So I shopped like I was shopping for alterna-Anna, this chick who landed in Hollywood and played poker with the stars. What would *she* wear?

I must have been deep in the delusion, because I bumped arms with a fellow shopper.

"Excuse me," the man said, giving me a super-creeper grin. The dude from the vegan café, with nothing in his arms and no reason to be up close and personal, not in this place.

I turned to look for Delia, who was across the store, flipping through rows of jeans.

"Is she your sister?" he asked. "She's very lovely."

I didn't say anything. I beelined for Delia and told her that we needed to leave. Now.

"Are you kidding?" she said. "After you've begged me all week to take you shopping? Are you sure you're not on drugs?"

"It's just—" I started, but by then the creeper was right beside us. He held his hand out to my sister, who ignored it until he dropped it by his side. But he didn't stop staring at her, like his inner carnivore had found the steak of his dreams. For all I knew, he was the one leaving notes on her door. I didn't like it, not one bit.

"I couldn't help but notice you," he said, sidling even closer. "Are you represented? Because I think I could do wonderful things for you," and I would have bet my last dollar that he wasn't talking about movies.

My sister, for her part, kept looking at the jeans, avoiding eye contact and acting as if this was business as usual.

"She has an agent," I said. "Okay?"

He ignored me. The cashier was checking something on her phone, oblivious. Then, without so much as a glance in the creeper's direction, Delia said in her most matter-of-fact voice:

"I think you can see that I'm shopping for a friend's birthday, and you can respect that this is something I intend to finish this afternoon."

No muss, no fuss. The creeper didn't leave.

She kept ignoring him, talking to me like he wasn't even there.

"These are great jeans," she said. "Have you tried them? I think they fit almost well enough to justify the price."

Finally, the creeper relented. He exited the store, still checking back to see if my sister was looking.

"That was awful," I finally said. "What was wrong with that guy?"

My sister shrugged like he was some pesky mosquito.

"If you ignore them," she said, checking the price tag on one of my dresses, "they generally go away. My shrink told me once that for some people, all attention is positive attention. I don't give creatures like that my attention."

What a strange way to live. No wonder she barely rolled her eyes when I mentioned the car parked outside her house the other night, or the crazy lady who was definitely *not* just confused about the address of some party, or when I wanted to talk about our mom's surgery. Either she was a Zen priestess or she was completely delusional.

"Now try these on," she said, pointing to the pile of dresses in my arms. "I want to be amazed."

9

For the next two weeks, it seemed like my sister was never around. She claimed to be auditioning for a pilot and reshooting more of the zombie flick, but I had a hunch she was trolling around with Roger. Dex would send me on errands on the *Chips* set to keep me busy, and then we'd hang out and wait for Delia in the evenings. There was no way I could forget about my family, but I did start to forget about school. I forgot about it so epically that when I got an e-mail from Mr. Haygood, subject line: *FINAL?*, it took me a good two minutes to figure out whether or not it was spam. It wasn't. Mr. Haygood wanted me to "stay on track," as August was "rapidly approaching."

"Shit!" I said, and then, "Sorry. I mean crap."

Dex shrugged his shoulders. "What gives, young one? You gonna let me in on why the only books you read are about serial killers?"

The question threw me enough that I told Dex my first lie. I said, "I'm supposed to be writing a final paper for my history class about Los Angeles and some event that changed America, so I picked Charles Manson." He gave me a funny look, and then I added, "And I'm supposed to find out everything I can about all the people who were involved." Dex got that peculiar squint around the eyes that adults get when you can tell that they're not sure what's happening in schools anymore, and then he smiled and said he'd help me brainstorm. One thing I know about grown-ups—they'll believe anything is a real assignment if you say it with conviction. I could have said, "I'm supposed to be pretending to be a Manson girl for my drama class and writing it up," and he probably would have gone along with that as well.

For my part, the only real work I'd been doing was reading for Roger, and I had kind of hoped that Dex wouldn't notice what I was reading, since when Dex was around I was supposed to pretend that Roger didn't exist. Although calling what I was doing "reading" for Roger was probably wrong, because he'd sent me an e-mail the other morning that said, "JUST BE THE GIRL. DO NOT KILL ANYONE." Ohmigod, like he really had to *add* the second part. He explained in a follow-up e-mail that he wanted me to spend a few days trying to see the world like one of the Manson girls. I had about a million things I thought about writing back to him, like, "I JUST GAVE A THIRTY-FIVE-YEAR-OLD EX-CON A BLOW JOB. DO I GET PAID EXTRA?" but given what he thought of me, he'd probably just send me a check for fifty bucks and ask for details.

Here's the funny thing, though: the minute I made up some weird answer for my history final, it stopped seeming like a stupid idea and started seeming like a good one. Maybe Delia knew something I didn't, that sometimes even something that started as a lie could become the truth before you knew it. At any rate,

I knew for absolute truth that Delia would kill me if Dex found out about the Roger thing. Once I told Dex about the paper, he said that he owned a copy of *Valley of the Dolls,* and I should watch it because it was about LA and starred Sharon Tate and was her biggest role. In fact, he'd watch it with me. So the next night we hunkered down with cheese popcorn and real Doritos from the normal grocery store.

What Dex failed to mention was that *Valley of the Dolls* is a terrible movie, and not even in the fun way that might cause a person to run around quoting it and making fun of the weirdest scenes. It's long and boring and the acting is terrible. Everyone is beautiful and on pills and sleeping with everyone else, and it's still so dull that I almost fell asleep. The story follows three women who are trying to make it in entertainment and meet Mr. Right, and they get addicted to pills, or "dolls," for a variety of reasons. Sharon Tate plays this dim-witted, sweet actress named Jennifer who falls in love with a nightclub singer who has a mysterious hereditary disease that shows up just when she reveals that she's pregnant. Sadness follows. The moral of the movie is supposed to be that the struggle to become famous, or even just wanting to be famous, is better than what happens when a person reaches that goal. Kind of like *Gatsby,* but trashier and infinitely duller. Success just makes everyone miserable and pill-happy.

Mostly, though, I watched Sharon Tate. I'd never seen her in a movie before. There were plenty of pictures on the Internet, most linked to stories about her murder, or memorials, but even those let you forget that she was a real person. On the screen, she looked like a giant Barbie doll. She wasn't an edgy kind of pretty, and even though she was skinny she was soft around the edges, fleshy, the way even the thinnest actresses sometimes look in old movies. Her first scene in the film she's dressed as a showgirl with a giant feathered headdress, and the camera pans from her ass to her boobs to her face in a series of shots. A few scenes later, she's on the phone with her horrible stage mother who reminds her that she's nothing but a body.

Nothing but a body.

The line bothered me, because when I was reading about the murders, so much more seemed to be written about the Manson girls, and Charles Manson, than about the victims themselves. Sharon Tate was just a name, or a beautiful blonde, or an actress, or the wife of a director, or another woman who really became famous only when her life was over. When she went from being a body on a screen to a body in a bag. I wanted the movie to bring her to life, but the camera seemed intent on making her nothing more than a beautiful face and a banging body. It didn't seem fair, not to her, at any rate.

But it would have been a lie to say that Sharon Tate was the only person I was thinking about. Roger had probably had me professionally hexed, because every time I saw Sharon Tate, I thought about Paige Parker. Paige looked kind of like Sharon Tate. They were both tall with dirty-blond hair and enormous boobs. Paige wasn't quite as glamorous, but she tried. Even in gym class she wore pink sneakers with little crystals on the side, and she had a pink phone with rhinestones as well. But they both had that thing that pretty people didn't usually have—a needy look, like they cared what other people thought. Like they wanted to be liked.

The weird thing was, I didn't really have an opinion about Paige one way or another outside of Doon. Paige had started at my school last year, and she took ballet with Doon. Doon hated her like a week of snow-day makeups at the end of the year. I mean she *loathed* her. If you asked me, Paige didn't have much of a personality to hate at all. She was more like Sharon Tate, pretty, but pretty boring. But friendships were kind of like poker games. The fact that Doon hated Paige trumped the fact that I didn't care about her one way or another. I went along with Doon when she talked about how awful Paige was, that she was a slut, a *whore,* that she hoped her dog died and she got fat. That was a lie, I had more than just gone along with Doon, but I didn't want to think about it.

"What did you think?" I asked Dex while the credits rolled.

"About what?" he said. After the first ten minutes, he'd been working on his pilot and only half watching the film. He didn't really look up from his computer to answer, which meant he was probably in the middle of fixing a scene or something. I was learning how Dex worked: when to talk to him, when to give him another minute, when to suggest a doughnut run.

"That movie," I said. "Why is it a cult classic? Because Sharon Tate was in it?"

"Probably." He finished typing and closed his computer.

"I guess it works for my paper. But I didn't like watching Sharon Tate. It's too depressing."

"More depressing than reading yourself blind about the Manson girls?"

"Yes. But it shouldn't be, right? Does that make me a terrible person? And half the time I can't even remember the names of the other people who were murdered. I can remember Abigail Folger, because it's like the coffee, but other than that? It's like they just evaporate. Why are the murderers the famous people? If Sharon Tate weren't really beautiful and already famous, I probably wouldn't remember her name either, right? That's messed up."

"Indeed it is."

"That's it? I thought you'd have something smarter to say."

Dex gut-laughed, which made me smile even though I hadn't meant it as a joke.

"From a narrative perspective," Dex said, "maybe it's because the stories of the victims are already over. And because they hadn't done anything wrong, there's really nothing left to learn from their lives, right?"

I wasn't sure that he was wrong, but it seemed like a terrible thing to say.

"But the story of the murders doesn't really make any sense. It's crazy how these girls killed all these people, isn't it? And they look all smiley and hippie-friendly in their pictures. It's just weird. I thought girls only killed their boyfriends and husbands or rapists. Definitely not pregnant ladies. What's the lesson there? Women are secretly batshit?"

"Secretly?" Dex said, giving me his best faux-teacher tilt of the head. "Anna, what ever made you think that women are nicer than men? Has high school changed that much?"

I thought about Paige Parker again, and then I made myself stop.

"I guess not. But it's kind of different, isn't it? And why do you think they're always talking about how pretty these girls were—not Sharon Tate, but the killers? I think they look crazy. Look at this: 'Some thought Susan Atkins was the prettiest.' What does that have to do with anything?"

"It doesn't. But Sharon Tate was fine."

I kept going back to that part of the murder, a bunch of okay-looking girls killing the really beautiful one. Not because it was creepy, but because it wasn't so terribly hard to imagine after all. I had to remind myself that murders hadn't been planned like that. The Sharon Tate part was an accident, a twist of fate.

"This paper. You going to write anything about race?"

"I think it's just supposed to be about the girls."

"But you know they were a bunch of white supremacists, right?" Dex propped his feet on the table and leaned back.

"Kind of. I hadn't really been reading that part."

And then I felt embarrassed, like a big, shallow, white-girl disappointment.

"Charles Manson thought he was going to take all his

white ladies to some hole in the ground and then rule all the black people left after the great American race war."

"Seriously?"

"How long have you been researching this?"

"I don't know. A couple of weeks."

"You need to be reading some different books."

He was probably right, but I knew that Roger wouldn't care. All he would care about is that my sister looked beautiful and haunted and had some artsy, made-up past. If I mentioned a race war to him, he'd probably start cursing me in Polish.

"Do you think Olivia Taylor is ever going to pay me back?"

"Olivia Taylor? Not a chance."

"Seriously? But she's rich."

"You think rich people stay rich by giving away their money?"

"But I don't have any money. And my dad is going to kill me when he finds the charge for that stupid bag. How is it that I've allegedly stolen a thousand dollars and now I don't have any money and everyone is mad at me?"

"Young one," he said. "You are going to have to ponder that yourself. Doughnut?"

Dex knew even better doughnut shops than my sister. He told me that he only ate the ones she brought to be nice, but the really good stuff, the crazy flavors, were at Do-Joe, which was in an even more sketchball part of town than the places where Roger filmed. But the doughnuts were otherworldly. I was hooked on a bacon-and-salted-caramel twist.

"I gotta do my work, kid," Dex said, and that meant it was time for me to pretend to read my book. I tried not to be obvious while I watched him on the couch.

If I thought about it just right, I could pretend it was Jeremy sitting there, reading one of the meditation books he toted around and smiling at me and asking how I was every once in a while. Jeremy, who yesterday afternoon had watched a video of Barbara Hoyt with me that we found together on the Internet. She was the Manson girl who ate the hamburger that was supposed to kill her, and I'd told Jeremy that she had testified against her former friends during the trials. She hated them so much that she still showed up to make sure Leslie Van Houten didn't get parole, forty years later. But here's the scary thing, when we watched the video, Hoyt looked every bit as crazy as the crazy girls. If you had told me that she was one of the killers, I would have said, "Of course, she's clearly out of her mind." She giggled about the trials and acted like she'd just made it to the finals in some idiotic reality show.

"Remind you of your cult days?" I asked Jeremy.

He did his best dead-eyed hippie impression and said, "There were no fries with my burger," and he sounded just like Barbara Hoyt. The guy could act when he wanted to, and even though it didn't even make sense, we cracked each other up the rest of the afternoon asking for burgers and fries.

I told myself that I wasn't falling for Jeremy just because he was beautiful, because then I would have been as bad as anyone else out here, right? Dex moved his mouth while he was reading the lines he was writing, for possibly the world's stupidest television show, and I kept wondering if there was some planet on which Jeremy was on some other couch, thinking about how when I turned eighteen he could fly me out to LA to live with him. Mars or Jupiter, maybe. Pluto. Not even a planet. Because I didn't look like Delia. Beauty was such an unfair advantage. In the great balance scale of life, whatever I had to offer was always going to come up short next to someone like her. Everything was so much easier for her, and she didn't even have the gratitude to stick around for her awesome life. It almost made me want to break the bad news to Dex: "My sister is probably cheating with her ex." Or at the very least: "My sister is lying to you."

That would have solved at least one of my problems—I can just about guarantee I'd have had a plane ticket back east.

10

Reading about the weird and savage Hollywood that came out at night was starting to get to me. When my sister dropped me at her place, I would lock the doors and then move a chair in front of them. Since our shopping trip, I felt like I should at least try to stay out of her hair in the evenings, but it wasn't easy. I didn't want to admit that I was more spooked by the night, that the wind could sound as sinister as a hand rattling a doorknob, that I felt like at any moment there could be a pounding at the door, and I'd be huddled in the bathroom again, party or no party. I hated that I never sat on her porch and watched the moon, the way Delia talked about doing when she was alone and wanted to feel at peace.

One night my sister was in such a hurry to get out the door that she left her computer up and running, her opened e-mail spread across the screen just daring me to read it. I resisted the urge to eyeball the messages from her obviously lengthy history of Internet dating, but I opened the ones from Roger. And I wasn't spying on her because I was nosy. I was nervous. Too much reading about the secluded nature of 10050 Cielo Drive, how people down the hill from the house said that they had heard nothing, but others reported that the screams had carried for three or four miles. And then there was the fact that the same car kept idling outside the house at night. I saw it once, a boxy red Honda that sped away when I peered out the front window. My sister said they were probably just lost, but I knew better. If she didn't have the sense to be scared of the people around her, I did.

Roger's e-mails to Delia were about as short as the ones I got from him, and just as badly written. *It is like blood, this hurt I have for you. You and my art are the same, ripped from this place I do not know. How would I be without either? I wonder. I have no answer.* Crappy English, but I knew creepy even in translation. And Roger spoke the universal language of sketchball. Fluently. The last one he had written Delia early last week: *You are like a haunted place I cannot exercise. I hate and am drawn to at once.* It took me a minute to get to *exorcise,* which made the whole thing funny but not. And my sister never wrote him back. Not once. The last one had some weird quote about "the devil making the light more real" attached to the bottom. I closed her computer and hid it under a pillow. For all I knew Roger was hexing us both.

When I was a lot younger, my mom took us to church all the time. We went to this super-evangelical church until I came home one day singing, "I'm no kin to the monkey," and my dad said that was the end of that. The churches we went to after that were a lot less scary, but I still remembered the things we'd been warned about at the church: Satanists, Ouija boards, reading the wrong book or listening to the wrong song and accidentally letting the devil in. My mom, who was otherwise pretty new-age friendly, didn't think anyone should mess with Satan, and the more I read about the Manson case, the more I didn't think anyone should either.

At night, my sleep was all messed up. I had nightmares about the white nightgown soaked red, these happy, smiling vegetarians who thought nothing of putting a knife in the belly of a pregnant lady. And they probably weren't any different from the long-haired actress wannabes at Whole Foods making sure that their meat was cruelty-free. I worried that I shouldn't have been reading about the murders at all, that I was catching some sinister wave and something might happen to Birch, or my mother. Maybe my mom was right in keeping me a whole continent away from her while she recovered. I felt like telling my sister and stupid Roger to forget the whole thing. It's not like Olivia Taylor was going to show up and pay me for the bag, plus interest. The thousand dollars I owed felt more like a million.

My sister almost caught me reading her e-mails the morning I told her I'd had enough with playing *Home Alone*. I slammed her computer shut and practically winded myself running to the sink to get a glass of water when I heard her keys at the door. Even though the clock blinked seven forty-five, she had the messy hair and flushed cheeks of someone who had been up since before dawn, working out. She flopped onto the couch and stretched one leg into the air, close to her nose, then the other.

"I can't stay here anymore." I sat beside her and talked to the floor so I wouldn't lose my train of thought. "You shouldn't leave me here at night. And you shouldn't be here either. It could be dangerous."

She opened her computer and ignored me for at least two minutes. I almost checked her ears for earplugs.

"Why?" she finally said. "There's nothing up here. You're too big for a coyote to eat. Don't be so dramatic, Anna. Did you think you were going to become rich and fall in love with a girl named Daisy when you read *The Great Gatsby*? You're as suggestible as Cora."

"I am not."

"Yes. You are." She typed as she talked, pausing to delete, type, delete. "But you can come over to Dex's if you want to. He has a couch and I don't think he'll mind."

"Thank you."

Before shutting the computer down, she logged out of her e-mail account. That was a first.

"I get jumpy when Mercury is in retrograde. Yesterday Roger shot me on the steps of an apartment building where a stalker had killed an actress, a young one. She opened the door, and that was it. It's the case that gave us the stalking laws we have now, so I guess that's something good to come out of it, but it's really eerie, being in all these places that look so, I don't know, regular." Delia's eyes narrowed as she talked, like the body was right in front of her.

"I think the whole thing is creepy. Roger is creepy, and he doesn't know what he's doing."

"Roger has money and Roger is paying me."

"So? I think he's driving by your house at night. I do. He even told me I should try to be like a Manson girl, you know, for research. I know he's paying me, but he'd probably pay me to eat dog shit, too, and that wouldn't make it okay."

"What are you talking about?" Delia said, laughing for real. "Why would he do any of that? He sees me every day. He doesn't need to stalk me; driving by my house would be redundant."

I wasn't buying what she had to sell, not with that pitch.

"Anna, are you having an easy time paying back that money you owe Mom? Or your dad? Assuming that we forget that you're living rent-free and eating my food? Does money just rain from the sky?"

"No."

"Well, it doesn't for me, either, okay? I can work five jobs one year and have nothing the next. In this town, unless you are insane, you say yes to everything within reason."

The last time I mentioned the stalker, Delia repainted her just-manicured nails. This time, she took a pair of tweezers out of her makeup bag and plucked at the stray hairs growing beneath her brows.

"It's not worth it if you wind up dead."

"Dead?" she said. "You really do have an imagination."

"I know about the note," I said, playing a card I probably should have kept hidden.

She was quiet for a good five seconds before she answered.

"What note?"

"The one Roger left on your door. He thinks you're a whore. I mean, it doesn't take Sherlock Holmes, does it? He's trying to ruin your relationship with his stupid movie, and he secretly hates you at the same time. I'll bet he hired that lady to bang on your doors at night. Don't you remember that awful thing that he said to you when you broke up?"

Delia slammed her fist on the table.

"I told you never to bring that up. People say stupid things when relationships end. I'm over it. And it's none of your business. None. Get it? It's not Roger driving by, okay?"

She was lying. I could tell because her lips were moving.

"How do you know?"

"I just know. It could be a million different things. It could be press, right? Ever heard of them? They might have gotten wind about Roger's film. I have a feeling it's going to be huge."

I gave her a good, hard "Not on this earth" stare.

"Okay, I have a feeling it might be the actress that I beat for the zombie role. She probably decided to see what life was like without her meds and is taking it out on me. Once she's back on them I'll be fine. Happy?"

She wasn't going to tell me the truth.

"How is that better?"

"It isn't better, but she's done this kind of thing before and she drifts on to the next person who beats her out. You're making a mountain out of a molehill. Just ignore it. I can't afford the emotional energy to make this an issue. My relationship is suffering. I need to start making money soon, or I'm going to be back in Atlanta working retail, okay?"

"Fine," I said. "I'm not trying to make you mad. And I'm sorry I looked in your purse, okay?"

"An apology doesn't change anything, Anna. One more strike and you're on the next plane to Atlanta. Do you hear me?"

"Yes."

I had no idea what was really going on in her head. And while I definitely didn't want to blow my invitation to stay with her in Dex's condo, I knew for a fact that she needed to start taking the crazy around her a little more seriously. She could get as mad at me as she wanted to, but I was doing her a favor. Someone needed to wake her up.

"Why is everything always about money?" I said. "Can't Dex just hire you?"

"No, he can't. They don't want to see old people on kids' shows."

"It's not a kids' show, and you're twenty-six. That's not old."

Then she lifted her face and pulled a lone black hair out of her chin. I almost threw up in my mouth.

"It is a kids' show, and for a kids' show, I am old. Those are the facts. I don't really have any more time to make it. I have to keep swinging. I *have* to."

And suddenly she looked determined. Creepy-determined. I always thought of things coming easy to my sister, of life handing her whatever she wanted. Two years ago she was almost cast as a Bond girl and filmed a sitcom pilot that never aired. She worked with Roger, but she was definitely doing him the favor. Now she was strictly B movies and reality TV, with Roger's stupid film suddenly at the top of her priority list. Maybe I just didn't like to think that Delia could fail, but for the first time I could see that she'd thought about it. Thought *hard*. Even with something as stupid as the herpes commercial, there were probably a hundred other girls who'd be just as geared up to pretend to have herpes.

"I hope you get herpes," I said.

My sister finally cracked a smile in spite of herself.

"Me too," she said. "And if not, there's always gonorrhea, right?"

"Or the clap. Or is that the clap?"

I couldn't wait to pack my bag and sleep in that big, insulated condo building where you could hear your neighbors walking heavily across the floors above you, their weird sex noises muffled through the walls. I was triple-locking the doors and never leaving again.

11

By July, I'd spent most of my summer reading about people doing things so horrible that they seemed almost unbelievable. On the other hand, in this very same world there were things so amazing, so completely unlikely, that they sounded just as made up when you tried to tell them to another person. How could I text Doon, "Jeremy Taylor whisked me away from the set today to spend the afternoon with him. Just him," without sounding like a pathological liar? A delusional lunatic? Still, that's exactly what happened. When Dex and I arrived on the lot, we didn't even make it out of the parking lot before Jeremy came up and asked if he could "borrow me" for the morning. *Borrow me?* He could have flat-out stolen me for the next two months and I wouldn't have complained.

"I thought about you this morning," Jeremy said. He hooked his thumbs through the belt loops of his plaid shorts. The shorts plus the pink polo shirt he was wearing meant that the "Chips" had been "playing golf" on deck. I had on a flowered sundress patterned with oversize red flowers and emerald-green vines, one of my sister's choices from the consignment shop on Melrose. I felt absurdly overdressed, but Delia was right, Jeremy didn't seem to notice. "Well, to be honest, I was thinking about my grandfather."

"Oh," I said, not exactly sure whether that was a good thing or a bad thing. "Where does he live?"

He opened the door for me, and I climbed into a fortress of a vehicle, similar to Olivia's but even larger. I buckled my seat belt and willed myself not to act as nervous as I felt.

"He died a few years ago," Jeremy said after he started the car and slowly drove us out of the studio compound. "He was a great character actor in the seventies. If you've seen any of those old gangster films, he's the skinny one with the droopy eyes."

I was drawing a complete blank. I hated gangster movies.

"I'd probably know him if I saw him."

"Definitely. He was hilarious. I still think about him almost every day."

I'm pretty sure that he was thinking about him right then, because he got quiet and for a while we sat there in silence, moving through a part of LA that I hadn't visited before. As much fun as it was to be on the set, I liked the neighborhoods outside the make-believe world of Hollywood, the thirty different LAs hidden inside of LA. And the neighborhoods could change so fast that if you weren't paying attention, you could close your eyes and miss one. I was worried for a minute that Jeremy was like my sister, that he was disappearing into a bad mood that was somehow going to wind up being my fault, but then he started humming along to the opening chords of a song that had just begun to play. He turned the volume up.

"Who is that?" I asked, pointing at his stereo. "If I didn't already know every song they ever recorded, I'd say that sounded like Freekmonkee."

"You like Freekmonkee?"

"Um, yeah. That would be an understatement. My best friend, Doon, knows more about them than their own parents."

"Cool. Josh hates them."

"He hates Freekmonkee? And you let him live?"

"He's working on his rap CD. I guess they're the wrong kind of Freek-ee."

If my dad had made a comment like that, I would have groaned, but Jeremy's jokes were cute even when they bombed. And the thought of his brother making a rap album was actually hilarious, though I was pretty sure that being the first to laugh at that idea was not a strong move.

"So what is this?"

"It's the new Freekmonkee. *Lost in Space.* They have the same label as Olivia, so she got me a copy."

"Get. Out. Get, get, get, get *out.*"

I turned the music up louder before realizing that I should have asked first.

"But the first single isn't out until next month—I just heard Karl Marx say so. On a podcast, I mean. Is this a CD or just the music? How many songs did you get?"

I was babbling like a deranged toddler.

"It's ten songs. There's a promo case back there somewhere. Here." He pushed a button and skipped to the next song. "This is going to be the first single."

I had officially died and gone to heaven. Karl Marx's low voice half chanted, *We're all just part of the void. Travelers on a lonely path. Lost in space. Lost on Earth. No looking back, no looking back.*

"This is amazing," I said. "Amazing. Can I play some for my friend?"

Jeremy shrugged, which I took as a yes. I recorded the next verse and texted it to Doon.

He smiled, and if it weren't almost too crazy to allow in the realm of possible, I think he put his hand on mine and squeezed.

"Killer song, right? Every song is that good." He moved his hand like he was going to give me the *Chips Ahoy!* salute, but stopped himself.

I gave him my very best "Hey buddy, old pal" smile, so he'd know that I wasn't crazy enough to think that he'd really be attracted to me, that his hand on mine was an accident we could both forget.

"Look," he said, leaning across me and pointing out the window on the passenger side, "That's where we're going." He pointed to a stretch of rolling hills just off the street. We were outside the heart of Los Angeles, but other than that, I had no idea where we were. "Holy Cross Cemetery," he continued. "It's where my grandpa is buried."

I had no idea what to say. If you had asked me where we were going that day, I think a cemetery would have been about one millionth on the list.

"Really?" I said. "Do you go and talk to him?"

"Sometimes. Sometimes I just go because it's peaceful and they don't allow photographers. Low stalking factor. When I was a kid, my grandpa took us there because we loved Dracula. You know who Bela Lugosi was?"

"Was he Dracula?"

"The best Dracula."

"I know who he was," I said.

"Did you know they buried him in his cape? Josh and I used to plan how we would try to come back one night and see if he was still there. We were gonna steal the cape if no one was around. Obviously, never happened."

"It's kind of a funny thought," I said. I had spent so much time watching him play a kid that I almost forgot he had been an actual kid.

He parked the car, and we went to walk the grounds. I hadn't really spent any time in a cemetery, and maybe it was the kind of place that would be scary at night, but during the day it was beautiful. Los Angeles stretched out below as we passed through beautifully twisted iron gates. The hills had shrines carved into them, the votives inside both burning and burnt out, and statues of the Virgin Mary kept watch over the dead. I didn't know much about Catholics, but I did know that they were crazy about Mary.

In places, the landscape was like something out of Middle-Earth but without the hobbits. At the top of one of the hills, two trees grew out of a hole cut in the side of the minimountain, and under the trees a shrine had been hollowed out. Inside the shrine, ten or twelve candles in long cylinders had been lit and left to burn.

"It's beautiful," I said to Jeremy, who was walking ahead of me but had stopped. "And so quiet."

"I know," Jeremy said. "I think my grandpa is probably happy here. My grandma is pretty loud," and we both laughed like I knew *exactly* what he was talking about. "I remembered something the other day, and I thought you might think it was cool."

We started walking down a gently sloped hill pocked with smooth granite graves that vanished into the grass if you weren't looking. There was a cemetery in downtown Atlanta that I had been to with my mother once, and it seemed like even in death, Southerners were trying to outdo each other. Every grave was bigger and showier than the one before. But this was the exact opposite. Whoever designed it had made sure the gravestones almost disappeared into the ground, but the weird thing was that it made me think about death even more.

"Are we going to your grandfather's grave?" I asked.

"Definitely," Jeremy said. "I always light a candle for him when I'm here. But I'm looking for something." He scanned the ground and finally pointed to one of the identical gray-black stones that we'd been walking around. "Sharon Tate," he said.

Once, when I was singing in chorus and it was hot outside, I had been standing too long with my knees locked and before anyone knew it, even before I could figure out what was happening, I had this feeling like I was on fire and drowning at the same time, and I passed out completely. The next thing I knew, someone was giving me water and propping me up, trying to decide whether I needed to go to the hospital. When Jeremy pointed to that gravestone, I had the same feeling, like something in the ground had buckled and I was going to collapse.

"Are you okay?"

"Fine," I said, kneeling in case I fell. "It's just so real."

I said "real," but that wasn't the word I was looking for; the word I meant was "sad." The kind of sad that would swallow you whole if you sat beside it too long. The gravestone marked four bodies. The top read "In Loving Memory of" and the left side continued with "Our loving daughter and beloved wife of Roman, Sharon Tate Polanski." The dates she lived were separated by the thin slivers of a cross, 1943–1969. Beside that were the dates for her mother and, at the bottom, her sister. But as haunting as it was, the name that knocked me down was just below Sharon's, "Paul Richard Polanski," followed by "their baby," and no dates beneath the name. No dates below this tiny person who both was and wasn't, but who had a name. I thought about Birch and the way he had kicked inside my mom when her belly was so big that I could line up Cheetos on it, the way he already had a name, and a face that we could see in his little ultrasound pictures, and how much I had been looking forward to meeting him.

"I'm sorry," Jeremy said. "I don't know why I thought this was a good idea. Do you need some water? Should I call Dex?"

"No," I said. "I'm fine. I really am. I'm glad I saw this."

And I was, because it was important. Because I needed to keep those murders as real and sad as they actually were, or there was no point in any of it.

"But can we go see your grandfather?"

"Sure," Jeremy said. "And we can say howdy to the Count while we're at it."

"If he's there," I joked, trying to pull myself out of the space I was in.

"Your color's coming back," Jeremy said. He gestured at the bottle of water he'd been carrying. I took a sip, and my mouth flooded with saliva. I willed myself not to pass out.

"I've never seen someone's face really turn white. That was wild."

"Great," I said. "Good to know."

On the ride home from the cemetery, I wrote the name Paul Richard Polanski on the sheet of paper that I had taken to carrying around with me, next to the name of his mother, Sharon Tate Polanski, and alongside Jay Sebring, Rosemary LaBianca, Leno LaBianca, Steve Parent, Abigail Folger, and Wojciech Frykowski. The names of the dead, which, like the gravestones themselves, could be lost all too easily in the clutter around them. I refolded the piece of paper and put it back in my pocket.

"What's that?" Jeremy asked.

"A list," I said. "Some names I need to remember."

He smiled and looked at me like I was a puppy.

"It's cute that you make lists and carry them around."

"Really? My mom complains that it ruins the laundry when they disintegrate."

"Can I ask you a question?" he said. We were stuck in traffic, but he looked at the convertible in front of us instead of my way when he asked, "And you don't have to answer. Did you really steal five hundred dollars from your parents?"

He didn't ask in a judgy way, like my sister, but I could tell that he wanted to know. I started to formulate a lie in my mind, but just as I was about to tell it, I realized that if I started down that road, I was going to wind up exactly like my sister. So I told him the truth. I broke the whole scene down for him in cinematic detail, so that if he decided that he liked me, that he wanted to keep hanging out with me, at least he'd know who he was dealing with.

I started at the beginning. The week before I took the card, my mom and dad had shanghaied me with a "family meeting" at my favorite Starbucks. I told Jeremy about how when they first split up, if either of them was late for a pickup, I would sit in the corner and listen in on people's first dates, or the baristas bitching about who they thought was throwing up in the ladies' room. I loved to put on my headphones and pretend to listen to music and spy. My parents decided it was a good neutral spot when they first separated, when they yelled constantly about "their needs" and who was doing what wrong and screwing me up for all eternity. Starbucks introduced the public shame factor. They learned to hate each other politely and with the volume dialed down.

"My dad and mom only communicate over e-mail," Jeremy interrupted. "When Josh and I were kids, they would have their assistants trade us off, kind of like we were secret documents. Josh would joke that it was because if they caught us with the other one, they'd have to kill us."

He said the last part in a spy-movie Russian accent, and I laughed.

"I'm pretty sure that if my parents could have afforded assistants, they would have been all over that."

I could remember the details of the meeting exactly. My dad had worn a pink shirt, the button-down kind that his new girlfriend, Cindy, probably bought him. She's a stylist, which means that she gets paid by adults to dress them in age-inappropriate clothing and then tell them that they look "hip." Atlanta is full of tight-assed, bleached-blond women who look twenty from behind and turn around to reveal their Botoxed, eight-thousand-year-old, veiny-handed glory. Those were Cindy's clients.

"My dad met her on the Internet, the same Internet he was always warning me about," I said to Jeremy.

"Parents," he said. " 'Physician, heal thyself,' right?"

I nodded.

My mom had looked tired, but then she always looked tired. She had left Birch with Lynette, which meant that she was fiddling with her boobs to see if they were going to explode.

"Mom!"

"Oh," she said. "Sorry. I forget sometimes."

"You forget all the time."

She closed her eyes for a minute and then opened them. I don't think she even heard me.

"Anna," my father said in his sad, authoritarian voice. Pink shirt, soy-latte Dad, I cannot take you seriously. "You have to start treating Lynette with respect, and Cindy as well."

Poor, poor step-dults. My parents both looked so earnest, like they really cared whether or not I pretended not to hear Lynette when she wanted me to play Cinderella for an hour, or that it hurt Cindy's feelings that I didn't want to go with her to buy overpriced purple jeans for some third-tier hip-hop star. I had almost convinced myself that I could leverage the situation into a new phone, when my mom came out with this beautiful and well-rehearsed number:

"And because your father is starting his own business, and I'd like to stay home with Birch, we won't be able to afford your school anymore. We have a thousand dollars allotted for your activities for the year. Five hundred for the fall and five hundred for the spring. It's really a lot, if you think about it, but that's only if we take you out of Lakewood and put you at McKinley."

My dad was staring right through me to the table behind us.

My mom checked her right boob again.

One of the baristas raised her overplucked eyebrow at me, like even she couldn't believe this was going down at Starbucks.

"We looked at the test scores, and they're really not that different at McKinley. It's close to the house, and you can walk home if you need to." My mom was giving me the same look she gives a chicken when she wants to see if it's done or not. "We know that you have friends at Lakewood, but you'll make new friends."

"You make new friends," I said. "I like my friends."

I had complained about Lakewood every morning my mom dragged me there, but suddenly it seemed like an island in the Caribbean. Lakewood was small, and there was a park on the campus where we could go outside to eat lunch. The teachers at McKinley looked like weekend pedophiles, and the cafeteria might as well have been a prison. I'd heard stories from Doon. I didn't need my mom to give me the hard sell.

"Now, Anna," my dad countered. "This isn't easy for us to have to say."

"Then don't. You don't have to say anything, do you? You just want to because you have some anorexic teenager buying you pink shirts, and you're too lazy to work now that the baby is born. And he's a toddler now, in case you hadn't noticed. He'd be happy if you went back to work. I wouldn't want to stay around that crazy house all day, why would he?"

That made her forget about her boobs for a minute.

"That's enough, Anna. I don't expect you to understand how much work it is to take care of you and Birch."

A woman at the next table craned her head to get a closer look, and I didn't even care.

"Include me out," I said. "You don't take care of me. You take care of you. And *stop* touching your boobs."

"I'm sorry," she said. "I was thinking about Birch."

That was it. I was done with both of them. Poor Birch, who was still stuck on my mom's boobs half the day, when she could easily have kicked him off and given him a glass of milk or something normal. He was going to have thousands of dollars in therapy bills. Millions. Good luck when they realized they only had five hundred dollars for that when he turned thirteen.

I was telling Jeremy all of this, the same way I'd run over the scene about a million times in my head, when I realized something that I hadn't before. I realized that maybe, when we were at the Starbucks, my mom might have already found the lump in her breast. She might not have just been touching her boobs to see whether or not they were full, the way I'd seen her touch them about a million times since Birch had been born. She might have been touching her boobs because they were breaking her heart. And there I was, not helping things one little bit.

"You okay?" Jeremy asked. "You went missing."

I had gone missing. And as much as I liked him and wanted him to like me, I wasn't ready to tell him about my mom.

So I told Jeremy the rest of the original truth, that I had taken the five hundred dollars because I figured if that was all the money they had saved for me, at least I could be the one to decide how to spend it. It might have been real stealing to take seventy-four more dollars from Lynette's wallet, but I figured they wouldn't want me getting to LA and thumbing a ride. Not even they would think that was a bad use of money, in the end.

I stopped again because what I'd said sounded like the whole story, but it wasn't. I'd left out the part that I'd made my mother swear not to tell my father, the real reason my mom probably first got it into her head that I needed to change schools, the thing that made me most like a Manson girl—though after seeing Sharon Tate's grave I knew Roger was an actual mental patient for even starting with the comparison. I might have been a lousy person, but only an idiot like Roger would think that made me the same. I wasn't. Not even kind of.

Still.

"There was one other thing," I said. "This girl. Paige Parker. My friend Doon hates her because the guy she likes likes Paige more." The whole situation sounded stupid and lame when I said it out loud, but I closed my eyes and spit the rest out. "Anyhow, Doon said that we could text her anonymously, so we did. Stupid things that were supposed to be kind of scary, like 'I see you in your tutu, you whale.' Then they got meaner and we attached some pictures. Like, Doon wrote that everyone wished she hadn't been born at all and sent a picture of a gravestone and a gun."

I held my breath a second before I finished. "But even though texting Paige was her idea, I was the one who sent the worst picture. After Doon had gone for the night, I found a picture of a dead fetus from an anti-abortion site. It looked like something out of a horror movie, I guess that was probably the point, and I sent it to Paige and wrote, 'Your mom should have scraped you out early.' " I heard my voice start to shake and I closed my eyes tighter while I finished. "I didn't even do it because I hated Paige. I know that sounds crazy, but I wasn't really thinking about her at all. I was thinking about Doon and how funny she would think the message was, and that I couldn't wait to tell her. It was like, in my mind, what we were doing really didn't have a person on the other end, getting the texts."

I had no idea what Jeremy was thinking, and I didn't want to open my eyes and find out. "Anyhow, it turned out they weren't anonymous like Doon had said, and I guess Paige liked to cut herself and had her phone open to the texts while she was doing it, and her mom caught her. Then her mom called mine, and my mom *flipped out* about the abortion pic. My mom said that if she was wasting money for me to become a bully, then she was flushing money down the drain. I couldn't explain to her that I hadn't even meant it with the fetus picture, that even that was kind of Doon's idea too, but I knew that if I got her into trouble she'd never speak to me again. How was I supposed to know that perfect Paige Parker was a cutter? She was the popular one, what did she have to be mad about? After that my mom treated me like I was going to go buy a gun and shoot up the cafeteria. It was horrible. She wouldn't listen to anything I said. I know they acted like they were changing my school because of money, but I think they just gave up on me. Who wants to throw money at a lost cause, right?"

I'd told him the ugly truth, my entire crappy past life in Atlanta. The parts that were all my fault and the parts that were only kind of my fault. And the awful thing was, even when I was talking about Paige Parker, I was still more mad at her than sorry for her. Maybe it was meaner than I'd thought, but it was still just a stupid picture. It's not like I'd sent her an actual fetus. And now she was ruining my life from two thousand miles away. So much for Jeremy liking me. By the time I was finished we were back on the lot, I'd probably been talking forever. I opened my eyes to see what he was doing, but he was looking out his window.

"I'm sorry," I said. "I guess I should have given you the short version. You probably think I'm a terrible person now."

"No," he said, turning toward me. "I wanted to know. I can tell that was hard for you to say. Thanks for letting me know the truth. Someone told me the other day that once you say something it loses its power." He was starting to sound like Lynette or my mom. Not a great sign. "I'm glad you wanted to come with me. Is it okay if I drop you? I didn't realize the time and I have to get to a meeting across town."

Great. I had officially scared him off. Maybe there was a reason no one asked me about my life. I was like some prehistoric aunt that your parents forced you to visit once a year—blabbing like I'd just learned how to talk, carrying weird lists around in my pocket, and not even all that nice at the end of the day.

"Catch you tomorrow," Jeremy said, and he looked for a minute as if he might reach over to hug me, but didn't. I'd gone from sad puppy to untouchable. Double great. "It was fun, Anna. I'm glad you got to see my grandpa."

By the time I crossed the thirty feet to the entrance of the set, Jeremy was long gone.

12

The next week was busy on the set with shooting and reshooting an episode where, I'd bet my last dollar, Josh was deliberately flubbing his lines. At night, Dex wrote and I tried to finish up my research for Roger's movie. I told Roger that I was done pretending to be a Manson girl, it was too weird, and he raised my salary to fifteen bucks per hour and told me to focus on the details around the murders. He had the girl figured out, but he wanted more background.

My sister claimed to have two auditions and then I think she was meeting Roger, but I had started to assume that she only told me what she thought I wanted to hear. If I lied, it was usually because I had a reason, but I think Delia lied for the sake of lying—it made her feel like she had a leg up on everyone. She was a strange one, my sister.

Dex was rewriting his pilot, and I helped him decide which parts sounded best. It was a drama about a single mom, a white lady in New Orleans whose husband, a black man, had been lost during Hurricane Katrina. She was raising their biracial kid and trying to figure out whether her husband was still alive or not—because his body was never found. Dex told me that he grew up in New Orleans, and his mom raised him, and he wanted to make a show that would be like a giant thank-you to her. He also said this was the ninth pilot he had written in three years, so he wasn't exactly counting on anything.

I had stopped feeling like the 130-pound weight Delia had dumped on Dex's doorstep. Dex and I had gotten good at working side by side, and I found myself wishing that he and my sister would be forever. I even searched the top of his dresser for a ring, but I guess that was wishful thinking. When Delia showed up, Dex talked a lot more, but they bickered about how much she was gone. My sister bickered with everyone she ever dated, so that wasn't a shock or anything. In our family, conflict was a form of affection. Still, there was something easy about the times when it was just me and Dex, like we were family already.

"You still reading about Chuckles Manson?"

"I am. It's pretty depressing."

Dex laughed and thumped me over the head with the folded pages of a script, like, *Duh, genius, what'd you expect it to be? Up-lifting?*

"I know," I said. "I know." For longer than you'd think possible, I'd avoided reading more about the actual murders and just read about the girls, the trials, the crazy that came before and after. But now I was knee-deep in the awful thing itself, and it made me feel dirty.

"I have a question," I said. "Do you think he was psychic? I know he was crazy and all that, but how does a person do what he does? I don't mean just the awful part, but making all those girls do those things."

"Those girls had choices."

"Okay, they had choices, but Susan Atkins said that he could see right through her when he met her. And she wasn't the only one."

"Anna," Dex said, "never underestimate the power of telling a person exactly what she wants to hear."

He was talking to me like I was an idiot. And he was missing the point.

"But what about the *White Album*? He thought the Beatles were talking to him, like they had some kind of psychic connection. Have you read all the stuff that he thought was written directly to him? Did you read that one of the lawyers thought that Manson stopped his watch in the courtroom? Don't tell me I'm crazy, but sometimes it seems like it's more than a coincidence. Some of it's, I don't know, it's just weird. What if he was right?"

Dex sat up straighter and closed his computer. "You mean right about hiding in a hole in the ground and starting a race war by having a bunch of crazy white people kill other white people? Was he right about every garden-variety racist comment that came out of his mouth? Oh, yeah, and did you miss that part of *Helter Skelter* where he called Hitler a 'tuned-in guy' out to 'level the karma of the Jews'? That dude wasn't exceptional. He was paranoid, actually insane, and straight-out racist. Is that what he might have been right about?"

My face had probably gone blotchy and red, shamed by the stupidity of my brain-mouth connection. Everything I wanted to say kept coming out wrong, and now I sounded like some dumb bougie suburbanite, so white that it had bleached my brain. I couldn't handle two of my sister's boyfriends thinking I was no different from a Manson girl.

"No," I said. "You know that's not what I mean. It's just creepy, that's all. Have you read these lyrics? I mean, 'Sexy Sadie'? Did you know that's what Charles Manson called Susan Atkins? Sadie. That's weird, right?"

Dex shook his head and walked to the other side of the room. Next to his bookcase, there was a cardboard box full of old vinyl albums. He closed his eyes, held his hand in the air, and then reached into the box dramatically, like he was drawing numbers for the lotto.

"Here we go," he said, pulling out an old LP from the back of the box. "Beastie Boys, *Licensed to Ill,* perfect. So let's say that Charlie wakes up in 1987, Reagan's in office, there are homeless people everywhere, he's still a white boy, and black men are still plucking his nerves, but he's about to talk to one of the great frat-party bands of the decade. The Beastie Boys."

I started laughing, because it did sound stupid.

"*Licensed to Ill.* Clearly that refers to a race war. The Beastie Boys, being white and from New York and not having discovered Buddhism or feminism yet, are letting Charlie know that he has license to do whatever his little cracker heart desires. 'Brass Monkey.' Well, that funky monkey probably needs to be taken down, but maybe, because it's brass, it's strong and it's going to rise up first, while he hides in some subway hole, right?

'She's Crafty.' You know Charlie probably's gonna use that on at least five ladies that he found at the Greyhound terminal. 'Fight for Your Right to Party'?"

"All right already," I said. "Maybe that just proves you're as crazy as Charles Manson."

We were both cracking up when Delia came through the door. She'd auditioned for the reality show earlier in the day, which was supposed to be about young actors in Hollywood trying to make it in the business.

"What are you clowns doing?" She took a box of tofu curry out of the refrigerator and ate it with the door open. "It feels *soooooooo* good in here. I think my air conditioner is on the fritz. I was *dying* on the way home."

She had another friend, another producer, who had encouraged her to try out, and I could easily imagine my sister, face earnest against some white screen, her name and shaved-down age in bold letters underneath, talking about how hard it was juggling a boyfriend, an ex, and a delinquent half sister. I wondered for a minute how many sketchballs Delia really knew, if there might not be a coven of crazies stalking her apartment, waiting to see if she'd crack. She moved around the kitchen like she was still auditioning, striking a pose against the sink, the countertop, the silverware drawer. Maybe threats didn't seem real to her because nothing did.

Dex went into the kitchen as well and kissed her even though she had food in her mouth.

"Nice," my sister muttered, still eating.

"How'd it go?"

"Terrible," she said. "They kept asking me about our sex life."

"And I'm going to pretend I'm not here," I said. "But just in case it matters, try to remember that I am."

"You wouldn't have believed the other people there. One woman wasn't wearing any underwear, and don't ask me how I knew but suffice it to say that everyone knew. Everyone. I don't know what my friend was thinking. They asked me how I felt about orgies."

"Gross," I said.

"I don't know if it's gross," she said. "It's more Roman than anything, but it's not my thing. Can you imagine if I took Dex to an orgy?"

Dex looked like someone had thrown up in his mouth.

"Have you been to an orgy?" I asked.

"No," she said. Lying. "I lived with a girl once who had one while I was filming in Canada. She failed to mention that it was on her list of plans. Let's just say that I found some of the evidence in the laundry room when I got back. I Lysoled the place and kicked her out the next week."

"So it *is* gross."

Delia ignored me. I knew she thought it was nasty, deep in her heart, but she never liked to admit that anything scandalized her.

"She was being dishonest."

What's that saying? "We always hate the things in others that we see in the mirror"?

"I'm starting to despise auditions," she said. "They won't call me back. I think I was the oldest woman there anyhow."

"Seriously? How young was the youngest?"

"I don't know," she said. "Nineteen?"

"Did they ask her about orgies?"

"I have no idea, I wasn't in her audition."

"Can we drop it with the orgies?" Dex said. "Maybe you can both forget that we have a child in the room, but I'm having some trouble."

"I'm not a child," I said. "Besides, I read about orgies most of this afternoon. Did you know the youngest Manson girl was, like, thirteen? That's younger than me. I'll bet she did more than hear about orgies."

"Great," Dex said. "I feel better already."

"Can I ask a weird question?" I didn't even know I had a question about orgies, but what the heck. "Do you think that people actually like having orgies, or do you think they just like being able to say that they were in an orgy?"

"And, *scene*," Dex said. "You sure you don't want some ice cream? A lollipop? To go roller-skating?"

"Ice cream," I said. "Definitely ice cream."

My sister shook her head and narrowed her eyes.

"Sex talk for ice cream. Kids today can work the system."

I shrugged my shoulders and smiled, but I was actually

being serious with the question. One of the funny things, reading the Manson family members talk about all the crazy sex, is that they were all like, *Yeah, that sex thing, kind of overblown, kind of didn't really happen like that.* It was almost like people wanted the crazy sex thing to be true even if it wasn't. Mostly, when you read what the Manson family really said about those weeks before the murders, they were short on food and hungry, not horny. But talking about the sex was evidently more interesting than the actual sex. Not that I knew anything about sex myself, but sex with a bunch of dirty hippies not being awesome seemed *totally* possible. The story was better than the stinky, hungry truth.

It's not like that would have been a first.

13

Dex said one of the fastest ways to make money in LA was to be an extra on a sitcom—totally legal for minors, and the unions made sure the pay was sweet. He wrote me into a *Chips Ahoy!* episode, where I played the quiet half of a nerdy sister pair whose boat comes across the Chips' yacht just before a hurricane hits. I got to wear glasses even bigger than my regular ones, and some crazy plaid miniskirt and kneesocks, and my one line was "Does not compute, buttercup," which I tried to say like a computer, but I think I just sounded like the nervous lunatic I was. Dex said I was great, and even Josh gave me a high five when the scene was over. "I love those socks," Jeremy said. "And the glasses. Classic."

"Yeah," Josh said. "A few more cameos and you'll be the next Olivia Taylor." He was cracking himself up.

"*Shiiit,*" Jeremy said. "I forgot about Olivia."

"Lucky you," Josh said without a touch of humor.

"I've gotta get out of here." Jeremy looked at the time on his phone and then at me. "Want to come with?"

Jeremy and I hadn't talked much since the day we went to the cemetery, so I assumed that he had written me off as a terrible, possibly pitiful human being best kept at arm's length.

"Sure," I said, trying hard to sound cool, but I think I accidentally used my computer voice instead.

"I have an idea," Jeremy whispered. "Top secret."

I pretended to lock my lips and gave him the *Chips Ahoy!* salute. If there was one thing I knew how to do, it was keep a secret.

Once we were in the car, Jeremy told me his sister was leaving town for Vegas, where she was sponsoring a series of parties on the strip. He was supposed to feed the snake and iguana while she was gone. The way he saw it, I could get back the purse I'd bought her and return it for cash, right a wrong, and the best part was that she was so loaded up with crap and unopened swag that she wouldn't even miss it.

"Have you seen her place?" He signaled and practically stopped driving as he rounded the corner to her street, but then he picked up speed. "I'm just warning you, it's not what you think."

"Okay," I said. But what ever was?

Olivia Taylor lived in a super-posh subdivision with a friendly but armed guard who greeted us at the gate before we drove to her bungalow. It wasn't a mansion, which I guess I had been expecting, but was definitely too big for one human being. The outside had a rock garden with benches, a small, squarish fountain, and an atrium with a clogged pond and a few sluggish fish bobbing on the surface.

"You ready to see how the other half lives?" he said, smiling like he knew something that I didn't.

A faint beeping noise droned from inside Olivia's house, and when Jeremy opened the door, a catatonic-eyed Pomeranian clawed halfway up my leg like it had lost its actual mind. The beeping was much louder and shriller inside. After flipping the switch on a light that wouldn't turn on, Jeremy punched the keypad on her security system until the alarm stopped. The dog hobbled down two steps before peeing in a puddle between its legs. Who knew how long he'd been holding it.

"Jesus," Jeremy said, picking the dog up and rubbing its head. "She forgot Mr. Peabody. Poor bastard."

The inside of Olivia's house was dark, and after three more useless attempts to find a working light, Jeremy opened the wall of curtains in the living room, letting in enough sun to show that Olivia had probably left in a hurry. Once my eyes adjusted, I could see that the downhill went far and fast. White furniture, black floors, black fireplace, white chandelier. It was like someone got all their decorating ideas from staring at a checkerboard. And then, along the sides of the house, boxes and bags, bags and boxes. Olivia Taylor was a high-end hoarder. I recognized the shopping bag from our excursion, tossed atop a pile of the same that led into the kitchen. Box upon box of Chinese takeout containers littered the counters. This was the picture the paparazzi needed. Piles of unpacked clothes cluttered the sofas, a dog-gnawed piece of pepperoni pizza sat abandoned on the floor, and the air smelled like animal piss and vinegar. For a hot star, she'd left an even hotter mess.

I didn't know what to say, or what I was supposed to do, so I asked Jeremy if we should clean up.

"No," he said. He pushed a stack of cotton-candy pink and baby-blue leotards onto the floor, sat on the sofa, and stared at the pizza box on the coffee table. Then he let out the kind of sigh that parents make when they're so disappointed, they've actually given up, the kind of soul-gutted exhale that was a million times worse than any kind of mad. "It's her mess. But someone needs to clue her in that she left the dog and her electricity is off. I should have known this place would have gone to shit. She always said that Vegas was for washed-up reality stars and ex-groupies. Guess she'll fit right in."

I thought about sitting down next to him and putting my hand on his leg, attempting the kind of "It's okay!" gesture that beautiful girlfriends make in the movies before their boyfriends kiss them tenderly and wordlessly express their thanks and understanding. But I wasn't his girlfriend. Still, we were in an empty house together, and even though it was trashed, there was something that made me feel like that had to mean something. I pretended he was the much older version of Birch and sat next to him and said, "I'm sorry. It's really nice of you to look after her."

He shook his head.

"Maybe that's how it seems," he said. "I used to think so. It would be nice it if helped, but it doesn't. But then there's the dog."

The dog was standing over the pizza and licking the pepperoni. Every few minutes he let out a rancid fart. People food wasn't doing him any favors, but the poor bastard was practically dry-humping a piece of stale crust now that he'd had a chance to pee. Jeremy shook his head and took the pizza away from him.

"I wonder if she even owns dog food," he said. I was sitting close enough to smell that he had probably washed his hair that morning, close enough that I could have reached over and traced the three freckles lined along his jaw like a wide triangle. He stopped staring at the mess and put his hand on my shoulder, and I thought for a minute that he might kiss me. I really did, and then it seemed like he'd awakened from a trance, and instead he stood up and kicked the pizza box off the table, kicked it so hard and far that it landed next to the shopping bags lined against the windows.

"Fuck," he said. "She's still my fucking sister."

"Careful," I said before I could help myself. "You don't want her thinking we came and trashed the place." For a minute Jeremy didn't say anything, and then he started to laugh. Even more than the thought of kissing him, his laughter felt like a gift. Like I registered, and I mattered.

"We couldn't have that, now could we?"

He wouldn't have believed me, but I knew exactly what he meant about Olivia. And then, like someone had written it into the script, the iguana bolted from Olivia's bedroom across the floor, its feet and long green tail slapping the floor like a toddler playing the drums. I couldn't help it, I was cracking up.

"Iggy!" Jeremy chased him to the corner. "Iggy, if this were not so completely depressing, it would be hilarious. You realize that, don't you?" Iggy wriggled out of Jeremy's hands and ran back into the bedroom. Jeremy closed the door behind him. "Who am I kidding? It's a comedy of sad."

The dog had burrowed into Olivia's clothes and rested his head on a pair of her bikini underwear. Jeremy talked to him like he was the dog's therapist. "And you," he said, "you actually miss her. You might want to think about your choices, little dude."

Then it seemed like as fast as the whole thing had become funny, it wasn't anymore. The dog rolled over and let Jeremy rub his belly.

"You mind doing me a favor, Anna? Could you hold your breath and dig through the kitchen closet and see if there's anything in the way of kibble that we could feed this animal? I'm going to give Olivia a call and see if she even knows that she left Mr. Peabody."

"Sure," I said. "No problem."

"And if you can find Iggy and get him in his cage, he'd probably thank you, you know, if he could."

"I'm sure even iguanas have their ways," I said, and he pointed a "gotcha"-style finger at me.

Part of me wanted to hear what he was saying to his sister, but I didn't want him to think I was being nosy, so I decided to hunt for Iggy first. I'd never seen Olivia's bedroom. For a minute, I thought about something I'd read about the Manson family, that before the murders they broke into people's homes, sometimes while they slept unaware, and rearranged their furniture without taking anything. "Creepy-crawling," they called it. I'd thought that the whole point was to scare the unsuspecting residents when they woke up, but walking around Olivia's house, I wondered if there wasn't a thrill to poking around the house itself. Going through someone's drawers could be as intimate as reading their diary, and I was about to see not just Olivia's room, but also in some weird way, a part of Olivia herself.

Before I opened the door, I thought about episodes I'd seen of *Hoarders* where even the bedrooms were overrun, where some crack team of investigators found the outline of where a human being could sleep on a bed otherwise piled to the ceiling with newspapers in triplicate and mold samples that had to be identified by outside laboratories. Another part of me imagined it might be an even more sexed-up version of my sister's bedroom, with padded walls and a secret sex-dungeon entrance. But it was neither. It was messy, for sure, but most of it just looked like a regular-girl bedroom, maybe even the bedroom of someone younger than either of us. Her comforter was ballet-slipper pink, and her bed had the kind of lavender canopy over it that I had begged for when I was eight. She hadn't made the bed, but she'd last slept next to an oversize stuffed iguana, and three or four other stuffed horses were tucked beneath the blankets. Iggy had perched himself on the back of a well-worn plush unicorn. I snatched the lizard before he knew what had happened, and once I got ahold of him, he relaxed and felt softer than I'd imagined. I could almost see why Olivia liked him.

When I went back into the living room, Jeremy was cleaning dog shit off his shoes and talking to his sister on speaker. I don't know what they'd been talking about before, but whatever it had been, she was furious.

"Would you please quit being a douche and get my electricity back on? I'll pay you for it when I get back."

"You can pay for it now," Jeremy answered. "You can look up the number."

"Don't," she said, like the word had teeth, "use that AA bullshit on me. You're not above this. You spent three nights in jail, if I remember correctly. How would you like it if that little truth was magically revealed to the press? Save your self-righteousness for meetings. I don't buy it."

Three nights in jail? That was the first I'd heard of that one. I couldn't tell if Olivia was telling the truth, or if the truth bothered Jeremy. If it did, it didn't bother him enough to take the phone off speaker. He shook his head and threw the cloth he'd been using in the garbage, and then he pointed to the iguana and gave me a thumbs-up.

"We've got Iggy," he said. "Now if you could tell me where you keep the dog food."

"Who's 'we'?" she asked. "Did you bring someone with you? I don't want your whores in my house. *Helloooooooo,*" she yelled cheerfully.

"It's Anna," he said. "You met her. And she's not a whore. She just found your iguana and put him back in his cage, so you might want to thank her." He slumped forward onto the counter where he'd laid his phone down, and shook his head like she could see him. "You're so angry. I don't get how you do it."

"I'm angry? How are you *not* angry, is the better question. How are you not outraged every second of your life?

"Anna," she said, her voice lower and suddenly sweet, "you know he's in AA, right? You know that in that stupid cult they have a rule that you have to do one nice thing every day and not get caught. My guess is that you're that thing for Jer-Bear here. Otherwise, from what I've seen of you"—and she might as well have been looking me up and down when she said it—"you're not his type."

"Enough," he said, in a voice so adult that it sounded like it belonged to someone else. "No more. The crazy thing is, Olivia, most days I try to do something nice for you, and I don't get caught because you don't even notice."

Then there was a silence like someone had slapped her across the face. Then the *beep-beep-beep* that she had left the conversation.

I wanted to disappear as much as I'd wanted anything in my whole life. I didn't care about the stupid purse anymore, or about helping Jeremy clean Olivia's apartment, or that her electricity was off. I didn't even care that I'd been stupid enough a few minutes before to think that Jeremy had brought me there because he really liked me. If Olivia had called me a hag, it wouldn't have felt any worse. *Not his type.* I didn't have to speak "bitch" fluently to know exactly what she meant. She meant ugly, and the word felt a thousand times more embarrassing than if she'd paraded me around in my nonmatching underwear. I wanted out of there, but I didn't know how to ask.

Jeremy had found the dog food and placed it by the door. Beside it was the bag from the store where I'd bought Olivia the purse.

"I found this." He lifted the bag toward me. "The receipt's still in there. It has your dad's name on it. I'll bet you can return it."

I took the shopping bag, but I couldn't look him in the face. Olivia's dog licked my ankle, and when I reached down to pet him I could feel how small and fragile his head was beneath all that fur, that he had a slight shake even when he was trying to be still.

"You can't pay attention to her," Jeremy said.

"Sure," I said. "No. I'm not."

More than anything I wanted him to stop talking, and almost like he could read my mind, he offered to take me back to the set. Mr. Peabody sat on my lap and we listened to music as we rode. I didn't recognize any of the songs, but they were low and sad, like they'd been dipped in the darkest of blues. Maybe it was the music, but when we got to the studio, Jeremy touched his hand against my face before I got out of the car.

"I'll see you later," I said, and before I could stop myself, like a total idiot, I said, "Thanks."

He looked at me like I was sadder than Mr. Peabody. At least he had the sense not to say you're welcome. And at least I had the sense to leave.

The rest of the week I played sick. I had to stay at my sister's place, because otherwise Dex would know that I was faking, but I couldn't go back to *Chips Ahoy!,* not until Jeremy had at least a week to forget that his sister had all but called me a hag. Delia said he probably wouldn't even remember, but that was only because she hadn't been on the receiving end of the beat-down I'd taken. I'd rather have risked Delia's psycho neighborhood than endure further humiliation. Not even a contest, really.

Delia brought me a stack of movies from Dex's place, including one that he'd snagged from the set: *Kandy Kisses: From Olivia Taylor to You, the Real Olivia Taylor Story.* "In case you get tired of working on your history final," she said. I couldn't tell whether Delia was being nice or just messing with me. I'd seen the movie twice with Doon when it first came out. We even talked her mom into taking us to a midnight screening "slumber party" the night that it opened. At the time, Olivia Taylor had seemed like the prettiest, nicest, funnest person you could ever trade stickers with, but now I knew that she was a spiritual wolf in Malibu Slut Barbie's hand-me-downs. Then I remembered that the twins were in the movie, and that more than anything made me load it up.

The movie came out right when my parents were first having problems, and part of the reason that I loved Olivia Taylor so much was that her own dad had never been a part of her life, and some of her mom's lunacy couldn't help but leak onto the screen. Her family wasn't crazy in the same way that mine was, but it was definitely crazy. The movie opened with a group of fans, teenage girls, talking about how much they loved Olivia Taylor, how she made them feel like someone understood them, how no matter how sad they were, they knew that happiness was just a "kandy kiss" away. Then, surprise, Olivia Taylor came out of her bus, showering them with air-kisses and high-end candy, telling them that *they* were *her* inspiration. The movie followed three months of her tour, three months of her and her mom fighting about her costumes, her boyfriend, the size of her ass. Her brothers had just gotten cast in *Mouse Around the House,* a show that ran for about ten seconds and might have been even worse than *Chips Ahoy!* Still, it was pretty obvious that Mom had her eyes on the newbies, that Olivia was going to be on her own soon enough, fighting or no fighting. Right after the movie came out, the court case when Olivia sued for emancipation started.

But the funny thing was, in the movie, Olivia had so many friends. There was her best friend from her neighborhood, the girl she met in dance class and would *never leave behind,* who tap-danced (badly) through her "Rock Pop Rocks" number, not to mention a posse of managers, stylists, and choreographers who claimed that they were just a bunch of big love-balls orbiting

Olivia. Selfless fans with nothing but her best interests in mind. The movie closed with Olivia looking at the camera and saying, "If I can make one person happy, I've done my job. I just want to make the whole world a little sweeter." Air-kiss and fade to black.

Jeremy texted me as the credits rolled: "Does the iguana get to live?"

I wrote back: "I don't know. Do you call that living?"

Jeremy responded: "LOL. Hope ur feeling better."

And that was it.

I decided that I had camped out long enough. The next day I would put on my big-girl pants and go back to the set. It didn't matter that I still felt embarrassed, that I had no idea what I was going to say to Jeremy when I saw him. I didn't even know what I was supposed to do with the stupid handbag; the fine print of its receipt read: *Can only be returned for store credit.* Not even kind of helpful. But if watching *Kandy Kisses* taught me anything, it was that you couldn't trust what you saw, no matter how beautiful it looked. And if everyone was going to pretend to be a little better off than they actually were, a little more sure of their place in the world, I might as well join the party.

14

I was trying to make myself inconspicuous on the set, tucked in a hallway and reading a book that was supposed to be from the perspective of Sharon Tate's family. The book imagined how all of Tate's relatives were just going through the motions on a regular day when they got the news about their daughter, their sister. She was murdered the night before what was supposed to be her baby shower; presents had been wrapped: baby boots, blankets, a bassinet. And then the phone rang and their lives changed forever. The Manson murders took America by surprise, and in particular, this one family. I knew what it was to hate the telephone, to have this low level of dread every time the phone rang or a message showed up at the wrong time of the night. Since my mom told me she was sick, all news was potentially bad news.

Only most of the time, the news wasn't bad. I kept getting calls from my mom about how great her life was going. She'd found a circle of moms who would donate their breast milk to Birch (I cannot even get into how hard I almost threw up). She was meditating and imagining me with a circle of light all around me. *Like a bull's-eye,* I said, and she didn't even pretend to laugh. But she never apologized, never even admitted that she'd said the horrible things that she'd said. *Oh, Anna, you hear things that aren't there. I don't remember saying anything like that. In fact, I would never say anything like that.* The whole thing was making me crazy. When I wasn't worried sick that she was dying, I was ready to quit talking to her forever.

It would be wrong to say that I had a genuine premonition when Delia's number flashed while I was tucked in my usual corner on the *Chips Ahoy!* set, but at the same time I had this crazy sense that something wasn't right. Everyone had just finished the table-reading when my sister called, her voice cloudy, telling me to get to the hospital. It took me a minute to realize that she wasn't talking about Mom, she was talking about herself. She sounded foggy.

"Anna," she said. "Just get someone to drive you. Do not, I repeat, do *not* let Dex know. Just make something up."

"Are you okay?"

She started to cry. "No, I'm not okay. My nose is broken."

"Your nose is broken?"

"Don't say that, okay? Don't say anything. Just get here and take me home. I don't have money for a cab. I was mugged. Someone stole my wallet."

"Oh no!"

"Please," she said. "Just hurry."

I must have looked as worried as I felt, because Jeremy stopped milling around the food table and asked what was wrong.

"My sister," I said. "She got mugged. She's in the hospital, and she needs a ride back to her place."

"I'll get Dex. I just saw him."

"No," I said, and hated that this was going to make me sound like an even bigger sketchball, a sketchball-ette from a family of the same. "She doesn't want him to know. I think she's really medicated. She said her nose is broken."

"I can drive you," Jeremy said.

"Really? That would be amazing."

"Sure," he said.

"Thank you," I said. "I just realized, I don't even know what hospital she's at."

"What part of town was she in?"

"Downtown. She's shooting an indie film." And I even had the sense not to say "with her ex-boyfriend."

"I think I know."

Jeremy was a slow driver, which I guess I had noticed before, but it hadn't bothered me. I foolishly chalked it up to his wanting to show me the wonders of Los Angeles at a speed that I could appreciate. Now, when I needed to be at the hospital ten minutes ago, the fact that he was a terrible driver was becoming clearer with each stop on yellow and long pause as he rounded a corner. He was cautious. And by cautious, I do not merely mean "safe driver," but scared old man going ten miles an hour down the road. For the first few minutes I looked at the faces of the angry motorists as they passed, throwing us shade for slowing them down. How had I missed this?

"Do you need to call your mom?" Jeremy asked.

"I can't," I said. And then before he could ask why not: "I

can't because she's sick herself. She won't know what to do. No one ever knows what to do in my family."

He pumped his brakes as we came to a four-way stop. Then he waited well past when my sister or Olivia would have turned, meandering through the intersection. He was going to get me killed. Then my whole family would be in the hospital.

"I'm sorry about your mom," he said. "What does she have?"

"Cancer," I said, and I realized I hadn't said the word out loud since that first night. It sounded ugly and heavy.

"Anna," he said. "Why didn't you tell me? I'm really sorry."

"Remember how you told me that once you say something, it kind of goes away? It's not like that with my mom. It's more like if I don't talk about it, it won't be real. Like saying she's sick really makes her sick. That probably sounds crazy. Plus, my sister hates talking about it. My whole family is insane, you realize that, right?"

My mom's surgery was scheduled for tomorrow. Lynette had called yesterday to tell us that while they were optimistic, they wouldn't really know anything until they were inside her. She'd decided not to have both her breasts removed, just the one, and to have chemo and reconstructive surgery. Lynette said that she was depressed. Birch was fussy, and every time she nursed him she became inconsolable. *I think she'd really appreciate a call, some flowers, as much goodwill as you can send. Her mental state has me worried.* I gave her a call later and she told me how much she loved me and missed me and couldn't wait until I got home. How I was her baby, that she wanted her babies around her.

But I didn't want to be there the way I had when I first heard the news.

"It's the kind where she'll get better. Only she doesn't sound so good. I think she's getting really depressed. The more she tells me that she's trying to visualize her body becoming this healing space, the more I think she's worse off than she's letting me know. She was breastfeeding my brother, and she had to stop, and she thinks that my running out to LA just made it worse, so that sucks too. It all sucks. It's a big fat pit of suck."

"And this all happened since you came out here?"

"Yes."

The sad-puppy look again. Not what I had wanted. I did not want to be his good deed for the day. I wanted to be something more.

We parked near the entrance, and I heard my sister before I saw her. She was yelling at Roger, *"Only you would pay a poor person to mug someone and think they wouldn't actually mug them. You get that people aren't pretending to be poor, right?"* The hospital lights had a blue-tinged fluorescence, and Delia looked like something that had crossed over from hell. Her hair was wild; her face was swollen around a tent of a splint pitched on the center of her face.

"If my face is ruined, I will sue you for every penny I could have made in the best of all possible worlds."

Roger looked desperate. I dare say he was happy to see me.

"Ohmigod." I hugged her. She hugged me hard and started to cry a little. "What happened?"

"You can leave now," she said to Roger, and pointed at the exit.

"I cannot leave you. Not until you forgive me."

"If you don't leave, I'm going to start screaming, and I'm not going to stop."

Roger left.

Delia hadn't even noticed Jeremy, and he seemed to go unrecognized in this place where everyone had something more pressing on their minds.

"You got mugged," Jeremy finally said. "Have you talked to the cops?"

"They just left. So Roger, because he wants to be super Method and cinema verité or God knows what, he decides that he'll pay one of the homeless men, someone he just met this morning, to follow me. To give me a genuine scare. And the dickwad tried to take my purse, so I grabbed it and went for his balls. And he punches me in the face. He punches me in the face and says, 'God, you're a bitch.' He took off with my purse, and instead of chasing him, Roger says to me—and I could not make this up—'I'm so sorry. I never thought he would do something like that.'"

"Man," Jeremy said. "That's a problem."

"What am I going to do? They called me this morning to say that I got the herpes. I can't lose that. How can I work like this? I can't even fucking breathe."

Jeremy looked confused.

"A herpes commercial," I said. Delia sounded crazy, like

one of those old people who talk about people getting "the AIDS." I was trying not to crack up, and so was Jeremy.

"So is he a Method director or something?" Jeremy was looking at my sister's face, which was still beautiful around the edges.

"He's a Method asshole," she said. "And a freaking Brando at that."

Jeremy laughed. I wondered if Delia knew who he was. As "the twins" they got stopped on the streets a hundred times a day, but when you separated Jeremy out, he became less recognizable by factors of ten.

"Can you give us a ride home?" Delia asked.

"Sure," Jeremy said.

"And please don't mention anything to Dex but that I got mugged, okay?"

I wasn't sure which of us she was talking to, but we both nodded.

Jeremy drove us, tortoise-style, up the winding hills to my sister's apartment. As we climbed the last hill, the red Honda that Delia claimed I was hallucinating sat parked outside. I wanted to wake her up, but she was finally asleep and moaning in pain. I poked Jeremy and pointed, then shook my head so that he wouldn't say anything. The car sped away as we approached.

"That car," I whispered. "It parks outside her place. For weeks, it's been there. She gave me some BS story about an actress who wanted some part that she got, but I don't believe her."

Jeremy shook his head slowly. "Stalkers are no joke. Have you called the police?"

"And said what? A car drives by our house, one that my sister won't even acknowledge exists?"

"You can tell her that I saw it. You should contact someone. This is kind of a secluded spot."

"Tell me about it."

Delia woke up long enough to stumble through the doorway and collapse on the couch. Jeremy made sure that we had ice, Advil, and food.

"I don't feel great about leaving you here," he said. "Is Dex coming?"

"I think so. I hope so."

"Call the set if anything looks weird. Anything at all. I'm due back in an hour, but I'll wait around in my car to see if anything happens."

"Thanks," I said. "Seriously. That's really nice."

"It's no big deal."

And I could tell that he meant it. It wasn't a big deal, it was what any decent human being would do, given the circumstances. But decent human beings seemed hard to come by, and his was such unlikely packaging. For a minute I thought he was going to hug me, and instead of opening my arms, like a normal human female, I panicked. I bent down to scratch my knee, which kind of itched, because even more than I wanted him to touch me, I didn't want him to blow me off.

When I stood back up he was still there, and he rested his

hands on my shoulders and held them there. I could barely breathe. If I was supposed to do something next, I had no idea what it was. After what seemed like forever, he squeezed my shoulders gently and ran his hands down both of my arms. Even though he'd only touched my arms, the whole inside of my body felt electric, lit up. And just when I'd almost convinced myself that he was about to draw me close and kiss me, he had opened the door and was waving good-bye.

My sister was all but tripping on meds for the rest of the evening. The doctor said that they'd given her enough muscle relaxants to tranquilize a horse, but she'd found a way to stay awake and manic.

"When do you think the swelling will go down?" she kept asking. "I need to know what my face is going to look like. Google something." And then if she looked in the mirror: "It's the Elephant Man. I'm Jack Nicholson in *Chinatown*." And then: "How am I going to explain this to Dex? What if I don't look the same?"

And for just a minute, I had a nasty thought—well, then you'll have to see how the rest of us manage—but then I felt terrible for it.

"Roger expects me to show up for work tomorrow," she said. "What am I supposed to do? He thinks it will help with the shoot. In his sick little heart, this is better than he imagined. I feel like I'm in *Boxing Helena*. What if this is the last movie I'm even in? What if Roger is my only hope?"

"Then you're screwed," I said.

She started to laugh. "Okay," she said. "Thank you. Will you call Dex, tell him that you're going on location with me tomorrow?"

There were only two more weeks of shooting the *Chips Ahoy!* summer season, and I didn't want to miss a day.

"Couldn't Roger just pick you up? Wouldn't it look more normal?"

"And then what? Dex has to drive all the way over here to pick you up while I hide my face? That makes zero sense, Anna, and thank you for all of your sympathy after all I've done for you."

She yawned twice while she was ranting, which sort of broke the rhythm of how pissed off she was. If she even woke up tomorrow it would be a miracle. She looked like she was roofied enough to sleep for months.

"I'm sorry," I said.

The next morning Delia's face looked worse: more swollen, more purple, more hopeless. She took one look in the mirror, scarfed a handful of painkillers, and left Roger a message that she couldn't shoot until the next day. Then she went back to bed. I watched her phone ring. Dex, Roger, Dex, Roger. She slept through all of it. There was nothing on television, and the only book that I'd downloaded but not finished was Susan Atkins's autobiography. She was the Manson girl I least enjoyed reading about. Hers was the knife that had killed Sharon Tate and her unborn son, but on death row Atkins had evidently found Jesus and was super born-again. She reminded me of the girls I knew who would sleep with their boyfriends, then go get revirginized at some church camp, then sleep with their boyfriends again.

My sister would moan every so often, or wander into the kitchen, drink some water, take another pill, and go back to bed. After the first time, she stopped looking in the mirror.

Susan Atkins was like a lot of the other Manson girls—their lives were kind of screwed up, but definitely not screwed up enough to go out and start killing people. She was a middle child who craved attention, an expert thief, and when she was a teenager, her mom got cancer. I didn't like the way her life was making me look more Mansonian by the minute, but I kept reading. Her dad was an alcoholic and she did a lot of drugs and hated him, and she had a son by one of the other Manson family members, which made it even crazier that she could kill someone who was eight months pregnant. Only she claimed that she didn't kill Sharon Tate, or anyone else, that she just *pretended* to have killed them so that she could be the center of attention and so that she'd fit in with the rest of the psychopaths. If you crossed *Mean Girls* with *The Lord of the Flies* and weaponized all of them, then you pretty much had the Manson girls.

Leslie Van Houten, the ex–homecoming queen, begged to take part in the LaBianca massacre because her best friend had gone on the Tate rampage, and she felt left out. But Leslie didn't really like Susan. Death row was *soooooooo* cliquey, what was a girl to do? Susan Atkins said she found Jesus and pretty much spent the rest of her life needlepointing and trying to do good things, like get paroled. Maybe she was sincere. Reading her whole story was kind of like becoming part of the Manson family for an hour. She believed whatever she was selling enough that her story was almost convincing. The fact that her reasons for taking part in the murders were all so stupid made the book extra depressing. I kept waiting for the moment when she revealed all the awful things that had happened to her that she'd forgotten to mention, but mostly she just sang the same old song. *I wanted to be special. I wished Charlie and the other girls liked me more.* When I finished, I had such a headache that I stole one of my sister's painkillers.

Maybe it was because I took the painkiller and it made me as crazy as Delia that I did something that I could never, ever tell Doon about. I texted Paige Parker. Two lines:

"Sorry. But for real, I am actually sorry."

The afternoon that I took Lynette's credit card, her wallet had been laying on the dining room table, right next to an apology note written by my mother: *Dear Paige, I am sincerely sorry for whatever hurt I caused you or your family. I would never have intentionally hurt someone . . .* blah, blah, blah. What it should have said was, *Please don't sue my mother. Please!* because that's what she really meant. I threw it away before I bought my ticket west.

I didn't want Paige to think that the text was something that my mom made me send because she'd read some Internet article about making your kid be sorry. I wanted her to know that at that exact moment, maybe for the first time, I actually felt bad about what we had done. Not that it mattered. She probably deleted it and threw her phone across the room. At any rate, she didn't exactly rush to text me back.

The next day Delia woke up groggy and said that Roger was picking us up. She must have texted him in the night, because I hadn't heard her on the phone.

"Did you call Dex?" I asked.

"I called him this morning. He's coming over tonight."

I was worried for her. Worried that Dex would start to realize that my sister had more fantastic stories than the zaniest of pilots, that he wouldn't like her face, that I wouldn't get to go back to the *Chips Ahoy!* set.

"How did he sound?" I chewed on my thumb, afraid of her answer.

"You should care about me, not him," Delia snapped.

She was right, but she was also painkiller pissy, so I just shut my mouth.

Not even Roger could pretend that her face wasn't a mess. He'd probably been practicing some spiel in the car about how amazing she looked, how well she was healing, but it was definitely "worse before better" territory, and when he saw her, he froze.

"That's great," Delia said. "We've finally found a way to keep you from lying to my face. *Change* my face." She popped a pill and rubbed her head. "I'm still not clear on what we're doing."

Had it been any other day, I would have said that made two of us. But Delia was freaking me out, because her nose was so busted that not even her voice was right. As lousy an option as Roger was, riding with him was better than being alone with my sister.

"Where are we filming today?" she finally asked, but it sounded like despair, like one of those questions you ask after you've just had the world's hugest fight with someone that you're still going to see every day. My mom used to do that with my dad, before they finally split. Things would be totally biblical-apocalyptic between them, explosive arguing that not even my bedroom door and television could block out, and then when I went in the living room, my mom would look at my dad and say something like "What's for dinner?" in his direction, all dead and defeated. Like I was deaf. Like they were these amazing actors, which they definitely weren't.

"Darkroom," Roger said.

"Good. Maybe it will hide my face."

After that, Delia nodded off to sleep until we reached our destination.

"I could not get the actual space," Roger told me, "but this is nearby. William Richard Bradford killed, who knows, maybe fifty women, and before killing them, he took their pictures. He told them that they should be models. He was going to make them famous."

Sounded like someone else I knew, but I kept my mouth shut.

"He would cut off the tattoos, so they were, how is it you say, Jane Doves?"

"Jane Does," I said.

"There were pictures of over fifty women on his walls."

"So this isn't the actual darkroom?"

"No," he said. "I have friends who have another space. Do you think Delia . . . ?"

He didn't finish his sentence. I shrugged my shoulders. His guess was as good as mine as to what we were going to get when she woke up.

"Ohmigod," she finally groaned, pulling out a bottle of pills. "What the hell have I been taking? I feel like my skin is coming off my body. These pain pills are worse than pain." She passed the bottle to Roger.

"Percocet," he said.

"Just throw them out the window."

Roger rolled the window down and tossed them out.

"I didn't mean literally, you asshole!"

"What?" Roger said. "I can do nothing to please you."

"You can start by not paying to have me mugged and de-forming my face. Do you have anything for pain, Anna?"

"I don't," I said. I was trying not to get yelled at. My sister was mental.

"We are here," Roger said, pulling into the lot of a run-down apartment building.

Delia wouldn't get out of the car. "How do I know you haven't paid someone to stab me?"

"Please," Roger said. "I promise you. You will be beautiful. This movie will be beautiful. I have it now, the whole thing came to me last night. Like God had answered a prayer. This film will be my way of saying how sorry I am."

I didn't care how many sketchballs were loitering in front of the building, I got out of the car. I could see my sister and Roger arguing through the window, and even the silent-film version of their relationship was depressing.

"So you'll have a full script for me by Monday," Delia said, exiting dramatically.

"I will do nothing else until it is finished."

"Okay," she said. "You take a piss, you call me first."

"Can we please shoot?" Roger lowered his voice, like he was coaxing a rabid dog into its cage.

The apartment building was like a more populated incarnation of the Bates Motel. Long and slender, it probably had peepholes in every wall, cameras mounted in every corner. Roger unlocked the door and the inside was worse. Top sheet on the bed from the seventies (when it had probably last been washed); dead roach on the floor; the sound of someone's music pounding through the wall.

"Can you film with all that noise?" I asked.

"Sound is later," he said. "I am still gathering images."

I couldn't decide which was worse, the canned stupidity of *Chips Ahoy!* or the dressed-up stupidity of Roger's image-gathering. But I did know which gave me a bigger headache. A much bigger headache. I wished I had Pinky the Penis from the *Chips* set to hide somewhere in the room. I could have bunny-eared it over Roger's head when he started shooting my sister.

"What is so funny?"

"Nothing."

"I need two minutes," Roger said, and opened his back-pack. He pulled out stacks of pictures from inside, eight-by-tens of women, most beautiful, all young. Some looked like high school pictures, others like head shots, others like amateur porn. He taped them to the walls rapidly and without any seeming order. "These women, he took pictures of them before killing them. I could find pictures of some of the women but not all. So some are now Manson girls. Some are from the magazines. I think it is better not to be too literal."

"Is there a mirror here?"

"In the bathroom," Roger said.

"I'm going to fix my face," Delia said. "What's left of it."

About nine pictures from the end, Roger put a picture on the wall that I recognized. Olivia Taylor. It must have been from her early pop-star days. Her hair was still curly and she was blowing a kiss. Three pictures later came Susan Atkins. The music from above switched to a pounding bass, and I checked the door to make sure that it was locked.

"It is good, no?" Roger said, backing away.

I nodded. It was creepier than any slasher film, smile after smile of hopeful faces, faces beautiful enough to be easily loved, unloved enough to be easily fooled. For the first time in my life I was glad that I didn't look like that, that I wasn't the kind of pretty that turned a girl into prey.

"I can't cover the splint," Delia said, emerging from the bathroom. She had camouflaged the rest of the evidence of the mugging. Her face was heavily powdered and her eyes were wild. "Are these real?" She was pointing at the wall.

Roger had started to film her.

"I want you to look at the pictures."

It was impossible to look at anything else. Delia ran her hand across one of the middle rows, and then went from face to face for a while, stopping on a girl who seemed quietly beautiful, straight brown hair parted down the middle, a crucifix around her neck. The girl could have been Delia's younger, clean-scrubbed twin. Maybe she'd been glad to be approached by a handsome photographer. Who wouldn't want to have her face on someone's wall, right?

"This is *fucking* depressing," my sister raged, pulling the pictures off with both hands, crumpling them and then going back for more. "*Fuck* this wall and *fuck* this film."

Roger kept filming. He didn't smile, but I could feel the charge in the air. He was getting exactly what he wanted.

"Is my picture in that bag?" she asked. "Do you have a picture like that of me?"

She went over to his bag and dumped the rest of the contents. An energy bar, his phone, what looked like a pair of shorts for working out, a condom. Nice.

"We're done for today. Come on, Anna. My head is killing me. It feels like someone put an ice pick through my face. And I saw a liquor store across the street. Roger, you are buying me the strongest thing they have in that store. I am going to roofie myself, frat-party style, and then no one is allowed to touch me. Got it?"

"Of course," he said.

Delia flopped back on the bed, closed her eyes, and rubbed the skin around her nose. I felt like telling her that she should be careful not to get bedbugs, but I didn't want those to be my last words.

"We can go now." He had packed his camera and opened the door for us.

"What time is it?"

"Four o'clock," I said.

"Dex is coming at seven."

"Dex," Roger said.

"Yes, *Dex,*" I repeated. "D-E-X. It's his name, not a curse word, okay?"

"I said nothing." Roger wasn't above being smug with me, no matter how much he'd take from Delia.

"If I'm sloshed, you explain, Anna."

"Okay."

But I couldn't explain my sister, not to myself or anyone else. Dex had even texted me to make sure that she was okay. Then he called. I told him that her face was messed up and she didn't want him to see her like that. He told me that was crazy, and I agreed, but the person whose opinion really mattered was having none of it.

We got back into the car and drove across the street to the liquor store. I waited in the car with Delia, who was moaning like an injured animal.

"Why did he throw those pills out the window? I'm going to die of pain. Die."

She was talking with her mouth almost closed, because when she moved her lips it hurt more. Roger returned with a bottle of vodka in a brown paper bag, and passed me back a can of orange soda. Delia opened the bottle and drank straight from it, right there in the front seat of the car. A vagrant sitting outside the liquor store pointed at her through our window and gave two big thumbs-up. Delia didn't stop drinking and gave him a thumbs-up with her free hand. It was like the opposite of how they tell you to live your life everywhere else on the planet.

"How much of this do you think I can drink without ending up back in the hospital?"

"I don't know," I said. "But I'd slow down."

"Good idea," Roger said. He looked nervous but weirdly happy. I think he liked my sister unchained. He probably had her face knocked in on purpose and now he was scared and lying, but loving it.

"Can we go somewhere besides this parking lot?"

"Yes," Roger said. "Of course."

My sister talked with more and more of her mouth as the

drive went on, but her speech was running together. Roger drove us back to his place, the same crappy apartment that he'd lived in with my sister. I had repressed, trauma-victim memories of the place, of listening to them have weird, angry sex through the walls, of my sister crying. Roger dropped us in front of the building and I helped Delia up the stairs and through Roger's unlocked apartment door. For someone documenting murders in LA, he wasn't exactly taking the safety lessons home.

Once Roger came in, we sat on his decrepit balcony that overlooked a Dumpster, and I watched my sister drink more vodka, the scent of decaying food and urine not even kind of faint in the air.

"I can't breathe," I said.

Roger ignored me and so did Delia.

"Can I get something else to drink? I finished my soda."

Roger gestured at the bottle of vodka. My sister shook her head.

"She's not even sixteen, Roger," Delia said. "Don't start thinking you're Polanski. There's water on the counter." And I wondered why my sister was so sure of where he kept his things. Did she just assume, or was this where she'd been going those nights that Dex and I were watching bad TV?

"Ugh," I said. "Throwing up in mouth. I'll get some water."

I wandered into his apartment, which had giant movie posters in Italian and French on the walls, *L'avventura, La Dolce Vita, À Bout de Souffle*. The women on the posters were beautiful and foreign, larger than life in every sense of the phrase. I took a handful of chips and ate them while I poured a glass of water from the pitcher, which was exactly where my sister said it would be. When I went back outside, they were going at it.

"He is a beautiful director," Roger said.

"He's a pervert and a monster," Delia said. "I don't care what happened to him. And I really, really, really don't care how many times you've seen *Chinatown*, or *The Tenant*, or *Repulsion*, okay? So please don't give me his résumé against his ass-rapery. Because it's funky math."

While she was talking, the phone next to her kept ringing. I saw Dex's number flash, and then the time, 7:20, and Delia ignored it, like having a broken nose was making her deaf as well.

"Your phone," I said.

She looked at it, turned it off, and tossed it into her bag like she'd touched something radioactive.

"Your reactions," Roger said. "They are very American."

"Bullshit," Delia said, taking another shot of vodka. "You think European women like being raped? Not even in the most French film on the planet."

Roger leaned back in his chair and folded his hands behind his head.

"If you believe she was raped."

"I do. I do believe that she was raped. And they should drag his ass back to America and put him in jail." Delia tossed her empty shot glass from the balcony into the Dumpster and looked at Roger like she was daring him to say something. The more relaxed Roger acted, the twitchier my sister became.

"You do not like to believe," he said. "But some girls, thirteen, yes, some girls, perhaps they do want this."

"You mean," Delia's voice sharpened, "that a thirteen-year-old girl was asking for it?"

"Is it so impossible to imagine?"

"Any girl who would want that hasn't been taught what else to want. Or she's been taught to want it. Either way. *No.* Just no."

"He was grieving," Roger said. "Who can imagine how a person lives through what he saw? He lost his child and beautiful wife. It turned him ugly. Anna, you have read about this?"

I had. I had read about how Roman Polanski was pretty much a sketchball who knocked up a very pretty actress and then continued to be a sketchball. Supposedly, after they'd been married a while, he was driving up to Tate from behind and started to catcall at the hottie walking down the road before he realized that it was actually his wife. His mother was killed in the Holocaust, his wife and unborn son were horribly murdered, and he turned around and raped a young girl. It reminded me a little bit of *The Virgin Spring,* an art film that Roger made us all watch one Christmas. In it, a young girl is raped and murdered by two men as the kid who is traveling with them, a kid who can't even talk and doesn't do anything, watches. They then accidentally go to the house of the father of the young girl, and after he lets them come in to spend the night, the father realizes that they've killed his daughter. He murders them all, even the kid who didn't do anything, who couldn't even talk. I don't know why, but Polanski reminded me of the father, all of that death and then he goes and does the wrong thing. There had to be a reason, but it made no sense. Still, it seemed important.

"I have a question," I said.

"The answer is no." Delia was cracking herself up. She was seriously drunk.

"Why do you think it is that Roman Polanski does this awful thing and doesn't even feel sorry about it, but he gets to live his life? And you have these women, the Manson girls, who did this really horrible thing when they were young and stupid and on drugs, and they never get to spend one day not paying for it, even though most of them have spent the rest of their lives trying to do something to, I don't know, atone?"

"It is a good question." Roger crossed and uncrossed his legs.

I didn't feel like it was a good question; in fact, it was the kind of question that made me want to wash my own mouth out with soap. How could a person ever make up for the things that those women had done? And yet, when the dust settled, it seemed like all of the women who had been part of the murder had genuinely been shocked that Charles Manson wasn't right. Helter Skelter didn't usher in some beautiful new world, it just left the old one a little more awful. They'd been following some horrible, sadistic loser who didn't know any more about the end of the world than the sketchballs in the liquor store parking lot. Was it so impossible to believe that a person, having re-gained what little sanity she might have once possessed, would then feel outright awful about what she'd done? The easy thing was to say, *No, they were monsters, they had to be monsters to do something like that.* But what if the truth was more complicated? What if they weren't really as different as everyone wanted to believe? But it was the kind of thought that was impossible to hold, double impossible if I tried to keep it in my head next to the list of the victims, or the thought of that sad, flat grave-stone. Still, I had to ask: What if they were really and truly sorry? Did it matter at all?

"Because women, my dear sister," Delia said, "are fucked."

"Hypocrite." Roger was matching her vodka for vodka. Not only was I not going to get a useful answer to any of my questions, I was also going to have to take a cab home.

"Oh, screw you, Roger."

Then my phone rang. Dex. I slipped into the other room and answered.

"Are you okay?" he said. "Delia was supposed to call me hours ago. What the hell is going on? Is she just messing with me, or does she need help, because I can't figure it out right now. I really can't. And I'm starting to feel like a chump."

Roger's living room table was glass and steel, a window to the unvacuumed floor below, and the backpack he had carried to the shoot was open across its top. The faces that had been on the walls spilled onto the clear glass, on top of which was a young girl with a heart locket, lips parted and hair feathered away from her face. I didn't recognize her. She might have been one of the real girls, the ones found in pieces around LA. She was no one famous. On the other end of the line, Dex was fuming. Irritated, worried, and mad—not a great combination.

"We're at her friend's apartment. She didn't like how she felt on her pain medications, so she decided that vodka was better than Percocet."

"Uh-oh."

I slumped back into Roger's couch. The impossibly perfect Anita Ekberg looked down from the wall, back arched and ankle-deep in a Roman fountain.

"I don't think she wants you to see her face."

"Why not?"

"I don't know," I said. "I think she thinks that you might stop liking her."

There was silence for a good minute or so. I thought he'd hung up.

"Do you know where you are? Do you have the address?"

There was a stack of mail on the counter. I read him our location.

"I'll be there in thirty minutes. And please tell your sister to stop selling me short, okay?"

"Okay."

When I returned to the patio, Delia and Roger were both quiet, staring across each other into space.

"Dex is coming to get us," I said.

My sister stayed frozen. Roger repeated his name.

I had carried the picture of the girl with the heart necklace back onto the patio.

"Who is this?" I asked.

And because he's such a dirtbag, a sketchball among sketchballs, I swear he was smiling. "The Geimer girl," he said. "She was in some famous pictures, no?"

"No," I said. "I've never seen this. Am I supposed to know her name?"

"I am paying you this money to research, you tell me."

I passed the picture back to Roger and the three of us sat in silence, watching the garbage rot. Thirty minutes later I helped my barely upright sister into the back of Dex's car.

Dex was doing the right thing, the kind thing, but he didn't look happy. Once he buckled my sister's slurring self into the car, he gave me one of those "Are you freaking kidding me?" looks that do not bode well. Delia smiled a little, too tired and too out of it to open her eyes. I honestly had to stop myself from telling her to wipe that stupid grin off her face, like I was her mom or something.

"Thanks for answering your phone," he said to me. "She went on a film shoot today? Must be some kind of director." He was disgusted.

My sister moaned and cracked the window, rubbing her head against where the glass opened into the night.

Thirty minutes later I was cross-legged on Dex's couch, watching bad TV and thinking how only a mental patient like my sister could find a way to like Roger more than this.

That night I looked up the name of the girl in the picture, Samantha Geimer. No wonder Roger was smiling. She was a girl who had been photographed, and famously, by Roman Polanski two weeks before he pumped her full of champagne and quaaludes and raped her. Like everyone in LA, it seemed, she'd wanted to be famous: a model, an actress, a star. He convinced her to pose topless, which I couldn't even imagine. I hated taking my shirt off in the locker room, or at the doctor's office. I had breasts, enough that my bra wasn't just one of those lacy things that flat-chested girls get to be part of the club, but they didn't totally feel like a part of me yet. Having breasts was definitely better than not having breasts, but I still wasn't about to parade them around town. Samantha was thirteen years old when Polanski raped her, and thinking of the picture it wasn't just that she looked older, but that she didn't even look like someone I recognized as a girl, baby-faced and *Do me* all at once. The slutty girls that I knew went all-in, Olivia Taylor style, and the ones who weren't wore promise rings from churches and could list all the ways you were going to hell and the diseases you would catch if you let a boy too near your crotch.

My sister and Dex had retreated into his bedroom. He was a good boyfriend, the kind that came out to get her water and was okay with doing his work in bed next to her. But he didn't look happy. Once my sister was better, my guess was they were going to have a conversation, and not about her face.

I had watched so much television that I could feel my brain rotting in my skull, so I went into the bathroom and locked the door behind me. I took my shirt off and looked at my fake-flesh-tone bra, sensible but with a pink bow in the middle, and then I took off my glasses, so I could sort of see myself in soft focus. I pretended that the mirror was a camera, and I tried to imagine what it was like to strip for someone, what it would be like for someone to want that from you. I thought about Jeremy, and I felt dumb for thinking about him. My breasts looked more like something from a medical textbook than a porno, and it left me feeling the way I usually felt when I looked in the mirror. Unremarkable. Regular.

Then I started to think about my mom. She was all about the breasts after Birch was born. When he was four weeks old, she opened the door to sign for a package with her shirt completely open. I think the UPS guy was more traumatized than turned on, and Lynette said that she needed to cover up. Even her wife and partner in lady-power knew that she'd gone bananas.

"The breast needs to be desexualized," my mom ranted, unwashed hair wild around her face, nursing pillow strapped around her middle.

"Then you're the woman to do it," I said, and we all laughed.

"Our culture's obsession with seeing the breast only as a sexual object hurts everyone. Especially babies. Imagine what kind of world we would live in if women thought nothing about breastfeeding in public, not with all these wraps and covers, just breasts and babies. Is that too much to ask?"

"Yes," I said. "It is. I vote no."

"That's because you're thirteen," she'd said. "You'll feel different one day."

If by one day she meant never, then she was right.

I knew what my mom was supposed to be going through right now. Lynette had sent the details of Mom's surgery in an e-mail to Delia and me. They would take out as much cancer as they found, and so long as everything looked clear, they would remove the right breast and rebuild it with some of her other skin. She wouldn't be able to raise her arms, or hold Birch, or even hold the phone for a few days, and then it would be weeks before she'd heal and then there was chemo. I wasn't sure whether or not she'd be through with the chemo by the time I got home, but I hoped so. I touched my right breast and wondered what it would be like to lose something like that, something that was actually a part of you. No matter how terrible my mother could be, I didn't want her to have to go through that. No matter how much I hated her, I didn't want her gone, not even one little piece of her.

I wondered if Delia felt the same way, if maybe that's part of the reason she was acting so crazy, why she wouldn't touch her phone. Lynette had left a message, saying that Mom was doing well, that Birch was with friends, that we were all missed and that she'd call again tomorrow. By then, hopefully, they'd have the pain managed enough for my mother to talk on the phone. I didn't like to think of her in pain, laid up in some hospital bed, pushing buttons for drugs and moaning in the night.

Dex tapped on the bathroom door. "You okay?"

"Just a minute," I said, trying to fix my bra and button up my shirt as quickly as possible.

I went into the hallway, where Dex was looking at me, worried.

"Delia told me what happened."

"She did?"

He leaned against the wall, ran his fingers over his scalp.

"I never know how to help her," he said.

I didn't know what she'd told him about: our mother, Roger, the real reason she was mugged, the stalker she liked to pretend didn't exist. There were so many things he wasn't supposed to know. I wasn't about to take a guess.

"So how about you?" he said. "Has anyone asked you lately how you're doing?"

We both knew the answer.

"How are you doing?"

I shrugged my shoulders.

"Okay, I guess."

He reached across the hallway and hugged me, not in a pervy way at all, but the kind of long bear hug that my dad gave me when we were kids, before I turned thirteen and it seemed like he was suddenly afraid to touch me. It was probably half my fault that my dad checked out. I wanted to spend time with my friends more than him, he was such a sad sack and wanted to talk about my mom all the time, and his feelings. I didn't like it when he touched me, not because it was gross or anything, but because he seemed so needy. Not like a dad. And then he found Cindy, and I sort of vanished, became the kind of person he could forget while he went to Mexico for a month and not even feel bad.

Dex was strong and warm and he smelled like the deodorant he wore, clean and minty. I relaxed into his arms, and if I'd been less exhausted I might have started bawling, but I was suddenly so tired that I thought I was going to faint, standing up, right there under his ugly fluorescent hall lights. I had turned into one of those pathetic animals that we read about in science class that practically cracks up when someone treats it like it has warm blood, when its wire-monkey family gets replaced with something real.

"I'm so tired," I said.

"You need an extra pillow?"

I nodded.

"Just knock on the bedroom door if you need anything. And if your sister ever gets like that again, promise me you'll call me before she spends a day on a film set. Okay?"

"Okay."

I curled up beneath the pile of blankets on the sofa and slept eleven hours straight.

15

It had been a week since he'd taken me to the hospital when I saw Jeremy again. Delia and I had pretty much moved into Dex's, and she spent most of her time sleeping, massaging the area around her nose, and driving to acupuncture appointments to get the blood flowing and facilitate healing. When Dex was gone, she'd waste hours on the phone quizzing various friends of hers on their favorite plastic surgeons. I pretended not to hear.

During that time, if she wasn't thinking about her own appearance, she was working on mine. She started with my hair, showing me how to braid it into a kind of funky side ponytail, thinning it out so that it had a better shape when I wore it over my shoulders. She went through everything we'd bought together and everything I already owned and lined up outfits for me like I was a toddler. She insisted that the next time I saw Jeremy I should wear the slinky black top and cuffed jeans that we'd bought on our shopping trip. She even lent me a long, vintage necklace that she said would save me from looking like I was too dressy, or trying too hard.

"Trust me," Delia said. "That boy is not driving you all over town because he can't afford a pet. You need to step up your game and act interested."

"I *do* act interested!"

"You act like he has smallpox. I'm not saying to stop, be-cause it's obviously working, but you might switch it up a bit since the summer's almost over."

I trusted her because I had no other choice. There was no telling how Jeremy really felt about me, but she was right that in the unlikely event that he did like me, I needed counseling on what to do next.

"Perfection," Delia said, before sending me into the world to practice my new flirting skills (smile; make eye contact; quit calling myself a "troll from Middle-Earth"). "And don't forget to let your hair out of the ponytail when you get there and fluff it, okay?"

I nodded.

Josh and Jeremy were shooting when Dex and I arrived. They were dressed in these absurdly formal seersucker suits, and the butler was running around the set, jumping in fear of an imag-inary mouse. "For this," the actor who played the butler had told me the first week in his best British accent, "I went to the Yale School of Drama." The hair people had gelled both of the twins' hair identically to the side, and it was almost impos-sible to tell them apart.

"I didn't write this," Dex whispered.

"That's encouraging," I whispered back.

When the scene ended, Josh immediately started to brush

the gel out of his hair, cursing underneath his breath. The jacket he wore was on the ground within seconds, and one of the crew members scooped it up like it was what she'd been put on earth to do.

Jeremy headed straight for where I was sitting, suit and hair firmly in place.

"Anna. Where have you been? Do you never check your phone?"

Something Delia had done must have been working, because Jeremy Taylor was all hot and bothered, and I appeared to be the cause. I was so nervous that I twisted the necklace Delia had lent me tightly enough that I almost choked myself.

"What? I always check my phone."

He pulled out his own phone and shook his head.

"Undelivered," he said. "My bad. So after I left your sister's place—" He lowered his voice, looking in Dex's direction. "After I left, I was worried, so I parked my car and waited to see if that Honda came back."

"And?"

"It did." He talked with his hands, pointing ahead like we were in the car together. "I tried to follow it, but whoever was driving went really fast." His face reddened. I knew exactly how "fast" he drove, but it was cute that he was embarrassed.

"The car is always gone before I can even get the plate," I said, helping him out as best I could.

"But I got the number."

"Seriously?"

"And," he said, with the face of a conqueror, "I have a name and address."

I felt a little dizzy.

"And, we're taking a break so they can rewrite the rest of this episode. Even for this show, it's ridiculous today."

"You think?" I said, and we both started laughing.

"Come on," he whispered. "Let's go check it out. If they see us go they'll make me stay."

No one noticed that we were leaving. Josh's entourage had melted out of the darkness and onto the set the minute he wasn't shooting. The writers were huddled together with Dex in the center, the quarterback of a losing team. Once we were clear of the set, we jogged to the car, probably moving faster than we would be once the car started to roll.

"So how's your sister?"

"Worried about her face," I said. "I had an epiphany. I realized that my sister on painkillers is kind of like your sister on Vitaminwater."

Jeremy laughed. "Did you go shopping?"

"No," I said. "We went to this crazy film shoot. It was just. Crazy."

"Same movie she was on when she got mugged? Already?"

"Don't tell," I said, lowering my voice. "It's her ex-boyfriend who's directing it. So she doesn't want Dex to know because she thinks he'd get jealous."

"That guy was her ex-boyfriend?"

"Yeah."

He mulled it over for a minute. "I guess that explains it."

Who knew what he was thinking? If Roger explained anything about my sister, I didn't want to know.

It was late afternoon, and the traffic was heavy as we inched across town. Jeremy had one of "his people" trace the license plate, which was evidently less of a big deal than I thought it would be. A perk, he said, of having to deal with stalkers. The address wasn't terribly hard to find, block numbers on the side of a curb, but the house itself was far removed from the road, guarded by hedges and a wide gate. Jeremy parked his car a block away, and we pretended to be walking, slowly casing the joint like a pair of unarmed teenage idiot detectives. The neighborhood seemed deserted, like so many LA houses during the day, the swimming pools abandoned, the lawns perfectly manicured for no parties, no sitting.

"I think we could climb the side," Jeremy said, pointing to the sloping hill next to the gate. "And peek down from there. See if the car is in the driveway. If it's really the place."

"And then what?" I picked at the side of my nail, the way I did before tests.

"I don't know. We could knock on the door and tell them we've called the police."

"And that we've trespassed and then wait for them to do something even weirder?"

"Let's at least take a look. That won't hurt anything. There's no one around."

I looked at the embankment, at the totally inappropriate

open-toe sandals I was wearing, at the dirt and debris and po-
tential for sliding on my face. Then I thought about the chances
that the people on the other side of the gate would have guns,
dogs, surveillance cameras. I was like the opposite of a Manson
girl, unarmed, unprepared, and these were the opposite of Manson times. Now most homeowners were armed and jittery, just
waiting for the chance to pick off a kid who walked on the
wrong lawn at the wrong time with a bagful of something sinister, like Mountain Dew. Or maybe I wasn't so different from
a Manson girl, ready to execute some incredibly stupid plan
just because a boy I liked was telling me so.

"Just to be safe," I said, "how about this. You keep watch
and I'll climb up, and I'll let you know if the coast is clear."

"How about if you keep watch and I climb?"

I pointed to his clothes. "You wore your set clothes. And
we're due back in an hour. They'll have your head if they're
dirty. How are you gonna get dirty in the middle of the ocean?"

"I can take this off," he said, stripping off his shirt before
I could stop him. He was even more beautiful half naked. I was
going to climb a cliff for this boy, possibly get eaten by Dober-
mans and thrown in jail, and for what? To help my sister, who
didn't even want to help herself.

"Ouch," he said, starting to climb. "I guess we wear clothes
for a reason, right?"

"That's probably the idea."

It wasn't too far up the hill, a short climb, and frankly it
made the gate by the entrance seem a little bit silly, unless the

idea was to slow someone down on their way back out who'd decided to steal a car. From the top of the hill, it was easy to see the house, a flat-topped super-modern pad that hugged the side of a cliff. Three cars were parked beside the house. A blue BMW, its convertible twin, and a red Honda hybrid. The Honda was the one I had seen outside my sister's house, but that wasn't what made my breath catch in my lungs. The BMW and the convertible had the same magnets on the back, passes to some country club, which looked familiar to me, though I couldn't quite make the connection.

"Duck," Jeremy whispered, pushing me down against the embankment as a woman wandered out of the house, talking loudly on her cell phone. She didn't appear to notice us, though we were barely hidden, and it was obvious she was upset about something. Jeremy inched closer to me, pushed my head down a bit more, and made a sign against his lips to be quiet. Like I was really going to talk.

"I'm going to check the license plates," Jeremy said.

"Are you crazy?" I whispered as loudly as I could, but he just put his index finger against his mouth again to shush me, and every time the woman turned away from us, he moved farther down the hill. He was going to go inside the house. He was officially insane.

I'd read about how people think they can hear their own heartbeats when something really scary is going on, and I was pretty sure I could hear that plus every other weird thing my body was doing—blood rushing to my head, my mouth as it dried up, my palms beginning to sweat. I clutched my cell phone in my shaking hand, wondering if someone inside was going to catch Jeremy. He had disappeared into the open door when the woman wasn't watching.

The next five minutes must have been forever, because no sooner had Jeremy gone inside than the woman yelled into her phone, shut it off, and headed back into the house. For all I knew, she was getting ready to Taser Jeremy and drag him to some rich-person dungeon where she'd slice him up and serve him for dinner to her Paleo coven. Best-case scenario, she'd only call the cops. How would I ever explain this to anyone without the two of us looking like juvenile delinquents, the kind of sketchball teenagers that parents warn their children about becoming?

And then finally, moving a lot faster than he had on the way down, Jeremy opened the door and closed it silently behind him, and made his way up the hill. He was halfway to where I was waiting when the door flew open, and the woman emerged. Jeremy flattened himself against the hill, and she scanned the landscape.

"I have a gun, you know," she yelled.

I closed my eyes and tried to keep my body from trembling.

"I'm calling the police," she shouted and held her phone in the air.

Then she went back inside, maybe to get her gun, but we weren't waiting that long. Jeremy had made his way farther back up the hill than I had thought, and he squeezed next to me and whispered, "I left a note."

"You left a note? Are you insane?"

"And I moved around some of the things on the counter. Like you were telling me those people did in that experiment."

He was remembering everything wrong. There was no experiment, just the Manson family practicing their creepy-crawling, breaking into homes and watching people while they slept, moving their furniture around and leaving without a sound.

"What did the note say?" I asked.

"'Stop,'" he said. "They'll know what it means. They're not the only ones who can leave notes, right?"

Next to me, Jeremy felt warm, and I would have sworn that I could hear his heartbeat as well. And while I was lying there, waiting for the cops to show up and drag us away, I remembered why I recognized the stickers on the back of the convertible, "HH" and "SSI." It was the same car my sister had been driving around LA the week of the zombie shoot, before Dex came back into town. We were at the nameless producer's house, or he was inside. And if there was some jealous vixen stalking my sister, she may well have been the producer's wife. Whoever she was, I'd have bet my life that she had her reasons and that my sister knew exactly what they were. I had to remind myself to breathe.

Finally, what felt like a million years later, the woman drove the red Honda down the long driveway and away from us. Jeremy gestured at the car.

"Look," he said. "The plates match."

But I wasn't looking at the house anymore. I was looking farther down the hill, across the lanes of traffic that bisected this area from the area where my sister lived. I wasn't great with directions, but even from this far away, I recognized the gaudy lilac paint job on my sister's back porch, almost DayGlo in the sunlight. And then I looked harder at the house, and something clicked, some sixth sense that let me know something that I didn't need to see from the front for proof. That the windows in the front of that house were wide and open. That the clear view up and down the canyon cut both ways. The porno house. This had to be the porno house that my sister was always pointing up the hill and laughing about, an inside joke between her and herself, and I was just one more person on the long list of people to whom Delia liked to lie.

"It's not the car," I said.

"It is the car."

"It's not. We have to go back."

"They're the stalkers. We should go back in and move a sofa or something."

I looked at Jeremy, shirtless, earnest, and so tragically gorgeous, and I realized that he was treating this like a sitcom, like something that was going to have a neat ending where the doors opened and the good guys won. But there weren't any good guys, not from where I was sitting. No good girls, either.

"Please," I said. "I want to go back." My face was about to rain down a total loser cocktail of snot and tears. I started climbing back over the hill, no longer caring if anyone inside saw us. I just wanted out of there. Jeremy followed, saying something about how he knew lawyers who would know what to do next. He was still excited. Even TV people got excited when you did something that seemed like it would be on TV. Only it wasn't TV, because then I could have turned it off.

"Are you okay?" he said when we got back to the car.

"I'm not. I just want to go home."

"Your sister's place?"

"No. That's not my home."

"Dex's?"

"No. That's not my home."

Knowing there was nowhere to go just made everything worse. My dad had called last night, excited that he and Cindy were engaged, that the trip to Mexico had been, as he put it, a "success." He was mad that I used his credit card, but not as mad as he should have been. He was too excited about his future. But I wasn't.

When my dad first split up with my mom, during his weepy and needy phase, I was his best friend. We'd watch Turner Classic Movies all of Sunday, and my dad would explain who all the old actors were, why the movies were important. After Cindy showed up, everything changed. If I got a meal alone with my dad, it was like some kind of international peace treaty had been signed. I was supposed to be so grateful; she was supposed to be so generous. And now I was going to be stuck with her, forever. She was probably knocked up already and they were just slow-playing it for fear that I'd run away for good. That's probably why my dad suddenly didn't have any money. The only thing left for me in Atlanta would be my mom and Lynette and their house of sick and weird.

It felt like my mom, my dad, my sister, they could all just take one relationship, trash it, and go on to the next thing, start building again, and expect everyone else to be excited. To throw a freaking party. But what about me? I was the leftover from my mom's second marriage, about to get promoted to being the leftover from my dad's first.

"Anna," Jeremy said. "You're not okay. Should I just take you back to the set?"

I nodded my head because it was the only place left to go.

16

My last full week in LA, Roger shot the final scenes of his film in front of what used to be 10050 Cielo Drive, but was now 10066 Cielo. The drive to the site was long and winding, with spider-vein-like cracks in the asphalt of the road ahead. As we wound our way higher above the city, the sound of the traffic below became increasingly muffled. A "No Trespassing" sign hung close to the entrance, with a redbrick wall in front of the sign announcing the new address in large brass numbers. From the outside, it could have been some tacky Atlanta minimansion. The estate seemed proud of its new identity, like it was daring you to try to figure out what it used to be. Nothing remained from the original home except for the telephone pole, to the right of the gate, which Tex Watson had scaled in order to cut the phone lines. It loomed like a forgotten remnant of the murders, of the 1960s even, a stake in the ground marking a gruesome past, an arbitrary last witness.

Barely any of the research that I did made it into Roger's film. Since Charles Manson treated "knocking up ladies" the way other people did "taking out the recycling," Roger decided that referencing it directly would be too much. Dex had warned me about this when he had told me about the movie business. He said that anytime you worked on a movie, whether you were writing it or researching it or shooting it, you could never forget that the end product was out of your hands. If you wrote a screenplay about Charles Manson, you shouldn't be shocked if it wound up being about Willy Wonka. It still felt like a lot of wasted energy. But Roger paid me $600 more, which, with the money from my *Chips* appearance, was enough to pay my debts and even go home slightly ahead at the end of the summer.

The movie wound up being about a married couple. The wife was supposed to be my sister after her face got messed up, which you don't learn until the end is something that the husband did to her. You don't really see the husband much; he's mostly a voice that whispers in the air, which you think must be a ghost or a serial killer, but it's not, instead it's this actor who didn't show up until the last weeks of shooting.

"It will be like Cassavetes," Roger said. "*A Woman Under the Influence*. You think the whole time that she is crazy, wandering around like this, but she is being crushed, ground down by this man."

There were three parts to the film, these haunted scenes where the ghost version of my sister visits murder sites in Los Angeles, scenes where the broken-nose version of my sister tries to live a kind of regular life but can't quite hold it together, and then scenes with the new actor, the husband, where you see that the marriage, or whatever it is, is the real horror.

The final scene of the film takes place in a car, outside the old 10050 Cielo Drive, and the husband is whaling on my sister, really letting her have it. He's berating her for the way she cooks pasta, for how she keeps her mouth open when she breathes, stuff you shouldn't even notice or care about. Then he starts in on how she looks, that she's getting older, that the only thing anyone will ever love about her is her face, and that her face is starting to wrinkle and fade. And while he's giving her this part of the speech, my sister, who's a good actress, but not that good, starts to shake, really shake. And then, I don't know how it happened, but her nose started to bleed. I think she was trying so hard not to cry that it must have unloosed something, and the blood came down her face and looked so sad and horrible that I forgot that it was a movie, I couldn't look anymore. I waited for Roger to say, "Cut," to make it stop, but he was transfixed. The cameras moved in closer. My sister closed her eyes, and her movie-husband whispered, with perfect cruelty, "I don't feel sorry for you, bitch." It was the last thing that Susan Atkins had allegedly said to Sharon Tate, word for word, as she was pleading for her life.

Had it been anyone other than Roger, I probably would have thought it was a cool idea. Before the scene began, he explained to the actors that people walked around locking their doors and looking over their shoulders, mindful of the too-close footstep in the parking garage, the abandoned house with broken windows, the stranger in the shadows. But he had an epiphany part of the way through filming: he had been wrong in his original concept. The real danger wasn't violence like you saw on the television news, random and exciting—the real danger was the vampiric kind, the sort that you invited in because it told you everything you wanted to hear. Charles Manson could never have been Charles Manson if there hadn't been girls by the dozen, ready and willing, scarred by the silent cruelty behind those carefully locked doors.

"Which is not to say that you have not helped me," he said, nodding to me at the end of his speech. "You and these Manson girls, you are my inspiration. This is the incarnation."

The final scene was the first one that my sister had filmed since the splint had come off her nose. Where her nose had been perfect before, it had the slightest tilt toward the top now. She'd fix it later, I was sure of that, but for the moment it made her face more beautiful, it had the openness of a butterfly asking the world to be gentle to its first unfolding wings. She didn't know that I was watching her while she got ready to shoot, the extra time she spent looking at herself in the mirror. I could feel the tears, the ones that didn't come until the cameras rolled, mixed with blood. They weren't pretend.

You would have thought Roger had just finished filming *Citizen Kane,* the way he clapped after he said "Cut."

"You are more beautiful," he said, holding a towel to my sister's nose while she continued to cry. "You have made something real. So real."

My sister was inconsolable. Maybe it was the place, something in the air that remained. They may have built a new house, reseeded the yard, put fifty years or even a hundred between the address and its history. It didn't matter. Even in the warm late afternoon, maybe especially at a time like that, when it seemed like nothing savage could ever happen in such a quiet and beautiful space, the hillside still felt haunted.

"It doesn't even look like my face anymore," she finally said.

She was right, but it wasn't just the nose. My sister was scared. Her face was her fortune, and it looked different. Better, I thought, but not the same.

The actor was on his phone, calling his agent. He didn't seem terribly moved by any of it.

"I cannot ask you to forgive me again," Roger said. "And still I ask."

"It doesn't matter. It can't be fixed."

"I think you look better." I finally worked up the courage to say it, not just because I wanted her to feel better, but because it was true.

She had stopped crying and was looking at her face again in the makeup mirror she kept in her bag.

"It looks like a piece of modern freaking art. A fun-house mirror would be kinder."

"It really doesn't."

"This better be huge at Sundance," she said to Roger, and he nodded vigorously.

"Enormous," he said. "We have tapped into the collective unconscious of America. Its violence. I would break my own nose if I could take it back, but the film, it is beautiful. It is something more than it would have been. You have truly suffered for your art."

Please, I thought, please let her say yes. Please let him have to break his nose.

"You don't have to be such a drama queen," Delia said. "Plain old queen is bad enough." She winked at me, and just like that, she was back.

"I'm out," her movie-husband said, and we all shook hands and did a round of air-kisses and he was off to the next romantic comedy.

"We should celebrate," Roger said. "It is our wrap day, your last week in Los Angeles, Anna?"

"It is," I said. "I have to finish a paper."

"Papers are for next week. Tonight we toast."

"I don't want to toast. I *can't* toast."

"Relax," Delia said. "We'll go somewhere low-key. I think I need beer goggles to get used to my face. Maybe after a few drinks I'll look good to me again."

"You would seriously have to kill yourself if you were actually ugly, wouldn't you?"

"God, Anna, to hear you talk, you'd think I was the vainest person in the world. Did you see how I looked in that last shot?"

"Great acting," Roger interrupted, "takes great humility."

So it was going to be that kind of a night. I'd hoped they would drop me with Dex so that I could meet Jeremy for the *Chips Ahoy!* wrap party. The party started in three hours, so as long as Delia stayed sober enough to drive, or got drunk enough that I could sneak off, there was still hope.

Roger drove us to a tiki bar in Silver Lake, a hipster neighborhood that was near his home. I expected the place to be empty, but there were at least fifteen or twenty people, some working alone on computers, others sipping late-afternoon cocktails.

"I am a regular," Roger said. "Do not order alcohol and we will be fine."

The waitress who took our order was heavily tattooed, with black bangs and long, straight hair. She knew Roger and half smiled when he introduced me as a writer for his next movie.

"Make sure he pays you, kid," she said, winking like we were old pals.

"I miss this place," Delia said after her second scotch and soda. "Is it wrong if I just drink scotch?" She trailed her finger over the water beading on the side of the glass. Her eyes were still puffy from crying, and she hadn't reapplied her makeup. "Have they rotated the music? I hope not. I never get over this way. You'd think I would, but it always feels like forever in the car. But I miss the jukebox. I hope they haven't changed everything up. I'm going to go play something."

I sat next to Roger, who watched Delia cross the room to the jukebox. My phone chirped a message from Jeremy: "C U in 30, buttercup?" I was bronzing the screen.

Delia came back as Johnny Cash started singing "I Still Miss Someone." My mom loved Johnny Cash, would play his music anytime we surrendered media control. She and Lynette didn't listen to music as much now, except for kids' stuff, and the song reminded me of the summers when Delia was still at home, when my mom and dad were still together. Delia was softly singing along and looking at Roger, sharing some moment from their horror show of a love affair. It made me feel more lonely and more sad that she was singing to Roger, when it should have been Dex, or me, or anyone else.

And then one of those things happened that I would have paid a million dollars not to have seen, that I will spend at least the next three summers trying to forget. Roger leaned across the table and kissed my sister. French-kissed her, and not like someone who was even kind of, sort of confused about his sexuality. And while I am no expert on kissing, there was no unseeing that in her boozed-out stupidity, she kissed him back.

"You can't do that," I said. "What are you doing? Stop it. Both of you. Stop!"

I truly believe they had forgotten I was there.

"That was harmless," Delia said, avoiding my eyes. Roger looked about as sorry as a dog rolling in shit.

"It was not harmless. You would never do that in front of Dex. Why are you screwing your life up? Dex loves you."

He'd never said so, and neither had she, not around me, at any rate, but I knew that it was true. And if my lunatic sister had the sense God gave an ant, she would have loved him back. But it looked like she didn't, and didn't again. I thought that I knew what it was like to hate my sister, but I had been playing around. This was the real thing.

"What is it you would have me do with my life? Get married and have kids and give up on my dreams?" She chugged her scotch and gestured for another.

"What are you talking about? Who said anything about any of that? I don't care if you have zero or a million babies. I just want you not to make out with your ex-boyfriend. Are you going to lie to Dex now?"

Delia flipped her hand in the air, waving me off like what I'd said was the droning of some pesky insect she needed to squash. Forget her stalker, I was ready to cause some trouble of my own. I moved her scotch in my direction. She reached across the table and yanked it back. Roger seemed to think it was all hilarious. I was ready to let him have it as well.

"Or should I say, keep lying to him? No wonder that producer has some porno zombie leaving slut-mail on your front door. I'd *love* to see the kind of movie you made with him. I guess the only big surprise is that the rest of LA hasn't figured out your address."

And the way Roger quit smiling and fast, I knew she hadn't told him, either. Forget sister fights, this was going to be a sister war.

"Roger, go get me a drink," she said, pointing at the bar. "Now."

"Yeah, Roger, go get her a drink. You might want to wash your mouth out. She is the spokesperson for herpes, if you hadn't heard."

If we had been in a high school cafeteria, they would have been clearing tables and giving us room to rumble.

Delia lowered her voice and narrowed her eyes. "Have you been going through my things?"

"No."

"So." She leaned in closer. "What is it that you think you know?"

"I know that the red car came from that producer's house, and if it was from an actress, then you must have beat her out for some kind of role."

She pointed at an imaginary pile of my clothes, at some suitcase she was hallucinating. Like this was improv class and not her actual life.

"The minute we get home, you can start packing. I should have known, once a thief, always a thief. Do I need to check my credit card as well?"

"What is *wrong* with you, Delia? What if that guy decides to have you murdered?"

"You don't know the whole story," she said, scanning the bar to see if Roger was coming back with her drink. "You don't know anything, really. It's not him, it's his wife, okay? She thinks something happened between us that didn't, and I'm trying to give her the benefit of the doubt. She's unbalanced, but not dangerous. He says she's medicated and seeing someone about her issues. He even forwarded me an apology that she wrote during one of her therapy sessions the other day. Did you find that on my computer?"

"An apology? Why are you talking to her?"

She ran her finger in the bottom of her glass and licked the dregs off her fingertip.

"She thinks I'm the reason her awful fraud of a husband can't stand her, that we had some kind of passionate affair."

"Did you?"

"Hardly."

"You're lying. Once a liar, always a liar."

For a minute, I thought she was going to haul off and slap me. Her hand flinched and came down hard on the table.

"I'm not lying. You want the truth? The truth is, it's none of your business. He promised me a role in a film, a *real* film, and the film isn't even going to come out. What happened was immaterial. It was before Dex and I started dating, if you're putting together a timeline for the rest of your inquest. I have no idea how his wife found out; she must have found something he was shooting and come to the wrong conclusion. Whoever knows what goes on up there? I didn't even know he had a wife at the time—he said they were divorced, so if there's a liar in the equation, it's not me. Maybe, in your universe, that makes all of us disgusting people, but you know what, you just made my universe your universe. So maybe you should shut up and stay out of other people's lives."

I felt like I was going to scream or cry; there weren't enough words to let her know how selfish she was, how much she took for granted about who we both were. Even in an argument Delia had to remind me that hers was the bigger story, that no matter what I did, my life would never be interesting enough to measure up to hers.

"Why doesn't anyone seem to understand that this is my life too? You act like everyone is some kind of bit player in your drama, but I'm living my life as well. This is my summer too. Cora is my mom too. Birch is my brother too. That song you just played? That's my song. I love that song, and you just ruined it forever. And Dex is my friend too, not just your boyfriend. And maybe it's not interesting enough for the rest of the world to care, but I care. I like Dex. He's taken me to work all summer. I have friends on that set."

"Don't confuse actors with friends."

"Don't confuse my life with yours."

Roger was leaning against the bar, watching us. I wanted to mail the producer's wife a key to my sister's place and Roger's apartment and an informational copy of *Helter Skelter*.

"Why do you have to be so mean?" I finally said. "Just drop me at the set, okay? You can do what you want. I don't care."

"I can just drop you at the set. Like I've just let you live with me this whole summer. Like I've just shared my home, and my relationship, and jobs, and my life with you. And do I get so much as a thank-you? You want to get to the set? You call a cab like anyone else. Okay? And don't go looking in my purse for the fare."

I stormed out of the stupid tiki lounge into the dry heat of the early evening. An angry red sun parked just above the horizon, and I clenched my fists into balls and tried not to scream, tried to keep myself calm, tried to remind myself that I had left places worse than this one with less money in my pocket. If I never saw my sister again, it would be too soon.

17

The party was mostly over by the time I made it across town. My cab fare cost the better part of what I'd won the last week at poker, and Dex had already left to meet someone, probably my sister. Nice that she hadn't called to make sure that I showed up. Nice that she wasn't worried about me at all. Jeremy was laughing with two of the crew members, but when he saw me he waved and broke away.

"I thought you'd skipped town," he said. "Don't miss your last chance for a genuine Hollywood party." I could tell that he was kidding, that on his party scale, this one was probably lame squared. I still wished the cab had moved faster.

Josh was talking to a girl that I hadn't seen before, her legs wishbone slender and as toned as a dancer's. The two of them were laughing and looking at the giant *Chips Ahoy!* cookie cake with the twins' pictures etched across the surface. Then he pointed across the room at the steering wheel of the boat, where Pinky was wedged atop its wooden hub. The girl laughed and pushed him playfully on the shoulder, and he pretended like she'd really hurt him.

"I guess the fun is mostly over," I said. "I wanted to make it. My sister was filming. It's a long story."

"You didn't miss all the fun. This is LA. The real fun hasn't even started."

Going out at night wasn't on the list of things that I did on a regular basis. Maybe one of our parents would drop Doon and me at a movie, but not with boys.

"My sister will kill me." I thought about it another minute. "If I don't kill her first."

"Sisters are a challenge." Joshua and the girl he was with disappeared, but not before he dragged Pinky through the icing atop the cake and licked the creamy sludge from its tip like he meant business. "Brothers too."

"Have you ever gotten in a fight where the other person did everything wrong, and you still felt like you were the bad guy?"

We walked over to what was left of the giant cookie cake. Pinky had taken half of Jeremy's face, but Josh's sugary image remained untouched. Jeremy broke off his brother's nose and half his cheek and handed it to me.

"You're not weird about germs, are you?"

"No," I said.

"What did you fight with your sister about?"

"I don't want to talk about it," I said. And I sounded exactly like Delia. "She kissed another guy. Her ex-boyfriend. Please don't tell Dex. I saw her do it, and it was so stupid. He's the worst guy on earth. But then the whole thing became about what a dishonest, lousy person *I* am. Don't ask me how."

"Is he the guy who broke her nose?"

"Basically."

Even for me, the cookie was too sweet, or maybe Delia was right—I was poisoning my system and it was finally catching up to me.

"Whatever she said, I'd try to forget about it. Was any of it true?"

"I don't even know," I said. "Maybe I am a thief. I read something I shouldn't have read. Is that stealing? I only read it because she never tells me anything."

He shrugged his shoulders.

"I don't want to be an awful person. I feel like everyone thinks I'm this terrible human being, but when I do things, I'm not trying to be horrible. I'm really not."

I didn't tell him the worst part, that in the cab, on the way to the set, I got an e-mail from Doon. Usually we texted or one of us called, so I was kind of surprised to see a regular message from her, titled: "TALK." I almost didn't open it because sometimes e-mails like that are from Russian ladies who want husbands or African "kings" trying to give you part of their nonexistent inheritance. But I opened it. She told me that she was disappointed in me as a friend, that I only talked about myself, that since I had been in LA I didn't even ask how she was doing. Since I hadn't asked: her dog was sick and her brother was thinking of joining the army. She said that she wasn't going to be checking on Birch again because she wasn't my servant and that I should call my mom myself if I wanted to talk to him. She said that my mom was sick and missed me and that I was being selfish all around, and that she hoped when I came home I had plans to make some new friends.

It hurt a million times worse than the fight with my sister, a billion times, and I couldn't tell Jeremy about it because it was all true, even though that's not how I'd meant any of it. I'd thought that she'd have wanted to hear about TV sets and cool vintage shopping and Olivia Taylor, because to me it was a million times more interesting than anything happening in our sad neighborhood. Looking at the weird losers milling around the set, at the half-eaten cookie cake, the stupid fake penis now propped upright in the potato chip bowl, I wanted to scream.

"I don't think you're horrible. If it makes you feel better, you didn't miss much with the wrap party."

"I still wish I'd been here," I said. "Anything would have been better."

"Anything?" He offered me another piece of cookie cake, but I waved him off. "How late does your sister let you stay out?"

"Well, since we're not speaking, I'm going to say as long as I want."

"You up for something kind of crazy?"

"Is that a trick question?"

We left with the last of the crew members, who were heading to an after-party at one of the writer's homes. Delia had mentioned it, and she may well have been there with Dex already, spinning some version of what she thought I might tell him, waiting for me to show. I thought about letting her hang, seeing if she'd break down and tell Dex what she'd been up to, why we were fighting, but being around Jeremy made me feel like I should be the bigger person. Do the right thing.

So I texted her: "I'M ALIVE. LIKE YOU CARE."

"Are we picking something up for the party?"

"Better," Jeremy said. "Trust me."

We crept along the freeway until we turned off into a relatively deserted area of what looked like warehouses. They could as easily have been movie studios or places where serial killers stored their bodies—nothing on the outside gave away their contents. Jeremy slowed down and I worried for a second that we were lost, that he was, in fact, too nice to be a television star and it was all a cover for slicing ladies into pieces, and this was going to be both my last night in Los Angeles and on the planet.

"There it is," he said, pointing at a warehouse on the corner. The building was as nondescript as the others, except for the two gorilla-size men outside the entrance, guarding the doors. Jeremy parked the car and for the first time I could hear the music coming from inside, loud and heavy on the bass.

The gorillas looked like they didn't even see us, though one of them outstretched his hand and Jeremy high-fived him on the way in. The music was so loud I could feel it pulsing through the floor, and the hipster crowd was already thigh-to-thigh.

"What do you think?" Jeremy shouted.

What did I think?

The warehouse was cavernous, and along the sides were piles of garbage, spray-painted with glitter and sculpted into a makeshift moonscape. Boxes of Tide, Cap'n Crunch, old CD cases, crumpled paper bags, junk mail, you name it. I went closer and touched it, to see if was real junk or just junk made to look like junk. It didn't smell, but otherwise there was no way of knowing. Atop the garbage, around the room were what looked like taxidermied monkeys, holding American and British flags and wearing astronaut suits. The lights went out and the walls glowed with eerily graffitied letters: *FREEKMONKEE. LOST IN SPACE.*

"Get out," I said, and grabbed Jeremy's shirt like he was Doon, like he was my very best girlfriend in the entire world and just the person to not even kind of believe this was actually happening. "Get out, get out, get out, get out, get *out!*"

"I thought you'd like it," he said, smiling.

"Is this a release party?"

"Pre-release. It's Max's birthday."

Max Storer. The drummer. Which meant that it was August 10 and I had officially died and gone to heaven, and heaven was a shit pile covered in glitter. I guess it made as much sense as anything.

Next to the stage was a DJ booth, and manning it was a statuesque alien in an aluminum-blue wig, with silver moon boots and a skintight peacock-colored bodysuit that changed from green to blue and back again depending on the light. There was none of the dollar-store, club-kid glow-sticking—

everything glittered and glowed, but differently as the light changed. Even the garbage was beautiful.

"Where are the bathrooms?"

Jeremy pointed across the room.

"Find me and we'll go backstage," he said.

A tall blonde in a gold minidress walked past us, looked an extra second at Jeremy, and kept going. I headed for the bathroom. And even though I was in LA, at this super-exclusive event, when I crossed the floor it seemed like I could just as easily have been crossing our high school cafeteria, only with better decorations and prettier people. People were still giving you the once-over to see if they knew who you were, if you'd be worth getting to know. I saw the way that blonde sized Jeremy up with a "Maybe later" kind of side-glance. It wasn't that she didn't recognize him, it was more that he was the wrong kind of famous. He was cheeseball-TV famous in a room of rock-star cool.

In the bathroom, I gave myself a hard look in the mirror. I was wearing the shirtdress with pants that my sister had convinced me wasn't actually just wearing two outfits at once, so the first thing I did was take off my jeans, roll them into a ball, and cram them into my bag. I unbelted the black tunic, which now hung midthigh, and loosed my hair from its braid. I had forgotten my comb, so it was wild and just a little tangled. Someone had already glittered herself in the bathroom, so I made sure no one was looking and I swept all the leftover glitter into my hand, dusted it into my hair, and then shook it around to make sure that it was at least somewhat evenly distributed. I did the best job I could penciling in the area around my eyes, and then I took off my glasses. I would be able to see far away but not close up, so I'd just have to trust that I looked funky enough to blend and take my chances.

The inside was packed, and I had to squeeze my way through about ten feet of people before I found Jeremy. He was talking to some friends, other actors or musicians, and he introduced me as "a friend who was working on his show." It wasn't as good as "girlfriend," but it was definitely a step up from runaway thief. And before I could even worry about what to say next, the crowd began to roar and whistle, pumping their arms as the Freekmonkee scream sounded from the monkeys on top of the garbage heaps.

Karl Marx walked out onto the stage, half whispering the song I had heard in Jeremy's car. It felt like he had darkened the room and started a séance with three hundred of his closest friends, the sounds were that eerie and mesmerizing. The crowd settled down and then erupted when the opening chords of "Heart Not Beating" began. If I hadn't been worried about embarrassing myself in front of Jeremy, I would have held my phone up and recorded the whole thing, because even though I was definitely there and it was really happening, I was still having trouble believing it. I closed my eyes and gave myself over to the music, to a place that felt so pure that it seemed impossible that anyone could exist outside that crazy space, let alone be mad, or worried, or sick, or sad. There was just this perfect sound, and hundreds of people becoming a part of it, and I was part of those hundreds. When I opened my eyes, there were lights flashing across the warehouse, and people were ripping parts of the trash piles off, throwing them at each other and onto the stage. Most of it was paper and all of it glittered and it was like nothing I'd ever seen.

Jeremy shouted something, but I could barely hear him. I leaned closer.

"C'mon," Jeremy said. "This is the last number. I've got to check on Olivia."

The moon-booted space DJ. Olivia Taylor. Of course. I'd heard the twins talk about their sister's new career, making appearances at clubs on the Vegas strip. My stomach dropped for a second, but I decided to play it cool. Fear of Olivia Taylor was not going to make me miss the chance to meet Freekmonkee. I was Jeremy's friend. I worked on a show. I had as much of a right to be there as she did. Kind of.

Jeremy grabbed my hand and we snaked our way through the crowd. The side of a CD case hit me on the shoulder, and a laughing man in a rainbow Afro showered glitter over Jeremy.

"Thanks, man," he said, shaking his head from side to side. "Can you help me get this out, Anna?"

We found a space where there was enough room for me to comb through his hair and try to shake the glitter free, a losing battle if ever there was one. I imagined we looked like a pair of blinged-out zoo animals, huddled in some corner, one grooming the other. Freekmonkee left the stage, and for a second I was sure that I had destroyed my hearing; the echo in my skull throbbed almost as loudly as the music itself.

"This is not going to end well," Jeremy said as more of the garbage made its way onto the stage. I could see what he meant, but I just didn't care. It might have been destructive but it was magic.

Backstage, Olivia Taylor had removed her moon boots and was curled catlike against Karl Marx. He rubbed his hand up her leg, almost into her crotch, and she opened a mirror and lined her lips silver-blue while he talked.

"It's all waste," he said, his accent as perfectly beautiful as it sounded in the interviews I'd watched. "Waste and filth. Even these women, these perfect creatures." Now his hand was in her crotch, but if I'd had my glasses on, I would have sworn he was looking at me. "They look like something off of God's top shelf, and you know they have their fingers in their underwear, smelling their own filth like the rest of us."

Olivia grunted with what was either disgust or interest, I couldn't tell. She shifted her position and put a hand on Karl's knee. He brushed it aside.

"What happens when we've filled the oceans?" Karl continued, leaning forward. "Should we decorate our shit and send it to another galaxy? Is that our legacy? Is it so different from the trash we already send into the universe, the television programs that mean nothing, the endless, banal chatter?"

He wasn't looking at Jeremy, but I wondered if Jeremy

took that kind of thing personally, even if Karl was right, which he probably was.

"Can we lose ourselves in space," he asked, "if space is nothing but what we leave behind for the uglies to care for? Our garbage? The shows we've already seen? The pop star whose music has come and gone? Isn't that all now just part of the void?"

I was listening to him but watching the rest of the room as well. Leo Spark was in the corner, smoking a cigarette and tightening and loosening his guitar strings. He was taller than Karl Marx, and had on skintight jeans and a red silk shirt, his perfect, wavy brown hair falling over his perfect brown eyes. When Karl said something he agreed with, he would stop touching his guitar and point at him, then return to what he was doing. He had silver rings on three of his fingers, a band with diamonds, a skull, and the openmouthed screaming freek-monkee that each of the band members wore. If I squinted I could almost make them out, and I so wished that I could just put on my glasses, walk across the room, and gape.

The music coming through the walls changed, and the band members all stood up. Karl kissed Olivia full on the mouth, and then much to my horror, on his way back to the stage, Leo did the same. She kissed each of them back for at least as long as Delia had kissed Roger, and though I was trying not to stare, I couldn't help myself. As she was tonguing Leo Sparks, Olivia Taylor opened her eyes and looked straight at me. Even without my glasses, I couldn't miss it.

The band headed for the stage, and Olivia walked in my direction. Without shoes, she was exactly my height, and I scanned the room, looking for an exit.

"Anna," she said, and threw both her arms around me, and kissed me on both cheeks, like I was her freaking iguana. "I love that you're here, Anna. You and my fucking brother. I love this kid."

Then she turned to Jeremy and kissed him. He flinched like someone had scorched him with the end of a cigarette.

"Thank you for taking care of my babies," she said.

Then she looked at both of us and said, "I love you both so much. Love is the only way to cut through the garbage."

I wondered for a minute if she'd ever taken Leo or Karl back to her place, if maybe they'd gotten the idea for the waste-ridden moonscape after sitting for an afternoon in her bungalow.

Freekmonkee had begun their encore, and Olivia grabbed my hand and started to walk me back in the direction of the crowd.

"Do you love them as much as I do?" she asked, and she squeezed her fingers against my palm. When she pulled her hand away she'd left behind a small tab of paper. I held my hand close and squinted to get a better look at it.

Jeremy put his hand on my shoulder.

"Can you find a ride home?" Jeremy asked me, not even judgmental, but keys in his hand, like he was leaving either way. "I don't want to leave you, and I don't want to ruin your good time, but I can't take this scene."

And for a minute, just a second, I seriously thought about staying. If there were one more thing to add to the long list of things I would do over if I could, not leaving that very instant would be on it. I should have dropped Olivia's hand and bolted for the door. Instead, I waited. I waited so long, in fact, that by the time I was running to catch him at the door, I had almost lost him.

18

We drove from the party through a series of winding roads up a mountain, and Jeremy was driving fast, like an actual person. I didn't ask where we were going. I should have been happy, but instead, I was starting to feel just the opposite. I had this sinking feeling that somehow I had done everything wrong this summer, made all the wrong choices. I shouldn't have been at a Freekmonkee concert tonight, or even at some stupid wrap party. I should have been alone somewhere writing Doon the longest, saddest, sorriest letter about how I'd never meant to hurt her feelings. There was no reason for me to be in LA, with people I barely knew and a sister who only tolerated me. I'd missed out on my brother, on my actual best friend, on my real if not glamorous life. The feeling was terrible, the kind I used to get at the end of summer camp, like I was losing the thing I was experiencing even while I was still in it, like life was beautiful and there and passing me by. I knew then that I was going to cry, and I didn't want to do it in front of Jeremy. I didn't want him to think that it was about his sister, and I didn't know how to explain what I was really feeling.

"You want to hear the crazy thing?" He paused a long time. "Just before the wrap party, Olivia called begging for me to go to the concert. She and Karl had some kind of fight, she was convinced that her house was bugged, she sounded crazy. And then we show up, and there's that scene."

"Did you know she was DJing?"

"Is that what you call what she was doing? No, I didn't."

"But she seemed so happy."

"Happy?" He squeezed the steering wheel harder and leaned forward. "That's an interesting word for how she seemed. Probably not the first one I would pick."

I remembered the tab she had put in my hand right before we left, a tiny monkey head on a hole-punch-size piece of paper, and then I felt even dumber than I had when we got in the car. "Sometimes I wish I could do this whole summer over again. I miss my brother, and my stupid mother, and even stupid, stupid Lynette. Do you ever feel like you make all the wrong choices?"

"Definitely," he said, and then rounded a corner so sharp that the whole earth seemed to fall away. "Was this summer really that bad?"

For a minute I almost told him that the only thing good about my summer had been getting to know him. And that part was so good that it almost made up for the rest of the nonsense. He had little bits of glitter in his hair and he was so gorgeous that he all but glowed. No, my summer was not all that bad. Not by a long shot.

"It's not that," I said. "I just wish I could have had this summer without missing the other summer I could have had."

"I get that."

We drove for a while in the night, and I loved the way in Los Angeles, no matter how miserable you were, you could disappear into something beautiful. The ocean. The mountains. The moon as wide and hypnotic as anything in the Freekmonkee landscape.

"Can I tell you something in confidence?"

"Sure."

He waited another minute or two before continuing as we climbed higher and higher up darker and darker roads.

"I don't know if you're into that kind of gossip, but do you remember last year when there was a piece about Olivia being hospitalized while she was filming in Japan?"

"She was hospitalized for exhaustion," I said. "I remember. What, was it drugs or something?"

Jeremy shook his head. "Her dad lives in Japan. We don't have the same dad, and I don't think Olivia had seen him in, like, ten years. So she wanted to meet him again, and it was this big thing because she's even more popular in Japan than she is here. There are girls who have plastic surgery just to get Olivia eyes. There are contact lenses in 'Olivia gray.' It's freaky."

"That must be weird."

"It must have been, but it wasn't that. She arranged to meet her dad, who's now become this international businessman, at some super-exclusive restaurant. I guess that she wanted to impress him, to show him she'd done okay without him."

"To make him love her," I said. My arms felt chilled and I turned the air off.

"Sorry," he said. "I'm so used to sound stages. It's always cold."

"No problem."

He turned the heat on low and I wrapped my sweater over the ends of my hands.

"I don't know exactly what happened. I know that he made a pass at her. I don't think he tried to sleep with her, but he did something. My mom flew over and she told me not to go, but I should have. I was having problems of my own, and I didn't know exactly what was happening. Olivia's always been so dramatic. Even now I never know when she's really in trouble."

My last mental snapshot had been of Olivia Taylor, practically spread-eagle next to Karl Marx, acting like some sad groupie and not like someone who used to be the world's biggest teen star. It reminded me a little of Squeaky Fromme, who got the nickname Squeaky because when the Manson family was living on the ranch, the owner was a blind old man who thought that Fromme squeaked when he was feeling her up. Which, evidently, was a frequent enough event to get a nickname out of the arrangement.

You couldn't have a favorite Manson girl—that would be like picking your favorite finger to start with as they ripped off your nails. But the one I thought about the most was Squeaky. Squeaky Fromme should never have been Squeaky Fromme, and not just the nickname, the whole deal. She should have grown up to become Lynette Fromme-Something-or-Other, veterinarian. Or dancer. Or poet. I'm not excusing her behavior. I don't think she was awesome. I still think she was a psycho who picked the dumbest hippie method possible to try to kill the president. Still.

Squeaky Fromme was a dancer as a child. She was on *The Lawrence Welk Show,* a program for the deeply old now—but big in its time—and performed in front of crowds of thousands at the Hollywood Bowl with a group called the Lariats. She loved animals and was voted best personality in junior high. But by high school she was shooting staple guns into her arms at work and begging her English teacher to take notice. She was covering black eyes and burning her arms with cigarettes. She pleaded with neighbors to take her in for a day, a week, the summer. She asked a friend's parents to adopt her. Any wild guesses as to why? Anyone? Anyone?

I know there's nothing worse than having your father molest you, but the problem is that you hear about it so much, it's like Roger talking about amnesia or past lives in his stupid script. It's just one of those stories, even though it's not. When I was reading about Squeaky Fromme, that her dad was probably a monster wasn't even a big reveal—it was like the "no, duh" of the book.

But the thing that stuck with me, that really bothered me even though it was about a million times less horrible, is that from the time she was a little girl, really little, he wouldn't let her eat dinner with the family. She had to sit somewhere separate while the rest of them ate Spam or whatever it was people ate in those days. That detail felt sad to me the same way Olivia

Taylor's big, overstuffed, animal pit of a house felt sad. No wonder Squeaky Fromme found another family.

I read about a million reasons that the Manson murders took place. LSD. The sixties. Failed record deals. Racial unrest. Paranoid schizophrenia. And who knows? Who knows if they could have been stopped? I'm sure there's no simple way that everything could have been erased, made better. But if I had to write a memo to America on what to do to improve the future, on how to go back and correct the past, it would be simple: *Dear America: Please give your daughters sturdy bedroom doors that lock from the inside. And when they are hungry, give them a place at the table.*

It wouldn't solve everything, but it would definitely be a start.

"That's really terrible," I said, and it was almost like I meant Olivia and Squeaky Fromme together.

We kept driving and I thought about Olivia flying back and forth from Las Vegas, sitting alone with her sad dog and her iguana. Wondering if she was ever going to catch up to who she used to be, find a table where someone wanted her there just because.

"I think you have the coolest profile," Jeremy said finally. "I like that when I look at you I can't think of anyone who looks quite like you. You have a great face. An interesting face." It was the worst kind of compliment. Interesting, but not beautiful.

"Wonderful," I said.

"I'm serious. You probably want to be pretty, because everyone here does. But pretty just winds up looking like a hundred girls who look like a hundred other girls who are all trying to look like the same person because they saw her in some stupid movie. That probably doesn't make sense, but after a while, pretty doesn't even register."

When he was talking I could tell that he wasn't lying, and it made me wish that I were a better person, that I knew how to take a compliment.

He pulled up beneath a white skyscraper of a structure, and it took me a minute to register that it was the Hollywood sign. He parked the car and rolled his window down, so I rolled mine down as well. The air was surprisingly warm and smelled faintly floral.

"That's the observatory where *Rebel Without a Cause* was shot," he said. "I love James Dean."

"Is that why you drive the way you do? Method?"

Jeremy had driven us to a clearing at the top of a hill. I got the sense that there might have been other people not too far away, also parked to see the view. He turned the key in the ignition to let the music play, loudly at first, and then he turned it lower.

"I almost killed someone," he said. "That's what my sister was talking about. That's why I didn't go to Japan. I was out one night with Josh and we'd been partying way too hard. Righteous, ugly partying, the kind the photographers love, and I think they figured we were both in the same car, because the paparazzi followed Josh. I woke up in the back of the club and it was practically morning and my head was black, just black. So I got in my friend's car, his keys were in my lap and we sometimes did that, to throw off whoever might be stalking my ride. And I didn't have my license yet but that didn't matter to me at the moment, I was so sure I could handle the car. I was going down Vine, and this girl was crossing the street, and I came so close to hitting her, all I could see was this look on her face, how surprised she was. I could have been the last thing she ever saw. I did hit her, I guess, but it wasn't enough to go to the hospital or anything. So I called my publicist and they gave her some money, and by some great miracle, no one found out. My sister knows because she was there when I called my mom. She'll probably let it out someday, but I'm okay with that."

His hands clenched the steering wheel as he talked, and he stared out the front window at the great expanse of Los Angeles, lit from below by the hustle and bustle of the night.

"That's terrible. I'm so sorry."

"So I went into recovery," he said. "It's not an excuse for not being there for her, but it's the truth. I know my sister thinks it's a joke, but it isn't. There's a guy in one of my meetings. A really big actor from the nineties, and he was my sponsor for a while. He told me that everyone spends their lives wanting to be like us, and thinking this is it. The big dream. But the real trick is just learning to be regular."

I watched a woman leave her house about a hundred yards straight down the hill. She went into her backyard and lit a series of tiki torches, and they were beautiful, like fireflies.

"There's probably something to that," I said. If I hadn't known Jeremy better, maybe if I hadn't been with him tonight, I might have thought it was a jerk-off thing to say, like when really beautiful people say that beauty is only skin-deep. But I could see that it was almost as hard for him to blend in as it was for him to stand out. And even for those with the dream in their grasp, it was always in danger of slipping away.

"What are you thinking about?" He lifted the leather armrest that separated us.

"Nothing," I said.

I said nothing, because I knew that saying "I was thinking about Charles Manson" would be the absolute wrong thing to say when Jeremy Taylor was focusing his impossibly perfect face on yours. Even I had that much sense. But I *was* thinking about Charles Manson, about how, on top of everything, he couldn't stand the thought of being regular. The address where Sharon Tate was staying, 10050 Cielo, had just been vacated by a record producer who'd turned down Manson's songs. He'd said they'd never work, never break into the mainstream. Manson may have been driving that black, hippie LSD trip of a school bus around like it was a movable Technicolor orgy, but the stops he made were all about him. He wanted to be bigger than the Beatles. He believed he would be. It was all so much less interesting and more petty than the pseudo-psychic, Satanic, Beatles-referencing mania. There was no mystique to being told "You are not good enough," losing your mind, and taking your anger out on the messenger and the blessed. If he had been born thirty years later, TLC would have given him a reality show, and the world might have been a safer place.

"You *are* thinking about something," Jeremy said.

"I am," I said. "About a paper that I need to write."

Jeremy laughed, and when he touched me his palms were damp on my arm. It seemed outside the realm of the real and possible, but he was nervous. Before I could say something to get him off the hook, Jeremy took my face in both of his hands and gave me a kiss so gentle, and then so firm, that it made me forget that he kissed women for a living. He pulled back and smiled, pushed my hair off my face, and kissed me again.

"Stop thinking about your paper. Okay?"

"Okay," I said.

I wanted him to kiss me again, and he did.

"Is this because I'm regular?"

"It's because you're beautiful."

"I thought you said I was interesting."

"Interesting *is* beautiful, put that in your paper."

I didn't care that it sounded like a line out of a movie. I didn't care that no one would believe me, or that it would ruin it even to tell. I sat there under the Hollywood sign and made out with Jeremy Taylor like we were the happy ending of a really foul-mouthed romantic comedy. If a roving band of hippies had come out of the mountains and tried to cut us down, I am pretty sure I wouldn't have cared. And the only thing I can say is that it was nothing like I'd imagined. It was so much better.

"You go home tomorrow," he finally said. "Just when we're getting to know each other."

"I know."

He took his phone out and messaged me a number that he said never changed, in case I needed to get ahold of him and his cell didn't work anymore.

"Look me up next time you visit your sister. This is going to be my last season on *Chips Ahoy!* I haven't told Josh, but I can't do it anymore."

"What are you going to do?"

"I don't know," he said. "I think I'm going to apply to colleges next year, see if I'm good at anything." Then he smiled again and looked me dead in the eyes. "Or maybe I'll just do more of this?" Then he leaned his body into mine and kissed me again.

If those were his future plans, they were fine by me.

19

Jeremy dropped me back at my sister's house the next morning. I'd only stayed up all night once, when I was in summer camp, to watch the sun rise, but never with a boy and definitely not with Jeremy Taylor. He offered to drive me to the airport, but I needed to pack, to have a minute to sit and let the evening sink in, to make it real for myself before time or having to tell it to another person screwed up the moment, pushed it a little further away.

"If you change your mind about the ride," he said, "just call."

"I will," I said, waving as I stood outside my sister's apartment.

As he drove off, I tried to take a mental snapshot of the moment, the orange of the flowers blooming by my sister's doorway, the electric hum underneath my skin. Dawn shaded the sky a dusty pink, the same color the sky had been when the cab dropped me off by the set the night before.

Day and night had no real meaning in Los Angeles. Where last night ended and today began was anyone's guess. Morning was pinker and smelled fresher, but it didn't really signal the start of anything. I imagined that could be as disorienting as it was wonderful, that in LA life always just seemed there for the taking, even as it was passing you by. Every week you looked up and there was another blonde with a gun on the billboard—another pair of green eyes staring into space, begging to be noticed, then disappearing as mysteriously as they had appeared. Another night meant another club opening. Another grisly murder. Another love story.

And then I went to unlock my sister's door and realized that it was already ajar. My stomach dropped. Delia was careless, but not careless enough to leave a door open.

"Delia," I said, trying not to sound scared. Then louder, "Delia?"

No answer.

I pushed the door open and stepped back. The inside of my sister's apartment was trashed. Black-and-white photographs of what looked like naked bodies were on the floor. I still hadn't seen my sister.

"Delia!"

Something moved.

"I'm calling the police," I yelled, and tried to steady my hands to find my phone.

"Don't," a voice whispered. My sister's voice.

"Delia! Are you okay? What happened?"

My sister was in the middle of her couch, cocooned in blankets and staring at the wall. She shifted, rubbed her eyes, and continued to look intently at absolutely nothing.

"You scared me to death," I said. "You're kind of scaring me now."

She held an oversize cup of coffee between her knees, and she looked tired.

"What happened?" I asked. "That lady. Did she come back?"

"You could say that," Delia said.

"Where's Roger? Or Dex. Should I call Dex?"

"We broke up," Delia said.

"Oh, crap. Did you tell him about Roger?"

My sister laughed, that laugh that crazy people do in the movies before they sink their teeth into the flesh of the living.

"Nope, not Roger."

"Then why?" I asked.

"Look around," my sister said. "Take a wild and crazy guess."

By my feet was half of an eight-by-ten photograph that had been ripped in half. The part that I picked up showed the torso and bare thigh of a woman, wrapped around a man's very unsexy, pale, and hairy torso. The thigh had a small cursive *D* tattooed in the center. My sister's thigh. And the torso? Not Dex's.

"What happened?" I asked.

My sister closed her eyes like the question itself gave her a headache. "Dex and I went to the wrap party. Then we went out. Then we came home and that crazy bitch had plastered my whole door with pictures."

I felt scared and embarrassed for my sister.

She kept her eyes closed while she talked. "I would say that it took about two minutes for Dex to go from really worried to really, *really* pissed. We had an extra-super-shitty fight. Things were said, pictures were ripped, glasses were thrown." She gestured around her apartment as she talked, like she was directing the scene. "And now he's gone."

"You need to call the cops," I said. "She's dangerous."

"I'm going to move," Delia said. "I'll change my number. I called her asshole husband, again, and he's changed his number, so it's in the air. She's already wrecked my life, the ten percent that Roger didn't get. That's what she wanted."

I shook my head back and forth the whole time she talked. "That's not enough, Delia. What if she's violent?"

Delia handed me two intact pictures that had been face-down beside her.

"I can't call the police."

The first picture was of Jeremy walking around a kitchen without his shirt. I didn't recognize the kitchen, but I knew what he'd been wearing that day. The entire place must have been rigged with security cameras. And the second photo was of a girl with her eyes closed hunched down in grass on a hill. It might have been tough to prove in court, but Delia and I both knew that it was me.

"Oh *no*," I said.

"I'm not even going to ask," Delia said. "Because it doesn't matter at this point."

"Is she going to have us arrested?" I was feeling sicker by the minute. "Does this mean I'll never get into college?"

Delia laughed. "She's not interested in you. Truly. And don't beat yourself up too much, because calling the police probably wouldn't matter anyhow. I thought about it, and then I heard myself saying that someone was taping pictures of me and her husband on my front door. You think the police care about things like this? I had a guy follow me to my door once, like, the kind of thing where I ran inside and closed the door and called the police, and the cop who came over accused me of being delusional. You think anyone in this town gives an actual, honest-to-God shit about me? Guess again."

Dex did, I wanted to say. *That 10 percent of your life, you ruined yourself.*

But what was the point? It was nothing she didn't already know. And I cared. I actually did.

"We were trying to help," I said. "Not that it matters."

There were other pieces of Delia across the rug. I didn't know if she'd torn them into shreds, or if Dex had. Her perfectly manicured hand looked like something peeking out of the corner of a crime scene photo. It made me think of Olivia's hand, wrapped almost possessively around Karl Marx's forearm, before he unwrapped her and handed her off to his bandmate.

It seemed like everything in LA that was whole could be broken down and sold off in pieces. And maybe one day Olivia would wake up and regret her time with the band, the way my sister regretted her time with the producer. The way the Manson girls eventually regretted their time with Manson. Maybe the situations weren't the same, not even close, but from where I was sitting they didn't seem so terribly different.

"I did almost call the police, to see if they could find you," Delia said.

"And said what, that you abandoned me outside a bar in LA?" The minute I said it, I wished that I could take it back.

My sister shook her head. "I'm sorry. I don't want to fight. I don't want the summer to end badly because of last night. I shouldn't have kissed Roger. I wasn't thinking, and it was stupid. And God knows you shouldn't have to see pictures of your sister's sordid and ancient love life. Not that I'll ever convince Dex of that now."

Understatement.

She looked out the big open window while she talked, glancing up the hill every once in a while in the direction of the producer's house, and then back at the coffee cup between her knees.

"I know you can't stand Roger, but we have a history. I think it's partially that he's my ex, and that sometimes makes me feel like I have a grandfather clause for making out, not sleeping together, and I know Dex and you both would never understand, but it just doesn't seem like anything to kiss Roger. Then—and I know that he says he wrote a role for me, but the fact that Dex's pilot got picked up, and my nose is a disaster, I just wanted to wreck it first. He can't cast me just because he wants to, and even he knows things don't work that way. I won't be the person left behind. I can't explain what I did with that producer to him. I just can't. People like to imagine that they get a girl who's been depressed, or confused, or desperate, and it's so romantic and exciting, but they definitely don't want to imagine what she might have really done. Trust me. I know of what I speak. Tragic is interesting but only if there was no collateral damage, and there always is."

My sister was matter-of-fact, even when her life lay in pieces around her.

"Dex wouldn't have left you."

She looked at me now instead of the landscape.

"But he would have. He really would. Anyone can leave anyone. And you're probably right, he might not have left me this week, or even this month, but this is not a town built on lasting relationships. We'll probably talk again. He might care that I have an explanation for the photos, he might not. How could I tell him about Roger after that? What purpose would it even serve? I don't love Roger. It won't happen again. Who's really better off by knowing?" She gestured at the garbage at her feet. "I'd say he's already seen enough."

I didn't know why my sister did the things she did. I couldn't match the Delia on the couch up against the Delia in pieces on the floor any more than I could match the Manson girls against their crimes. Maybe she really did love Dex, and she was being stupid and afraid. Maybe she had slept with half of Hollywood, but it suddenly didn't seem like my business to be calling her a slut. I felt bad about the way Doon and I had joked about her. I wanted Dex to forgive her. I wanted her to get a second chance, whether she deserved it or not.

"Don't you still have to film with Roger?"

"I do, but I can control myself around Roger, believe it or not." She gave an eye roll of self-disgust. "I even told Dex that I'd been shooting with him, before we came back here, of course. And about Mom."

Mom.

I needed to pack, but I just wanted to sit down. My sister moved her feet and I curled up on the other end of the sofa.

"What did he say?"

"He said that I must really not trust him. Irony, right?"

"But you don't, do you?"

"I don't trust life," she said.

My sister tossed her baby-blue blanket in my direction. The fabric smelled faintly of vanilla, her perfume, and I felt for a minute like I was going to cry, like I wanted to bottle that scent and take it home with me, to keep a little part of my sister close, no matter how big a disaster she was. I felt that way when I smelled the top of Birch's head as well. He had that powdery baby smell, and I wanted to hug him so hard when he was sleeping that I sometimes worried I would break him. I could remember smelling him like that, but I couldn't get the scent, the same way I knew that by the time I was on the plane I would have lost that feeling around the smell of my sister's blanket.

Maybe she wasn't the disaster. Maybe I was.

"Are you ready to go back?"

"I'm almost packed," I said. "I pack really fast. I promise."

She shook her head.

"That's not what I meant."

I knew what she meant.

"I don't know. I kept thinking Mom would apologize at some point. And now Doon is mad at me too. I miss them all so much, and I want things to be like they were before, way before, and I know that's not even possible because it doesn't exist anymore. I just feel like Mom can be the nicest person and then the craziest too."

"Because she can be."

"But does the crazy make the nice not true? I read about all these awful families this summer, and I know ours isn't that bad. It's not like Dad's a pervert or Mom locks me in a closet, but sometimes I still feel like neither of them is really trying that hard. And then I think to myself, 'Well, it's not like it's their job to try,' and then I think after that, 'But wait a minute, yes, it is,' and then I just get so mad at both of them that I want to run away again, only someplace farther away and with more money. Don't look at me like that, it's not like I'm going to do it. I want to see my brother and I want to figure out how to survive this new, stupid school, but I also want my parents to just work a little harder at being my parents. And then I just feel like a jerk."

Delia waited before she spoke. "I think you can't expect more from people than they're able to give. And you're happier if you don't hate them for it."

I thought about it for a minute. It was the kind of thing people said that you knew was probably true, but still didn't help very much.

"And if all else fails," she said, "I can loan you my credit card and you can come back next summer."

"Seriously?"

"Seriously."

I gave her the hardest hug I've probably ever given her in my life, and she hugged me back just as tightly. I wanted someone to love her, too, to keep her safe.

"I almost forgot," she said, breaking away and getting her bag from across the room. "Dex said to give you this." She tossed a T-shirt in my direction. "Too Many Rich Crackers." "He said to wear it the first day of school and to think of him."

"Right," I said. "I'll make sure to have a backup form of social suicide, though, just in case."

Delia yawned and laughed at the same time, then went back to her place on the sofa.

"If you ever talk to him again, tell him thank you."

"I know he's a good guy," my sister said. "That's what makes it harder, believe it or not. I spent half my life swearing I would never end up like Cora."

Her voice was soft. I thought for a minute that she was going to cry.

"Jeremy and I were talking last night," I said. "He said the hardest thing in life is figuring out how to be regular."

"Because he's clearly an expert," Delia said. "And haven't I been nice in not asking you where your pants are?"

"You said this was a dress."

"Obviously, I was wrong. So where did you go? Did you two lovebirds have fun?"

I thought about trying to explain the whole night to her, but it seemed like it would just sound like the most fantastic lie.

"We did."

"Should we have a talk?"

"It wasn't *that* fun. Scout's honor."

I gave her the *Chips Ahoy!* salute and sat next to her on the sofa. The house was quiet and still, like the morning after a hurricane blew through town. Adrenaline was rapidly giving way to fatigue, and I slumped against my sister's side, which was softer and more pliant than I'd imagined. She wrapped an arm around me and rubbed the top of my arm, slowly and rhythmically, humming a song that our mother used for Birch. *Hush, little baby, don't say a word.* I was almost asleep when my sister stopped humming.

"Anna. I'm not trying to make you mad, so please don't take this the wrong way, okay?"

I woke up a little but didn't open my eyes.

"I know Mom owes you an apology, and I know the two things aren't comparable, but"—she paused, trying to be careful, I guess—"did you ever apologize to her? It's not that easy waiting on a couch all night for someone, even if you are furious at said person."

I didn't say anything and she started to hum again, but I couldn't fall back asleep.

"I'm not trying to be a jerk," she said.

"I know," I whispered.

20

My sister claims that I fell asleep again, but all I remember is sitting on her couch one minute, and the next finding myself in her car with my bags packed, looking out the window as I said good-bye to her apartment, to the summer, to Los Angeles.

On the way to the airport, my phone twitched. A one-word text appeared from a number that I didn't know: "THNX," followed by a picture of a tiny pink rabbit waving a sparkling wand dancing next to the letters. I scrolled through my address book when it hit me. Paige Parker had written me back. I won't lie, I'd hoped that it was Jeremy, but at the same time, those four stupid letters and bunny made me feel ridiculously okay. The universe seemed to be saying: *Thumbs-up, Anna, you don't suck all the time!*

"Good news?" Delia asked, raising her eyebrow like it had to be from a guy.

I rolled my eyes back at her and then she parked and walked me through the airport all the way to security. Delia hugged me and then handed me off to an airline official whose name tag read "Michelle." Michelle made small talk as she escorted me to my flight like a low-security prisoner. After I was safely buckled in my seat, she left to shuffle another kid from one place to the next. The walk from security to the gate had felt like a walk in a dream, slow and almost underwater. By the time I boarded, I was completely exhausted and yet too awake to sleep at the same time. The summer was really over.

I started my paper on the way home. The plane circled a wide arc around the city as it rose, the early evening's pink glow warming the hills of Hollywood. Farther off, the occasionally broken darkness of the ocean loomed, and Los Angeles seemed like something perched on the edge of the earth, beautiful and always slightly in danger of being swallowed whole.

Somewhere, my sister was telling or not telling Dex the whole truth of what she'd done the night before, and Jeremy was sitting in a meeting asking for the serenity to face another day. The plane might even have flown over the jail where Leslie Van Houten was doing life, guilty as much as anything of choosing the wrong friends. There were beautiful homes full of boxes and dog shit, the kinds of things that didn't make the gossip sites or glossy magazines.

Jeremy had texted me twice to wish me a safe trip home, but he hadn't called and neither had I. Part of me was sad, the kind of sad you get at the end of a really beautiful and tragic book. *Gatsby* sad. My evening with Jeremy was one night and it was messy and perfect, and it was probably best just to leave it alone, to accept that anything that freakishly awesome should probably just be sealed in the amber of memory and left undisturbed. That was poor Jay Gatsby's mistake—he had one great night with Daisy and tried to turn it into a whole lifetime. Then again, how could he not?

The lights in the cabin dimmed and I pulled down the shade of the window so that the woman next to me could sleep. She had on earphones and a face mask, and within minutes her head was tilted back taking in choked, openmouthed breaths. I put on my own earphones and read the second part of my assignment from Mr. Haygood: *What's so great about Los Angeles?*

Probably because I am a professional procrastinator, I pulled out the magazine that someone had left behind. Right underneath "What NOT to Say to Make Him STAY," in gummy pink letters, was "My Shopping Diet: Olivia Taylor Learns to Live Lean and Love It." The article was a page and a half, about how hard it had been for her to stop shopping at first, and how many other things she'd started doing once she got used to it. Allegedly, she'd started writing "nice notes" to her friends every day. But the craziest part was that there were pictures of the inside of her house, and it looked like an actual house. Someone had cleaned it out before the photo shoot, or they had the most advanced computer in the universe erasing every bag from every corner and hallway. The picture featured Olivia, Mr. Peabody, and Iggy, and she looked like the kind of girl you'd want to be in the kind of house you'd like to own. I closed the magazine and put it back in the mesh pocket.

It was almost too easy to hate on Los Angeles. The city was

a kind of apocalyptic tar pit, a freak show of broken hearts and half-fulfilled dreams, full of artists, liars, parasites, and roadkill, all of whom had just a touch of violence in their hearts. Even today, it was Manson territory without the Manson. But those hills and canyons were beautiful as well. Anyone could see how easy it was to write off the glitter, the fake boobs and hair, the way that the dumbest and worst seemed to rise to the top, that at the end of the day it was probably all just a big lie, but I still couldn't do it myself. I may not have wanted to stay, but I sure liked to visit. Maybe Los Angeles was like Gatsby's dream of Daisy, but for all of America. Instead of sitting on a pier and gazing at a green light across the water, now people just sat in their living rooms and watched the wide-screen, 3-D version of some life that was out there for the taking, if only they could get off the couch.

Los Angeles, I wrote, *is not really so different from the rest of America*. Los Angeles was Olivia Taylor spending the rest of her life trying to become Olivia Taylor again. And then I borrowed a phrase from Dex, who'd borrowed it from someone else. *Los Angeles is simply the illusion America most chooses to treasure. The Manson murders changed that, and America, but maybe not that much*.

And then something weird clicked, the way an idea can start to make sense only when you're in the middle of writing, and so I wrote what would become my paper on the airsickness bags in the pocket in front of me. I wrote about Jay Gatsby and Leslie Van Houten. They might have seemed worlds apart, but they weren't so terribly different. They both wanted to escape their families. They both believed in something that wasn't half as awesome as it seemed to be at first, and believing in the wrong things ruined both of their lives. Had the Manson murders really changed America? Or was Manson just America gone wrong all over again, but with women in the headlines? I was either getting an A or going to hell.

As I finished writing, I thought about *Valley of the Dolls* and the long line of beautiful women, from Daisy to Sharon Tate to Olivia Taylor to my sister, who made books and films and music come to life. In the middle of *Kandy Kisses,* Olivia Taylor smiles at the camera and says, "If I could blow the whole world a kiss, I would." Then I almost started cracking up, because I remembered the afternoon when Josh was making fun of his sister, and he puckered up and said, "If I could blow the whole world, I would," and he and Jeremy almost laughed themselves off their chairs. I knew Daisy was just imaginary, but I also wondered if the real girls, or women, or whatever, weren't sometimes just as make-believe themselves. I thought about the wall of women's faces in Roger's movie, the new girls and the old. By the time the flight attendants turned the lights back on, I had a draft of something.

My mom was supposed to be meeting me with Lynette, and I wondered if she would still look like herself when she picked me up from the airport, if she'd let Birch stay up past bedtime to meet me as well, if she'd come at all. Lynette had promised that they would both make it, even though my mom was still more tired than usual from the chemo.

A calming voice announced: "Please fasten your seat belts and prepare for landing. All electronics should be turned off and properly stowed."

I closed my eyes and for just a minute I felt how much I'd missed my mom, and I wondered if she missed me as well. It almost didn't matter that within ten seconds of seeing her she would probably be driving me insane, or that for all I knew she wouldn't be there at all, she'd just be the lame sound of parroted excuses escaping from Lynette's mouth. But even that didn't matter. In the moment, with my phone off and the landing strip ballooning in the window, anything was possible. I might turn on the phone and Jeremy would have called, begging me to go back to California. Or Doon would have texted to say that she hadn't meant anything she'd said, that there was no need to apologize, that we would be best friends forever. I could imagine my mom healthy and Lynette and Birch standing next to her, and my dad back from Mexico, all waiting for me at the gate with one of those cheesy signs and flowers: *Anna, we've missed you. Welcome home!*

My mom asked me about a million times over the summer why I ran away. If it was because LA was so fabulous, or I liked my sister better than her, or if I was dealing drugs or whatever weird conspiracy she'd read about on the Internet that week. But the truth of it was, I didn't really have a plan past getting on the plane. Even when my sister showed up, which seemed like the thing that had to happen, that should happen, part of me was still kind of surprised. I guess, at the end of the day, what I wanted most was to feel that moment when you're on a plane and every-one around you is in their own world, anxious to stand up and open the overhead bin and get ready to start the life they've only ever dreamed of, or reenter whatever life they left behind: that moment before the plane hits the ground, when the air starts to hum and it seems like if the impact doesn't kill you, the possibili-ties are almost too much to bear.

Author's Note

Why the Manson Girls?

I never set out to write a book about the Manson girls. In fact, I'd been at work on this novel for some time before the book told me that it wanted to be about the Manson family—and my first thought was that it couldn't. The material was sensationalistic and a little clichéd, and who wanted to give another American psycho more attention anyhow?

Before I wrote this novel, my first thought about the Manson girls, like that of many people, was "Yuck, the Manson girls? They're still in jail, right?" I wanted to write a book about Los Angeles, girlhood, and what the American dream might mean to a kind of lost, basically decent, deeply cynical fifteen-year-old girl. I definitely didn't want the book to be about Charles Manson—and I don't think it is.

To be honest, I didn't even enjoy researching the Manson girls all that much. I kept looking for the key, the really horrific thing that must have happened in their lives that turned them into killers, a poorly wired circuitry that might excuse such colossally shorted-out humanity.

What I found was that most of them had screwed-up lives

but low-level screwed up—their biographies suggested they could have gone on to become perfectly functional adults had they encountered a different group of friends (and had they had a few years of good therapy).

The Manson girls were lost girls who made bad choices. *Really* bad choices. And in some cases, most cases actually, wound up being really, really sorry about those choices.

What does one do with that?

Rather than mirroring the Manson family, I decided to write a novel that put the focus on emotional violence—the kind that doesn't leave the obvious scars. I wanted Anna's "crime," as it were, to be invisible but damaging. I wanted her to be forgivable.

Anna is a "regular" girl who finds her way home. I think that the Manson family continues to fascinate because—as hard as it is to imagine—the Manson girls were once "regular" girls as well.

Acknowledgments

I suppose there are books still written by the artist, toiling alone, wrestling with her genius—but this was not one of them! This book was written catch-as-catch-can, during toddler naps, in the waiting room of auto shops while the oil got changed, fifteen minutes at a time before I started the official day, and on occasion in large chunks, thanks to the generosity of Bruce and Judy Umminger, Mike Mattison, and the most caring Pam Murphy and Julie Reed.

One of the great advantages of being a late bloomer (that is to say, someone whose "first novel" is published after one has been writing for years) is that along the way I have collected some truly wonderful writer friends and brilliant readers, whose insights were instrumental in drafting, redrafting, and finally finishing this book. Thanks first and foremost to Margaret Mitchell, a friend and fellow writer extraordinaire, who read more versions of this than I could count. Thanks especially to Bob Bledsoe, Romayne Dorsey, Dana Johnson, Michelle Ross, Meg Pearson, Mike Mattison (again), Bruce Umminger (again), Jim Elledge, Dionne Bremyer, Sean Jepson, Christine Sneed, David Groff, Sarah Dotts Barley, Yael Sherman, and Neeti Madan for reading drafts, offering insight, and being most excellent cheerleaders. And speaking of cheerleaders—thank you, Kate Gace Walton, for your wonderful Web site, Work Stew, which inspired me to get back on the horse as a novelist after putting that dream aside. Thanks to Greg Frasier for helping me place an early section of this novel. Thanks to Bernadette Murphy, Alexandra Cordero, Linda Rattner Metcalf, McCalla Hill-McKaharay, Amy McIlwain, Lisa Connell and Jason Keesling, Elaine McSorley-Gerard, Dave Mandel, Aelred Dean, Jan Tolbert, and Katherine Hamburger-Schneider and April Umminger for always lending an ear and encouragement when I needed it most. GURU mamas, you know who you are, and thanks for your support and insights. Thanks also to Josh Black and Thomas Jones for their early help with research and to Jill Sutton for photos. And to Philip Pascuzzo for the amazing cover design.

Extra-special thanks to Neeti Madan for being the best agent ever—fabulous friend, wonderful reader, tireless advocate. I cannot say what a pleasure it was to work with Sarah Dotts Barley, the brilliant, lovely editor who helped make this book strong in ways that I couldn't have predicted. Thank you. Thanks to the others who have made this experience of bringing a book into the world a dream come true—Amy Einhorn, Sarah Castleton, Madeleine Clark, Marlena Bittner, Sheryl Johnston, Liz Keenan, Molly Fonseca, Karen Horton, and Szilvia Molnar. I couldn't be more excited to be on the Flatiron list. Thanks to Caroline Abbey and Donna Bray as well.

Thanks also to my big extended family—Judie Mattison,

John and Lynne Mattison, Miles and Judy Renaas, and Katrina, Will, and Geneva Rutherford, and more Ummingers, Aherons, and Bryants than I can list—you've all been so encouraging and interested. This is a book—ultimately—about family, and I am blessed to have lived long enough to be able to see and truly appreciate how much love I have in my life. I couldn't list everyone who's offered an encouraging word along the way, but every bit of kindness mattered. (Do I sound like Jewel? Help!)

And finally, thank you, Mike and Maggie. You are my great loves and make it all worthwhile.

Recommend
American Girls
for your next book club!

Reading Group Guide available at
www.readinggroupgold.com